3

To Von and Samuel

Paige Cothru

Cover Picture:

Woodall Mountain
Highest Point in Mississippi
Tishomingo County
Elevation: 806 ft.

UPON
A
DISTANT
HILL

A Christian Novel

The Second in the Patie Corbin Christian Novel Series

By

PAIGE COTHREN

Upon A Distant Hill

Copyright © 2007

Swinging Bridge Publications
1332 Hwy 15 South
Woodland, MS 39776

ISBN 978-0-9798378-0-7

UPON
A
DISTANT
HILL

Paige Cothren

OTHER BOOKS
By
PAIGE COTHREN

Let None Deal Treacherously

Seeking to Know Her

Walk Carefully Around the Dead

An Academy Called Pain

So Great the Pretender

The Echo of Silence

Home Sweet Homochitto

The Cry of the Camel

At the End of the Swinging Bridge

At What Price Law

A Lamp Unto My Feet-A Light Unto My Path

CONTENTS

Introduction 1

Chapter One   In Godly Retrospect........................... 5

Chapter Two   Shock and Awe................................. 15

Chapter Three   Muscadines and Madness.................... 27

Chapter Four   A Courageous Grief.......................... 37

Chapter Five   A Pressure of a Different Kind 51

Chapter Six   A Casket and a Confrontation 63

Chapter Seven   Beyond the Metal Screen 77

Chapter Eight   Two Invitations of a Worrying Kind....... 91

Chapter Nine   What It Was, Was Football................. 105

Chapter Ten   When the Lights Went Off 119

Chapter Eleven   A Lesson in Faith......................... 133

Chapter Twelve   Why Do Thangs' Like This Hap'en, Preach?.... 145

Chapter Thirteen   A Dog Named Jake.......................... 157

Chapter Fourteen   A Man Unknown 169

Chapter Fifteen   A Curve Ball Thrown....................... 183

Chapter Sixteen   Sorghum................................... 197

Chapter Seventeen   Another Lesson 211

Chapter Eighteen   The House on the Hill..................... 225

Chapter Nineteen   Pulled into Controversy 239

Chapter Twenty   A Second Wind............................. 253

Conclusion 265

A Personal Note 267

Other Books by Paige Cothren....................................... 269

Upon A Distant Hill

INTRODUCTION

Patie Corbin found the Justice Center without much trouble. But he didn't stop. He drove past it, continued on for a mile or so, pulled into the parking lot of an automotive service center and then stopped. Resting both hands on the top of the steering wheel of his SUV and his head upon his hands, the old athlete turned preacher prayed. Like Hannah in I Samuel, his lips were moving but no sound came from his mouth.

Lord, he meditated, when Paul was weak, he wrote that you made him strong. Lord, I'm weak. Please make me strong and please go before me. Please prepare Phil's heart. And help me remember, as you taught in Philippians, that I'm to be anxious for nothing and help me to *really* understand like you teach in II Chronicles through Johanziel, that the battle is yours, not mine.

A few minutes later the pastor lifted his head. He opened his truck door more energetically than he would have ten minutes earlier and walked smartly into the store. After using the restroom, he stopped at the counter, purchased a small packet of Listermints, and popped one into his mouth. Then he got into his vehicle again and pointed it back toward the Justice Center.

"May I help you?" the uniformed lady behind the large desk asked.

1

She did not smile.

"Yes, you certainly may," Corbin replied, acutely aware of the fact that the weak smile on his face was there only through an act of his will. He did not want to do what he knew he must do, every fiber of his being straining against it. "I would like to see one of your inmates, Phil Appleby."

"Does he know you're coming?"

"No, Ma'am."

"May I have your name?" she requested, still unsmiling.

"Patie Corbin. I'm a preacher."

"His minister?"

"No, Ma'am. Just a minister who knows Sissy, his daughter, and knew his wife."

"Please be seated," the officer commanded, pointing to a chair at the side of the desk. "It will be a minute."

"Thank you. Ma'am," Patie replied, trying desperately to maintain some force in the tone of his voice. He didn't want to sound uncertain—nor weak—nor afraid.

Fifteen minutes later, Patie heard his name called. He looked up and saw a middle-aged man, slightly stout, standing behind the desk to one side, looking at him. The man held a door open. The preacher placed the magazine he had been reading back onto the table by his chair, stood, and walked through the open door. He smiled at the officer. The officer did not smile back.

The door opened into a short brightly lit hallway. The guard pointed, "This way." A few feet down the hall, the guard held another door open and followed Patie into a small room with a table in the center of it.

"Reverend," the man said, his voice softer than Corbin expected it to be, "I'll have to search you."

Patie nodded.

"Would you empty your pockets, please, including your coat pockets and your shirt pockets. And please take your coat off."

The pastor complied. He placed everything, including his small pocket Bible on the table.

When the guard saw the Bible, he smiled. "You carrying a mighty good book, there, Reverend."

"Thank you, Officer—oh—Morgan," Patie acknowledged, glancing at the name tag on the man's shirt. "It's one that I discovered I can't live without, as the Lord told the devil."

"Amen," the guard responded. "I have mine, too, right here." He patted his buttoned shirt pocket.

"Sounds like you really know the Lord Jesus," Corbin asserted.

"Sure do. Gave my life to Him more than twenty years ago now. And I've never regretted it."

"Amen," Patie laughed. Suddenly, in the midst of all the gloom of the jail, God had sent him a light. "Thank you for sharing that with me."

Following the pat-down by the guard, and upon his instructions, Patie, quickly stuffed everything back into his pockets. By the time he finished, the man was holding another door open. Patie walked through it.

He had visited the scene before. In Bay St. Louis, Mississippi, more than four years earlier in real life, *and* on his favorite secular television program, "Law and Order." It was the visiting room, where the visitor could talk to the prisoner through a heavy wire screen.

"Sit here; Preacher," the guard gently commanded, pointing at a chair resting before a screened opening. "We'll have Mr. Appleby out in a minute or two. He'll be on the other side of the screen, of course."

Patie nodded. "Thank you."

The few minutes which the preacher waited gave him an opportunity to reflect upon his short visit with the Christian guard. He noticed the man had called him "Preacher" a moment ago, rather than "Reverend," as he had done earlier, a change which Patie appreciated. Something about being called "Reverend" bothered the new preacher! Corbin was shaken from his thoughts by the sounds of an opening door on the other side of the screen followed by the rattling of chains. He twisted around and looked into the contorted face of Phil Appleby, a man who three days earlier had threatened to kill him and *had*, in fact, three days earlier murdered his own wife.

CHAPTER ONE
IN GODLY RETROSPECT

Patie wasn't aware of the amount of time he sat on the end of the swinging bridge in the warm summer Mississippi dusk. Nor was he conscious of the chirping insects, nor the occasional distant call of a whippoorwill, nor the gurgling waters of Bear Creek a few feet below him. His mind was racing like a wild unbroken stallion running across West Texas plains, unfettered and without obvious destination. Self-condemnation kept attempting to force its way into his thought processes, although, as quickly as it happened, he would consciously try to reject it. The stomach churning sickness roaring inside of him told him that everything which had happened to Betty and Phil Appleby was his fault. And yet the word of God and the Spirit of God graciously challenged that accusation. Biblically and theologically and mentally and practically, he could reason he wasn't responsible. The Bible clearly teaches, he reassured himself, that every man is responsible for his own sin—and theologically—well— theologically, man's sins may only be transferred to one Person, The Lamb of God—Jesus. Mentally, Patie knew Phil Appleby was responsible. Reason told him that! Practically, he wasn't even there when it happened. How could anyone hold *him* responsible? "How can *I* hold me responsible?" He asked out loud, experiencing a momentary flash of peace flowing out of the question.

"Well, if that's true, Lord, and it is, why do I still feel so miserable?" Corbin prayed out loud, glancing up to the sky as though he were expecting an audible reply. He would certainly have welcomed an audible reply! Oh, how he wanted one—for the first time, really. Since becoming a Christian, faith had been enough for him—faith, empowered by the ministry of the Holy Spirit, assuring that God exists; faith that Christ was the answer for man's sins; faith that God hears His children's prayers; faith that God answers prayers; faith in the authority and inerrancy of His Word. Tonight, though, he would have welcomed the audible voice of God.

Darkness was quickly enveloping the bridge when he finally stood and faced back across the creek where his SUV was parked. He could barely see it in the dimness and he could see no other vehicle, which meant he was still alone, although he would not have cared. The pain inside of him was too great to worry about the agony which twisted his face, a contortion of which he was not even aware. So preoccupied was he with sorrow that he wasn't conscious of the dried tears on his cheeks, or the deep furrows now etched across his brow or the furious squint in his burning eyes.

Holding tightly onto the bridge rail, his mind traced back to the time earlier when Dimples had brought the tragic news to him. Standing there, his head bowed slightly, he remembered what she had said. Thrusting his hand suddenly into his trouser pockets, he groped for the note which she had handed him, and he had, without thought, crammed into his pants. It was wrinkled and crinkled when he extracted it. Unfolding it almost reverently, he squinted against the fading light to read it for the hundredth time. Scribbled on the note was the fact of the murder, the daughter's name and phone number and the phone number of Betty Jo's brother, with whom she had been living. Written beneath that was the name of a funeral home in Birmingham, followed by the word "probably." Apparently that decision had not been made when the call had come.

Staring at the name of the funeral home and the word "probably," Corbin almost smiled. He imagined Dimples asked for that information, which may not have yet been finalized.

Slowly the pastor walked across the swinging bridge. The motion and rhythm of his steps moved the structure slightly, bouncing in sequence to his strides. His mind continued to race, moving mushily through the pain to *what* he needed to do—and *when*! Most of all he needed to call Betty Jo's daughter. He would do that as soon as he got back to the cabin. And he would need to go to Birmingham—if the daughter and brother would allow it. They might not want him there! And what about Phil? Had the police arrested him yet? Should I try to talk to him?

Patie had planned to move his clothes and other personal items from the cabin at the park into his house—since his furniture had come. If the daughter will allow it, should I go to Birmingham tonight? I can't move to my house tonight, not with all this. If I do go to Birmingham, what about Wednesday night Bible study at church? That might not be a problem, though. Surely one of the elders can handle that!

Whether it was the Holy Spirit inside of him or a normal settling of his emotions through the structure of his personality, perhaps both, by the time the preacher had walked the hundred feet or so to the other end of the bridge, his mind had begun to recapture some territory from his emotions. Rationality had begun to replace turmoil, understanding and faith in his God replacing self-condemnation. Before stepping off the bridge, he prayed again. "Lord, I just realized that I could wallow in total self-pity and self-abasement on this bridge all night if I allowed myself to do that. But I'm not certain I should! If I did anything wrong, please show me. If I should grovel at the daughter's feet, please, please let me know it. But until then, Lord, I am one of your blessed redeemed sinners, by your grace and forgiveness. 'There is therefore now no condemnation in me, Lord,'" Patie confessed, quoting Romans 8:1, "not because I deserve it, Lord, but because I know I am in Christ Jesus. Please help me stand up like your servant and do exactly what you want me to do." With a faint smile forcing its way through the somewhat sad expression on his face, he muttered, "And amen, Lord. Amen and amen. But I think I still need to talk to Jess."

Reinforced now by his fresh re-commitment to the notion that he had to be strong in the Lord in order to victoriously handle everything he would be facing in the next few days, and with a slight rush of new energy, Patie walked quickly to his vehicle, cranked it, and drove to his cabin. A few minutes later, he stood before the open refrigerator door trying to decide between orange juice and a Diet Coke. Pouring a large glass half-full of orange juice, he walked into the small bedroom, flipped his loafers off and strolled into the living room. Depositing the glass on a table beside the easy chair, he dug his cell phone from his pocket and started to call Jess. Suddenly he stopped, a new thought interrupting the process.

"No" the preacher murmured, "I'd better call the daughter first. I may need to tell Jess about that conversation." He stuck his hand back into his pocket for the note.

Corbin had found himself lodged between two desires many times in his life, before and even after salvation. But other than the day he prayed to receive Christ as his Savior in Jess Gingrich's office, when the forces of darkness in him battled furiously against the force of light, he could not remember an inner struggle more intense. He had to call her—ah—. Quickly he glanced back at the note. The daughter's name was written on it. *Sissy*. He had to call Sissy. He had to call her. He needed to call her. He wanted to call her. And he was going to call her. But on the other hand, he dreaded calling her. Obviously she would be extremely distraught and his phone call might exacerbate that— And, too, be prepared, she might blame him for her mother's death.

Patie closed his eyes. "Lord, I'm about to make a phone call to Sissy. Please let her be there and soften her heart. Let her receive what I have, in your name, to say to her. And, Lord, please help me take, with love in my heart, whatever she might have to say to me."

Corbin took a deep breath, a quick drink of the orange juice in order to dampen his dry mouth, and dialed the phone. A pleasant sounding deep male voice answered, "Clayton's residence."

"Is this Mr. Clayton?" Patie asked, quickly grasping the family's name. Dimples had not written Sissy's last name on the note.

"No, this is Dr. Stephen Devonshire. I'm the Clayton's pastor."

"Oh, Doctor," Patie quickly replied, "I'm Patie Corbin. I'm so glad to get to talk to you. I'm glad you're there."

"Thank you , Patie. I'm glad to get to talk to you. Thank you for being used of the Lord in Betty Jo's life."

"I'm just grateful that He used me, Doctor. May I ask you a question?"

"Certainly."

"Is Sissy there?"

"Yes. She and Jamie are here. They're in the bedroom right now. They'll be back out here in a few minutes. They asked me to answer the phone."

"Jamie is her husband?"

"Yes," Dr. Devonshire answered.

"Doctor, is Sissy alright? I know she is in extreme pain—but—do you think she would be willing to talk to me?"

"Oh, I think so, Patie. Sissy—and Jamie, too—are committed Christians. I had the privilege of leading them both to the Lord—and baptizing them."

"May I ask you, Dr. Devonshire—the name of your church?"

Corbin knew this wasn't the time to get into church doctrine and he certainly wasn't trying to do that although he realized Dr. Devonshire might misunderstand his motive for asking. Dr. Devonshire, though, would apparently be the person, understandably, ministering to the family. He desperately wished that the pastor hold strong scriptural views, especially concerning the Person and work of Christ, forgiveness, and the ability of the Holy Spirit to comfort God's children.

"Cedar Heights Baptist, Patie. Southern Baptist."

Patie felt a deep sense of relief. He knew what Baptists believe and he agreed with 99 percent of it. "Oh, thank you, Lord," the new pastor breathed into the phone. He secretly wanted Dr. Devonshire to hear his exclamation. Dr Devonshire did.

"I'm sorry, Doctor," Patie apologized. "It's just that I didn't know what—"

The Doctor interrupted him. "I understand, Patie. If the roles were reversed, I'd be asking you the same question."

Patie thought he could hear a touch of elation in the pastor's voice. Two men pastoring churches in two different denominations, although Corbin's church was independent, but both held one faith, one Lord, one baptism and even one view of Scripture. He had learned that pastoring a church in a particular denomination reflects much of the preacher's beliefs. He learned at Dallas about Southern Baptist Seminaries and how they had re-adopted a strong view of Christ, His vicarious atonement, and Scripture.

"Sissy has just come back into the room, Patie. Would you like to talk to her?"

"If you think it's alright and if she doesn't mind speaking to me."

Patie realized the telephone sounded muffled, and he imagined Dr. Devonshire was holding his hand over it, talking to Sissy about him. A few seconds later, Sissy spoke. Her voice was very soft and tearful. "Hello."

"Sissy, this is Patie Corbin. I'm so, so sorry."

A few seconds passed before Sissy answered. "Thank you, Brother Corbin," she whispered, her voice broken and perforated with sobs.

There was strength in Sissy's voice. The sobs and tears could not extinguish the sound of it.

"Sissy, is there anything I can do?"

"I would like to talk to you, Brother Corbin. I would like to ask you about Mama."

"Now, on the phone, Sissy, or would you like for me to come over there?"

"I would like to meet you, Brother Corbin, but I need to talk to you now. I mean, I would like to hear about Mama—I mean—" she hesitated, "I mean—about her prayer to receive Christ—her confession about what she and Dad were doing—and about—about something else."

"I'll be glad to talk to you about everything, Sissy. You want me to give you the details about how she came to receive Christ?"

"Yes, Sir. Would you?"

"Oh, Sissy, I'd be happy to!" However at precisely the moment he started to talk, the preacher heard a sound on the telephone. A sound like a doorbell ringing.

"Brother Corbin, can you hang on?' Sissy asked, softly.

"Certainly."

The sound of the doorbell was followed by the sound of several voices. Patie reasoned that other family members or friends had come into the house. Momentarily, Dr. Devonshire spoke. "Patie, Sissy, will pick up the other phone in the bedroom. She wants to speak to some visitors, then she'll be with you. Shouldn't be more than a minute or two, if you can hang on. I'll hang this phone up when she picks up the other one."

"Certainly, Dr. Devonshire. Thank you."

Patie could hear the conversation in the background. The faint voices seemed to be filled with grief and deep compassion. He picked up his orange juice and realized just then that he had not eaten anything since lunch. Normally, he would be experiencing some hunger pangs by now, but not tonight. The trauma of the events and food simply did not seem to be compatible. Not tonight. And the sounds of grieving voices suddenly thrust his mind backward to his own mother's death. "Mom," he whispered, "I still miss you." Then, almost as an afterthought he prayed, "Lord, I know Mom can't hear me, but I know of no place in the Bible which says that you or maybe an angel can't pass that on to her. If It doesn't violate Scripture or Your will, would you tell Mom how much I love her?" Then Patie wondered suddenly, if in some way that might offend the Lord. He reasoned that it probably did not.

The pastor was mulling over that concept and swallowing a big drink of orange juice when Sissy asked, "Brother Corbin?"

As Patie answered, he heard the "click" of the other phone being hung up. "Yes, Sissy. I'm here."

"I'm sorry, Brother Corbin. I can talk now." Patie could still clearly hear the grief in her voice.

11

"Sissy," Patie offered, "we can talk later tonight if you need to be with—"

"No, no, Brother Corbin. I need to talk to you now. I explained everything to them. It's okay."

"Good," Patie responded. "What would you like for me to tell you?"

"Everything," she implored, "from the time you met Mama and Dad to the last time you saw her—and then about her phone conversation with you. Will you do that?"

"I'd be happy to do that, Sissy. It's a great story." So, starting with the note on his door, he told Sissy everything: his visit with her parents and the other couple; their walk back to his cabin; Betty Jo leaving the note with him and what the note said; their meeting behind his cabin a little after daylight and their meeting at the end of the swinging bridge. Finally he covered in detail Bettye Jo's deep emotional prayer turning her life over to Jesus and inviting Him to become the Lord of her life. By the time the tough old ex-athlete finished the story, small teardrops glistened in the corners of both his eyes.

"So, Brother Corbin, you really believe Mama was truly saved?"

"Oh, yes, Sissy. There's no doubt about it—not in my mind."

"Did she tell you what she and Dad and the other couple were doing?"

"She told me about sin in all of their lives and that she was sick of the sin in hers." Patie could not bring himself to say the words wife-swapping to Sissy. He didn't have to. She said it.

"That they were wife-swapping?"

Patie hesitated. Quickly thinking through the situation, he finally decided a "yes" violated no confidence nor Scriptural principle. He knew Bettye Jo would want him to tell Sissy everything. "Yes," he softly answered. "But, Sissy, you know the guilt for those sins ceased to exist when she prayed to receive Christ. He removed them from her as far as the East is from the West and remembers them no more."

12

"I know—I know," Sissy, her voice choked down to a whisper, answered, "and I'm so grateful. I know now for certain Mama's with the Lord."

"I believe that, Sissy, with all my heart."

"Dad said you met Mama that morning to start an affair with her. He said Mama told him that."

CHAPTER TWO

SHOCK AND AWE

Patie leaned up in the chair quickly then fell back lethargically onto it, his cellphone still pressed hard against his reddening ear, which suddenly matched the rest of his face. A thin film of sweat quickly layered his body and his astonished eyes narrowed into thin slits. For a moment his vocal cords tightened, adding to the frustration. His mind almost went blank, yanked under the waters of disbelief like a cork on the end of a fishing line pulled out of sight by a Mississippi catfish. And then the astounded preacher started slowly shaking his head, a sickening knot in the pit of his stomach destroying what little appetite for food he might have had. Through all the massed accumulation of physical change which had swept over him, his mind raced back to those moments at the end of the swinging bridge. Without thinking, he knew he had said nothing to Bettye Jo overtly which might have incriminated him, but had he indirectly, subconsciously, conveyed the notion to her? His mind raced like a cassette tape on fast forward. No, he screamed to himself, forcing the sound down his throat. I did nothing wrong! Maybe it wasn't smart meeting Bettye Jo where we did—when we did—but, I had no choice. It would have been worse to have invited her into my cabin and Phil finding her there. At least we were in a semi-public place. Three other women saw us on the trail. We weren't hiding. I finally reached the point in my life, he thought, where I could actually meet an attractive woman in a place like that, share Christ with her, and then lead her to Him without a single evil thought blazing into my mind—yet still get accused of doing something evil. No! I will not accept that! I did nothing wrong and I will not accept self-condemnation. I will not have the righteousness of Christ insulted nor His name profaned!

Patie wasn't even remotely conscious of how long it had been since Sissy spoke those emotionally shattering words—how long he had been silent. It seemed like five minutes. It was probably thirty seconds or less. He was preparing to issue his statement of defense to the grieving daughter when part of a Scripture verse literally exploded into his fevered brain, "...we have an advocate with the Father, Jesus Christ the righteous."

The preacher's mind, under the force of that great principle, began to de-accelerate. Some of the contortion left his face. Some of the strain and tenseness began to ease from his body. He reached over, picked up his glass and sipped his orange juice. Slowly he placed the glass back on the table and into his cell phone, he spoke Sissy's name as a question. "Sissy?"

A soft and meek voice replied, "Yes, Sir."

"Sissy, you're a Christian, aren't you?"

"Yes, Sir."

"Sissy, may I pray with you?"

"Yes, Sir."

"Father, you are the God of all power—you are the God of all knowledge and you are the God of all comfort. Please bless Sissy and all her family in this dark day of heart ache, with your knowledge, and comfort them, as only you can. Grant to all of them a deep peace of heart, mind, and soul, and refresh their spirits with the knowledge that Bettye Jo is with you and with the knowledge that Phil, through all of this, could possibly come to you, too. In Jesus name, amen."

Patie waited a few seconds before he spoke again. When he did, his mind was clear and he had emerged from the slavery of fear into which he had allowed the false accusation to place him. "Sissy?"

"Yes, Sir."

Patie almost smiled when he suddenly realized that the last four

16

times the young lady on the other end of the phone had spoken, she said the identical same words.

"Sissy, you know we Christians have a lawyer in Heaven to defend us. We have an advocate, Jesus. First John 2:1 tells us that. In context, that verse means that He defends us to the Father and against Satan when we sin. The verse teaches us that He is our defense. Are you familiar with the verse?"

"Yes, I am, Brother Corbin."

"Good. Well, having said that, I still owe you an explanation to your statement for truth's sake, not in defense of—"

"Brother Corbin, I didn't say I believe it. I wanted you to know that Dad had said it."

"That, too, was truth, Sissy, that your Dad said it. Thank you for telling me."

Sissy said nothing. Patie continued.

"The Lord is my witness. No bad thought, word or deed was entertained, either by your mom or me. Her heart was breaking over her sin and she wanted peace and forgiveness and she wanted cleansing. And by our Lord's wonderful mercy and grace, and like all the rest of us who repent of our sins and convey the ownership of ourselves to Jesus—SHE—GOT—IT!" the preacher forcefully declared, stressing the last three words.

A few minutes of silence passed, a quiet interrupted by the soft sobs of a heartbroken yet grateful young woman, grateful that her mother who for so long lived in sin, along with her Dad, had repented of her sin and was in Heaven with her Lord. "Thank you, again, Brother Corbin."

"You are so very welcome, Sissy. I need to ask you another question. Have funeral arrangements been made yet?"

"No, Sir. We're going to do that in the morning. I'll call you."

"Do you have my office number?" Then remembering she had called the church earlier, he said, "Of course you do."

"Brother Corbin? I've talked to Dr. Devonshire about this, and we both agree. We'd like for you to have a part in the service—I mean—if you

17

can!"

Patie's heart jumped but this time with elation. Before he even thought about his church responsibilities, he blurted out, "Of course I can, Sissy. Thank you so much for asking me."

"I'll call you in the morning, Brother Corbin."

Before the pastor replied, he heard his cell phone beeping, telling him he had another call. Quickly he told Sissy goodnight, punched a button and looked at his screen—it was Dimples. Before he answered, he glanced at his watch. It was eight o'clock. If he hustled, maybe he *could* move his clothes, kitchen utensils, towels, etc., to his house tonight. It shouldn't take over two trips. He would call Jess later, after he moved.

Patie was walking into his new house with an armload of towels, bath cloths and other bathroom articles when his cell phone rang again. He dropped the items on the bathroom floor, dug his phone from his pocket and answered it, drifting over to the kitchen counter for something to lean on.

"Patie, it's Ann Chester. Dimples told me you were moving in tonight."

"Yeah, praise the Lord," the preacher responded joyfully. The appealing tone of a pleasant voice sounded very refreshing to him—a positive influence tugging against the trauma which still lingered in his head. "I enjoyed the cabin at the park, but I'm really glad to get into my own place."

"You had anything to eat tonight?"

Patie instantly considered saying yes. But he didn't! He couldn't lie, but then he really didn't want company tonight. He wanted to finish unloading his SUV and then he wanted to call Jess. The call from Ann had surprised him and left him with no time to create an answer in which he wouldn't lie but still not have to entertain anyone. "No, I haven't." If having a visitor was inevitable, Ann would be a good choice, he supposed.

She seemed pleasant, intelligent, non-confrontational and so far as he knew, presented no problem—and from her question, it sounded like she might be offering food, which earlier did not appeal to him, but now sounded better.

"Well, Tyce and I have finished eating and had lots left over—bar-b-que ribs, string beans, fruit salad and pecan pie. I would love to fix you a plate."

"Oh, Ann, it's too late for you to feed a preacher. Don't worry about—"

"Patie, it's not late," Ann interrupted. "Let me bring a plate over there to you. It's no trouble—really."

Corbin looked at his watch. It was 9:30. Reluctantly, he agreed, guarding his voice so that Ann could detect no negativism.

"You ready for it now?"

"I'm ready."

"I'll be there in fifteen minutes."

The pastor, who had already brought his clothes in, darted into his bedroom, pulled his dress clothes off and slipped into a pair of jeans and a very loose fitting tee shirt. He stuck his sockless feet into a pair of jogging shoes and dashed back to his vehicle for another load. And then another. And then he heard Ann coming.

He met his neighbor at her car and opened the door for her. The female publisher leaned over toward the passenger seat and picked up two foil covered plates. She handed them to Patie, looked up at him, smiled, and breathed a soft "Hello, Brother Preacher."

Patie smiled back and replied, "Hello, Madam Publisher. How are you?"

Twisting back around to the console, she lifted from it a large styrofoam cup of grape juice. "Fine. How are you?"

"I'm fine, too. Get out and come into a finally furnished though very modestly furnished home."

Patie led his guest through the darkened rock infested front yard, but when the two of them reached the front porch, he slowed down, turned around and looked at her. He could not help noticing what she wore; a pair of medium-length white shorts, a purple shirt, tied off at the waist, and a pair of Nikes with no socks, making her look even younger. She was very attractive. Carefully and with forethought, Corbin walked up the steps beside her. A minute or two later they were seated at his table, two plates of food and a large glass of grape juice spread out before him; nothing to eat in front of her.

"Before I ask my blessing and eat this delicious-looking supper, want me to make a pot of coffee? You need something to sip on or would you like—"

"Let me make it."

Corbin grinned. "Hoped you would say that. Can't eat pecan pie without coffee."

Bouncing from her chair, Ann asked, "Where is everything? Oh, I see the coffee pot on the counter."

"Filters are beside the pot and the coffee is in my bare refrigerator. Let me say the blessing, so I can get busy here," the preacher responded. "Preachers eat first, ask questions later, you know."

Ann, standing next to the counter, smiled and lowered her head. Five minutes later, she had made the coffee and re-assumed her seat across the round antique dining table from Patie, who had already finished one rib and was starting on another.

"Umh, umh," the diner exclaimed, in the words of Andy Griffith, "Good ribs—good ribs."

"They are good, aren't they," Ann agreed. "I can say that because I didn't cook them."

"Where'd they come from?"

"Red Bay."

"Alabama?"

"Um hunh," Ann explained. "I had to go over there today calling on an advertising customer. Picked them up at a little bar-b-que place there."

"Boy, they know what they're doing on a bar-be-que pit," Patie bragged. "They cook anything other than ribs?"

"Yes—chicken, link sausage, turkey drumsticks, briskets, hot wings, and some deer meat. I always bring back a load of bar-be-que when I go over there."

"You go often?"

"Every other week or so."

"I'm a little surprised that you would have enough circulation in Alabama to be able to sell ads over there," Corbin remarked frankly, more interested in promoting conversation than gaining knowledge about Ann's business.

"Well, I—ah—I—own the newspaper in another little town east of there, Riverview."

Patie lifted his eyes from his plate of food and looked at Ann. She had dropped hers, appearing to be almost embarrassed by her declaration, it seemed to the preacher. "Oh, of course, I knew you owned other papers, Ann. It had slipped out of my aging brain momentarily. I didn't know you owned that particular paper, though."

Ann smiled. Her demeanor had changed slightly.

Corbin, noticing the change, thought, I've embarrassed her or she has something important on her mind. Surely I didn't embarrass her, though. He asked, "You cook these yeast rolls? They are really good."

Ann laughed. "No, I didn't cook them, either, nor the pecan pie. But the fruit salad and string beans are all mine," she answered, throwing her hands up in the air like a high school cheerleader celebrating a touchdown. "The pecan pie *is* homemade, though."

"Umh, unh, boy are these string beans and fruit salad good," Patie exclaimed, teasing Ann, but meaning it. They were good—as good as string beans and fruit salad can be.

"Thank you," Ann's face had re-assumed the more serious mien.

"Patie," she continued, "Dimples told me about the lady in Birmingham being killed by her husband, and—"

21

"She called you?"

Ann nodded. She had leaned back in her chair and the expression on her face indicated that she wasn't *absolutely* certain she should be telling Patie that Dimples had told her about it.

Patie, unaccustomed to small town friendships, was certain that Dimples should not have told Ann about it without his permission, at least. He disciplined the appearance of displeasure which the news brought to him from his face. His problem was with Dimples, not Ann. "Yeah, it was bad, Ann. Really bad."

"Dimples told me that you led her to the Lord Sunday night at the Swinging Bridge."

Patie looked hard into the face of his visitor. He saw compassion there, he thought, not morbid interest—or—could it be editorial interest? That thought surprised him. Surely not. Surely she wasn't morally dishonest enough to talk to him about the murder in order to get a story.

Now it was the preacher's turn to nod. "Except that it was early Monday morning, just a little after daylight." Patie looked carefully for an expression change on Ann's face. He got one.

"Early Monday morning?" she repeated. "How did that develop so that—"

For the second time in less than three hours Patie told the story of Bettye Jo's conversion. When he finished, he fixed his eyes firmly upon his guest and asked, "Why do you ask?" straining sternness from his voice.

"You mean about her getting saved?"

Patie nodded.

"Oh, I think it's a marvelous story. Not her death. Her giving her life to Christ before she was killed. I just kinda' wanted to hear about it, I guess—to hear again about the marvelous grace of God."

The suspicious preacher suddenly regretted his suspicions. Ann certainly seemed sincere.

"I can tell you are really troubled about what happened to the lady. Would you like to talk about it?"

22

Corbin had finished the meal—the first part of it. He had not eaten his pie. The coffee had stopped dripping so he knew it was ready. Saying nothing, he stood, picked up his plate holding six large "meatless" ribs, which looked as though they had been subjected to a battle with sandpaper, and walked over to the sink, conscious of Ann's eyes following him. He reached into a small box which he had stored in the cabinet under the kitchen sink and extracted a large plastic garbage bag and slid the ribs off the plate into it. He ran hot water over the plate rinsing it, his fork and knife, opened the dishwasher and placed them in the rack. Then he reached into one of the cabinets above the counter and took two identical mugs from it, each with the early Christian marking of a fish and Greek letters, Icthus. The entire time the preacher did that, he had said nothing, but his mind was racing.

Talk! Do I want to talk about my "problem?"

Looking back at Ann, he asked, "Ready for your coffee?"

By then, his new neighbor had begun to think that she might have offended Patie—or reminded him of something too sad to talk about. His question and the smile on his face when he asked it alleviated that fear. "Yes. Thanks."

No sooner had Patie poured the coffee, than a loud "Uh oh" tumbled from his mouth. "I have no idea where sugar, Equal, nor Sweet'n Low are. I don't think I've unloaded it yet. And I have no cream nor milk. I hope you can drink it black—or I'll go the car and get the—"

"I can—thanks."

"I can, too, since I'm eating this delicious looking pecan pie with it."

Corbin brought both mugs of the coffee back to the table and sat down. Before he took his first bite of the pie, Ann asked, "What do these Greek letters stand for? I've heard, but I've forgotten."

Patie smiled. "The letters actually spell "fish," but the word "fish" is "icthus." Icthus, the acronym, is created using the first letters of Jesus Christ, God, Son, Savior. Does that make sense?"

23

"Oh—yeah—kinda'. What are those actual Greek words?"

"You mean the actual Greek words translated Jesus Christ God Son Savior?"

"Yes."

"Iasous—Cristos—Theos—Wheeos—Sotar is the transliteration of them."

"I'm sorry, the what?"

"Transliteration. That means sounding the words out using English letters."

"Oh—okay," Ann grinned. "I'll take your word for it."

Patie laughed.

"Ann, a few minutes ago, you asked me if I wanted to talk about Bettye Jo, the lady who was killed. I haven't answered your question yet. You are right. I am troubled about her getting killed and a few hours ago I was beating myself over the head about it. I don't need to talk about it for me, but I'll be glad to tell you what happened, if you want me to do that."

"I'd like to know what happened to her—but—Patie?"

That sounded serious to the host, the way his guest phrased that statement in question form.

Corbin looked across the table at Ann and held his gaze there for a moment, waiting for her to continue. When she failed to say anything else, he quizzed, "Yes?"

"I just want you to know I'm asking as a friend, not a reporter."

"Great, Ann, I really appreciate that. I never really thought differently."

"I notice you said 'really.'"

Patie grinned real big. "Well, you can't stop being a newspaper woman any more than I can stop being a preacher. That makes both of us suspect when we start asking questions. Anyway—thank you for being such a good friend to me that your concern is more for me than for developing a story."

24

Ann looked a little surprised. "Well, I do hope I'm that good a friend to you, Patie—but I meant Bettye Jo. I asked as a friend of Bettye Jo."

CHAPTER THREE
MUSCADINES AND MADNESS

Patie jumped, lay there a second or two, rolled over and looked at the clock. It was 6:30 a. m. Did I hear a bump? He silently asked himself. Then he heard it again, a loud knock on his door. His front door. His *only* door. The thought hit him for the very first time. I don't have a back door to this place, stuck as it is back into these boulders. What if I had a fire in the front of the house? Humh!

"Preacher!" the loud male voice bellowed. "You 'wake?"

"Yeah," Patie called back. "Just a minute." He swung his feet out of bed, stood, and stretched. Slipping on a pair of Bermuda shorts, a tee shirt, and his old floppy houseshoes, he made his way out of the bedroom and into the large living room- kitchen area. Glancing at his coffeepot, he noticed it had not come on yet. He reached for the "on" button, but before he could punch it, it clicked on, issuing the distinctive "blurp" sound of its first perk. Walking swiftly to the door, he reached down to unlock it. It wasn't locked. He had forgotten to lock it last night. Oh, the wonder of living in a small Southern town, he pondered, as he swung the door open. He looked squarely into the face of Lester Junkin, who was holding a large aluminum pan and smiling.

"Preacher, you like muscadines?"

"Oh—mornin', Lester—oh—muscadines?"

"Yeah, muscadines. Good crop this year, seems lik'. Comin' in a little early, too. You lik' 'em?"

"Well, oh, yeah, of course, Lester, everybody likes muscadines, I reckon, don't they? Come on in," Corbin invited, holding the door open.

"Jest' 'bout," the visitor replied, walking through the open door, holding the pan with both hands. "Whur' ken' I set 'em?"

"I'll take 'em," Patie answered, reaching for the pan. "Thank you, Lester. Nothing any bettern' muscadines."

"'Cept scupernons."

"Scupernons?" the preacher asked over his shoulder, walking to his kitchen counter. "Are those the white muscadines?"

"Yeah. But they don't grow wild, not 'round here, nohow."

"Are these wild?" Patie asked, reaching into a cabinet for a large bowl.

"Un hunh. Growin' over Bear Creek. I git' me 'bout ten pieces o' wood 'bout 'lik' a' axe handle and I walk up and down Bear Creek evr' year 'bout this time—wal'—actually usually a little latern' now cause they a' little early this year. Anyhow, I walk up an' down Bear Creek, find muscadine vines 'agrowin' up in the trees on the bank. I throw my pieces o' wood up in the vines, knock the muscadines off an' when they fall into the water, I jest scoop 'em up."

By the time Lester had told the story of how he had gathered the muscadines, Patie had poured the wild grapes into the large bowl and was handing the empty pan back to his visitor. "How long you been doing it, Lester?"

"All my life—since I'se a little boy. Been doin' it all my life. You know how to make jelly, Preacher?"

The preacher tried not to frown, but he felt his face do it anyway. He hoped the large man hadn't noticed. "Make jelly?"

"Yes, Sir. Make jelly. Nothin' bettern' muscadine jelly 'cept maybe scupernon' jelly. 'Course you can mix 'em."

"You can mix muscadines and scupernons and make jelly from both of them—oh—mixed?"

"Um humh, shore ken'."

"So muscadines and scupernons are that much alike? I mean, that you can mix 'em and make jelly?"

"'Shore are."

"Humh," Patie pondered out loud, trying desperately to keep from grinning, which he was determined not to do . Lester had brought him a wonderful gift from a pure and generous heart. And he had worked for it. The two men had come from two totally different cultures, but I'm in his culture now, he's not in mine, the preacher thought, and I'm a minister. Corbin was determined to push any trace of a smile from his face.

"But jelly ain't the only thang' you ken' make from muscadines thet's good, Preacher."

At that moment, Patie realized he had been a bad host. "Have a seat, Lester, and let me get you a cup of coffee."

"Ain't got time, Preacher. You ' ken' make sumpin' outa ever' part of a muscadine 'cept the seed an' I hear tell some folks are even a' crushin' 'em up into a powder an' takin' it fer' health reasons."

"Like grape seed extract?" Patie asked.

"Hunh? Wal', I dunno'. I recken'. Anyhow, you ken' make a mus-cadine-hull pie outta' the hulls and muscadine butter outa' the pulp."

Corbin nodded his head, letting his visitor know he understood what he was saying. "I may have a little problem, though," he admitted.

"What's thet'?"

"I've never made muscadine jelly, Lester, and I've certainly never made muscadine-hull pie—nor muscadine butter from the pulp. Wonder what I could—"

"'At ain't no hill fer' a stepper, Preach," the farmer interrupted.

"How's that?" Patie asked.

"Wal', plenty o' women in the church would be mighty pleased to come out here and make all 'at fer' yew', Preacher. Or, iffen' yew' wuz' a mind to, yew' could go out to the school an' set' in on at' home economics class fer' a day or two, or at least ast' the teacher 'bout it."

The preacher squinted at his friend, looking carefully at his face.

29

He was almost certain he saw a slight smile on it. And when his early-morning visitor started down the steps, Patie was almost certain he heard a muffled laugh. Or could it have been a grunt? Over his shoulder, Lester yelled. "Need to put them muscadines in the refrigerator, Preach."

Patie watched his guest walk to his truck, get into it, and drive out his driveway. Suddenly a big grin swept across his face. "Umh hunh" he blurted out loud. "Here I am trying not to laugh at some of these country customs and I do believe some of my church members may be trying just as hard not to laugh at me." He laughed out loud at the thought of that. He would try to remember to keep that in mind from now on. He looked at his watch. It was 6:45 a. m.

Patie poured himself a mug of coffee, placed it into the microwave for thirty seconds in order to make it a little hotter and smiled. He could still hear Mom's voice almost as clearly as when she actually said it. "How in the world can you drink that coffee so hot, Son? It's boiling! You sure' didn't get that from me."

Sweetening it with a pink and a blue packet, he walked onto his front porch and sat down in the swing. The water from beneath his cabin sounded its normal peaceful gurgle as it flowed down toward Bear Creek. Two squirrels raced up and down the large hickory tree on the edge of his driveway. A quail whistled her mating call in the distance and a bobwhite, a male quail, answered a hundred yards away.

The preacher stopped swinging in respect for his God and prayed, thanking Him for his new home, his ministry, and a new day in which he hoped to glorify Him. By the time he opened his eyes and raised his head, thoughts of the funeral, Phil Appleby, calling Jess, and Ann flooded his consciousness. He would make plans for the funeral and visiting Phil and calling Jess when he got to the office—but Ann—that was another story.

Patie sprang up from the swing, walked smartly back to the microwave and re-heated his coffee. Then he lumbered back to the swing and sat down, a touch of concern attempting to capture his consciousness. Gently pushing himself back and forth, he meditated upon he events with Ann last night. Several parts about her visit had begun to bother him.

First, it was so natural. She seems to be a committed Christian, Patie thought, but we can't establish a lifestyle perforated with instant visits either here or at her house. At the very least it would give the "appearance of evil." Is it possible for us to be friends like Jess and I are? No, probably not, the preacher was forced to admit. Not like Jess and I.

The pastor had to admit he enjoyed her company. Part of him rejected the notion of her visit last night—but—part of him was glad. He had been surprised, though, when Ann admitted to having known Bettye Jo, although they had not known each other that well. They had met at a party at the state park several years earlier and had run into each other in town a couple of times. Once, when she and Phil were at the park, Bettye Jo had dropped into Ann's office for a short visit.

Patie was lodged in a vague psychological mist somewhere between enjoying the notion of being friends with Ann, yet knowing a relationship with her was extremely forbidden, when his cell phone rang. He stopped the swing, gripped his coffee mug and made a dash to his phone which was plugged into the charger and lying on the kitchen counter, "Hello."

"Mornin', Patie. This is Ann. Hope I didn't wake you."

"No, indeed. I've already had a visitor this morning. Brought me some muscadines."

"Do I know her?"

Patie laughed. "If that was a woman, it was a poor excuse for one—about like I would be. It was Lester Junkin."

Ann chuckled. "Patie, I called to apologize to you about staying so late. The time just kind of got away from me."

"And from me, Ann. Did I thank you for bringing the delicious food by?"

"Yes, two or three times."

"Well, thank you again. It was really good!"

"Thank you. You accept my apology?"

31

"Oh, of course, Ann. My goodness, you have nothing to apologize for."

"Thank you, Patie. May the Lord strengthen and guide you with the funeral and with Phil."

"Thank you. Be praying for me."

"I will."

"Umh," Patie moaned immediately after hanging up. "I don't know, Corbin. I don't know. Better be smart!" he counseled himself.

"Mornin', Dimples," Patie called out immediately after entering his office. He hadn't seen her but he knew she was there—for three reasons. Her car was outside; the door between the offices was open; and he heard her making noise.

"Mornin', Patie. You alright?" she asked, sticking her head into the preacher's office, her big eyes twinkling, but her perpetual smile having diminished somewhat. That meant she was worried.

"Fine, thank you."

"Don't forget Holie Preacher's Club this morning."

The preacher started to repeat her reminder but stopped—and thought. "Don't—forget—" The preacher started to repeat her reminder again but stopped. That's a strange statement. Where did that come from?

"Why do you say that, Dimples? I mean—why do you remind me this morning about Holie Preacher's Club?" Patie had slowly walked over to where Dimples still stood, her head protruding through the doorway.

"I thought you might really need it this mornin'."

"This morning," Patie repeated. "Why this mornin', I mean, in particular?"

"On account of last night."

"Last night?"

32

"Yeah, you know. Mrs. Appleby."

"Oh, you mean meet with the other preachers? Talk to them about it? Maybe get counsel from them?'

"Won't hurt," the secretary declared.

"No, it won't, Dimples. There's wisdom in a multitude of counselors—and safety, according to the Proverbs. You're concerned about me, aren't you?"

Dimples nodded. The twinkle had not left her eyes but the smile was gone. "Was the pecan pie good?"

Corbin thought he heard the question right but he wasn't absolutely certain. "What?"

"Did you like the pecan pie?"

"Did you make that pecan pie, Dimples?"

The secretary nodded again, turned quickly and moved back toward her desk.

Patie called out loudly. "It was great pie, Dimples. Thank you. And, Dimples!"

She stopped and partially turned her head. "Yes sir?"

"Thank you for something else. Thank you for being concerned about me. I'm alright, I promise."

Dimples said nothing nor did she look at the pastor. Patie suspected there might have been the sparkle of a tear in her eye.

"Dimples," the preacher called after her again. "Would you hold my phone calls, please, except from Jess Gingrich or from Birmingham?"

"Yes, Sir."

As soon as the preacher sat down, he picked up the telephone and dialed Jess. Dorothy, Jess's wife, answered. After a few pleasantries were exchanged, she said, "Hold on, Patie, I'll dial Jess."

A moment later Corbin heard the deep and comforting voice of his human spiritual father on the phone. " Pate. How you doing, my Brother?"

It took Patie a little while to answer that question, a fact which carried far more importance for Patie than Jess could ever have imagined. Fifteen minutes later, Corbin had told Jess everything, including his own internal struggle with self-condemnation, sickness of soul and spirit, and his wrestling with the teachings of Scripture concerning personal responsibility for someone else's sin, as in Phil Appleby's case.

"From what you say, Patie, and the strong tone of your voice, I would say you seem to have settled your doubts," Jess observed.

"I really have, Jess. By God's magnificent grace."

"Speaking of grace. I know you read Dr. Chaffer's book on grace when you were in seminary, Patie, but do you have a copy of it?"

"No, I don't. I would love to have one, but I thought you said it was out of print."

"It is. Has been for years. But I just bought another one over the internet. It's yours."

"No, Jess, that book's too valuable. Although I would like to have it, I remember what you told me my first year at seminary about the book's rarity. Lewis Sperry Chaffer sure nailed the Biblical teaching on God's grace. But I can't take that book from—"

"Hush," Jess teasingly interrupted. "You're my spiritual child and you'll do exactly what I tell you to do."

Patie laughed out loud. "Okay, okay, Papa. I'll take it. I assume you have another one."

"You wouldn't be getting it if I didn't," Jess chuckled. "I'll Fed Ex it to you. I guess Fed Ex reaches Tishrock, doesn't it?"

"It does. Thank you, Jess."

"You're welcome, Patie. Call me after you visit the husband."

Patie hung the telephone up, leaned back in his chair and took a deep breath. A gentle smile altered the lines of his face as he recalled his first meeting with Jess, his praying to receive Christ in the Eagle Pass preacher's office and all that Jess had done for him afterward. *I wonder if that turkey knows how much he means to me,* he thought. *Of course he does,* the preacher silently concluded. *Someone led him to Christ, too.*

Pushing himself out of the chair, he walked quickly over to Dimples' office. He could see her standing at one of the filing cabinets and he was about to ask her about Jack, her husband, when the telephone rang. The secretary pivoted around and picked up the telephone, glancing up at her boss. "Tishrock Community Church. Yes, m'am. May I ask who's calling? Yes, m'am."

Punching a button on her telephone, she looked at Patie. "It's Sissy Clayton."

"I'll pick up in my office, Dimples. Thank you."

Dimples nodded, punched the button again and gently declared, "He'll be right with you, Mrs. Clayton."

"Brother Corbin? This is Sissy."

"Yes, Sissy."

"Brother Corbin, I called to let you know the arrangements."

"Good. Thank you for calling early."

"I'm with Dr. Devonshire at the funeral home. Visitation will be from 6:00 to 9:00 o'clock tonight at the funeral home. The funeral service will be at 10:00 o'clock tomorrow morning and we'll go from there to the cemetery."

As Sissy spoke, Patie wrote the times and places on a note pad. "Could you give me the address of the funeral home?"

"Just a minute, Brother Corbin," Sissy stated. "I'll have to get that."

Patie heard the grieving daughter ask someone to give her the address. While she was waiting on that person and Patie was waiting on her, he marveled at the young woman's strength. Her voice was soft but also strong. He could hear the grief but he could hear her faith, too. What a joy, he thought, that she knows her mother is with the Lord. What an intensified tragedy this would be if she didn't know that.

A few seconds later Sissy gave the preacher the address. Then she quietly asserted, "Brother Corbin, if you can't make it here for visitation, we would certainly understand. I know it's a long way for you to come."

"I'll be there, Sissy. I want to be there. I may not be able to get there by 6:00 o'clock, but I'll be there by 7:00 or 7:30."

"Thank you so much, Brother Corbin."

"You're welcome, Sissy. Are you doing okay?"

"Yes, sir," the saddened young woman confessed. "I'm doing okay. I just thank our loving God that Mama was saved. And thank you again, Brother Corbin."

"Oh, Honey, when you thanked God, you thanked the right Person. To Him be the glory," Patie whispered, feeling his own voice soften almost supernaturally.

"Yes," Sissy agreed, the sorrow evident in her voice. "To him be the glory. Brother Corbin?"

"Yes?"

"Brother Corbin, I don't exactly know what to do about this. Ronnie Ogden called and said she and Fred were coming."

CHAPTER FOUR
A Courageous Grief

When he hung the telephone up, Patie sprang out of his chair and walked briskly to the window, shaking his head. Ronnie and Fred coming to the funeral! I'll say one thing for the two of them, Corbin thought, still shaking his head in disbelief—they have guts—or maybe a total indifference for righteousness, which is more likely. Probably coming to exhibit their own self-righteousness or maybe to declare publicly by their presence, "What we were doing wasn't wrong—at least not for us—maybe for someone else—not for us."

No sooner had the preacher entertained these thoughts than he regretted it. I can't read the intentions of their hearts, he reminded himself. They're going to hear the Gospel in the service. Maybe God has motivated them to come! Wonder if they know I'm going to be there? Wonder if they know I'm going to handle part of the service? He had not wanted to ask Sissy those questions—not under the circumstances.

Standing at the window, his hands thrust hard into his trousers pockets, he was considering these things when Dimples opened the door between their offices. "Patie?"

The pastor turned toward his secretary, "Yes."

"Maggie called while you were on the phone. She said you had asked her to call this morning.

Patie Corbin had always exulted in the fact that he had a "quick" mind. He had been told that by numerous people who seemed to know him best. But at that precise moment he could not invoke from memory what he had asked her to call about. He remembered her—and he remembered her problem—but he could not seem to recall why he had asked her to call back. "Did she say why I asked her to call?" Patie blurted out, not considering how stupid his statement might sound to Dimples.

"No, sir," the secretary replied softly. "I 'spect she thought you would know that." Her eyes were twinkling, a slight smile on her face.

Corbin thought about her comment for a second and laughed. "Yes, I think you are right, Dimples. That would be a reasonable assumption."

"Mills came home last night."

"What?" Patie acted surprised, knowing Mills was supposed to come home. Maggie, of course had told him the day before.

"Mills came home last night," Dimples repeated.

"He did? How did you know that? Don't answer. I know. This is Tishrock."

Dimples smiled broadly.

That's it, Patie suddenly remembered to himself. She was to call to let me know what Mills did—and what all happened. "Did she leave her telephone number?'

"Yes, Sir," the secretary answered, holding up a note from a note pad. "She said to call when you could."

"Before I do that, Dimples, we need to talk a few minutes."

"Want me to sit down?"

"Might as well," Patie responded, as the two of them moved to chairs.

Seated now, the preacher explained, "Dimples, I have to go to Birmingham this afternoon—to visitation tonight and— "

"Visitation's tonight?" Dimples interrupted, apparently surprised.

Patie nodded. "And the service is tomorrow morning at 10:00 o'clock. Sissy asked me to participate in the funeral service tomorrow. I'm going to miss our service tonight."

"Well," the secretary uttered quietly. "It can be mostly prayer time anyway. And Abe can handle it."

"Abe Goodson?"

"Un hunh."

"Good. I'll call him. I just dislike missing the first Wednesday church supper and service."

"Folks'll understand. 'Course, we'll miss you."

"I hope so, both of those," Patie grinned. "One other thing, Dimples. Pearl Sue was to bring Millaree and Fern to see me tomorrow. Would you call them and reschedule their visit. Either Friday or sometime next week?"

"Yes, Sir. Anything else?"

"Don't think so. I'll be back in the office Friday morning and I'll have my cell phone—if you need me."

"Maggie, this is Patie Corbin."

"Mornin', Brother Corbin."

"Did Mills come home, Maggie?" Patie realized he almost certainly knew the answer to that question. He had learned to trust Dimples' underground method of gathering information, but he could not tell his counselee that. He had to ask.

"Yes, Sir. He came home."

Reaching into his desk drawer and pulling Maggie's file out, he asked, "How was he? I mean, what was his attitude?"

"Well, it was alright, I guess. He didn't seem to be as excited about it as I thought he might be, or maybe as I wanted him to be."

The preacher quickly scanned through the still brief file. Of course he had seen her twice and the last time was only yesterday. He marveled in the fact that he needed to look at the file to remember everything Maggie had told him only hours earlier. But that wasn't all bad, he reasoned. Forces a counselor to carefully read the file before giving direction. That, in turn, means he had better record all important information on paper, not try to hold it in his mind.

"I need to ask you some questions, Maggie. I have your file out and I'm gonna' write everything down. It's gonna' take a few minutes. That okay?"

"Yes, Sir."

"Good. Well, here's the first one. Did he bring all his clothes home?"

"I think so. It took us a while to unload the car. If he left anything over there, it wasn't much."

"Good. Now, did he mention the other woman?"

"No, Sir."

"Did you?"

"No, Sir," she answered again quickly, authoritatively.

"Maggie, this question is a tough one and I want you to think very carefully before you answer. Why did you not mention her?"

Maggie hesitated. The preacher could hear slight sounds coming from her and he knew she was considering the question and the answer to it. A few moments later she spoke—or tried to. "Well—ah—Brother Corbin—ah—I—oh—should I have?"

"No, no, I didn't mean that, Maggie. I'm trying to look at what you were going through when he walked back into that house. It would have been very natural for you to have asked him what he told her about his coming home. But you didn't ask and that's good. Now, I need to know why you didn't ask. Was it to avoid an argument? Were you afraid he would get mad and immediately leave again? Was it because you were hurting so badly at what he had done that you couldn't bear hearing her name? Were you saving that question until he has been home several days, before asking it?"

Again Maggie delayed answering, and Patie knew she was care-

40

fully considering the question. And that, too, was good. God has given women special sensitivities concerning their husbands—supernatural, almost—insight growing out of Genesis 3:16, where God told Eve, among other things, "Your desire shall be for your husband."

The preacher smiled when he considered that declaration. A wife, though she may be facing an opposite direction, knows when her husband looks up and down the figure of another woman. And—she often knows much more about her husband even than she realizes—or than he knows about her.

"Well, I—oh—Brother Corbin, maybe a little bit of all of them but probably mostly because I didn't want to start an argument."

Patie was glad to hear her say what she did, not because her answer was the easiest one with which to deal—it wasn't. It might be the most difficult one. He was glad to hear her answer because it meant that she had considered the questions and *knew* the answer.

"That's great Maggie, I mean that you have identified the reason you didn't ask him if he told the other woman he was going home. But that other side of that coin is that you were afraid he would get angry if you asked, isn't it?"

The words quickly burst from Maggie's mouth. "I *know* he would." She sniffed at the certainty of it.

The preacher figured if Maggie believed that, Mills probably indeed might have grown angry. Maggie's belief would become an open female window through which the minister could view the inner workings of Mills' mind, emotions, and desires. After what the husband had done, left his wife for another woman and moved out, not only out of the house but out of town, he had no right to grow angry at his wife at the mention of the other woman's name. Maggie had, in fact, not mentioned the other woman but it was because she feared that he would become angry. And—if it were true that he would have, then there existed reasons for it. After all, if he were truly sorry and repentant enough to come home, he really ought to be broken-hearted over his actions, not arrogant enough to get mad. Patie

41

wanted to explain all of that and more to Maggie but he wanted to know for certain that she could handle the knowledge correctly.

"Maggie, we need to talk about this a little, but I don't want, in any way, to interrupt the relationship between you and Mills. You need to know these things , though, and I may say some strong things to you, things which you may not want to hear. Do you think you want me to do this?"

Maggie hesitated. Patie knew it would be a little difficult for her to agree to submit to his directions when she didn't know what he would say. It would indeed require some faith on her part, faith in him and his counsel.

A moment or two after the preacher asked Maggie the question, she answered. "Yes, Sir, I think so—I mean I don't know what you— "

Corbin gently interrupted her. "I know, Maggie. I know it's a little tough to subject yourself to an open-ended concept like this. I want you to know, though, that everything I say is designed for three things. First, to glorify our Lord. Second, to make you stronger. And third, to help strengthen your relationship with Mills. I will tell you nothing, or at least I'll try desperately not to, which contradicts Scripture. I ask you to trust me on that one. Can you?"

"I trust you, Brother Corbin."

"Good. Now, having said that, would you allow me to pray with you?"

Patie acknowledged four "vitamins" in Christian growth: Study of the Word; Fellowship with other believers; Witnessing; and Prayer. The Study of God's word purifies one's mind; Fellowship tends to increase our faith; Witnessing builds exuberance for the Lord; Prayer opens up the lines of communication between God and us through which He gives us many things, including trust and strength. Combined, these four activities help transform us more closely into the image of Christ.

There was another reason the pastor wanted to pray with Maggie, however. He wanted her to become a little calmer—and—he wanted to give her a few minutes to consider what he had said.

"Yes, Sir," she agreed.

Two minutes later, Patie had prayed. Then he quietly cautioned, "Maggie, it is critically important from this moment on, that you see yourself as a minister of the gospel, not a hurt wife, which, of course, you are."

Corbin hesitated for a moment. Maggie said nothing.

"The fact that you are a hurt wife, will, of course, control you if you allow it. You will want to see sorrow in him, as anyone would want and it may frustrate you if it doesn't come quickly. You may be tempted to try to force him into sorrow if it doesn't come quickly. But only God working into Mills' conscience will bring Godly sorrow. How you respond to him *can* provide an environment through which the Holy Spirit may work, though."

When Patie stopped talking for a second, more to catch his breath than anything else, Maggie blurted out, "I don't understand, Brother Corbin, what do you mean by that?" The preacher heard what he thought might be microscopic tones of embryonic frustration at the notion of what Patie was beginning to suggest. He did not want it to grow.

"Maggie, what I mean is this. You are a Christian. As a Christian, you have been made a minister and given a ministry." Then quickly, Patie began quoting II Corinthians 5:17-20 from memory to the hurting counselee, but speaking very slowly and emphasizing the key words, "new creature," and "reconciled us to Himself" and "given to us the ministry of reconciliation." When he finished, he waited a few seconds, then he asked, "Maggie, do you see what God is saying in those verses?"

"Yes, Sir, I do. But do you think He's talking to people like me? I mean—I'm the one who's been wronged! Why would God expect ME to try to minister to Mills? And how do I do that anyway? I don't know how to minister to him!"

The preacher had not planned to introduce the woman's past into the conversation unless absolutely necessary. It had become necessary.

"Maggie, my Christian sister," Patie almost whispered, speaking very slowly and deliberately, "we are all sinners. Did you know Rahab,

43

who is in the righteous line of our Lord Jesus Christ, was a prostitute? Look at Matthew 1:5 and read Joshua, Chapter 2. She was the great grandmother of King David. But she was forgiven. You, too, Maggie, have sinned, as have I. Do you not remember telling me you had been unfaithful?"

Patie waited for an answer. He received none. Still he waited. Finally, he whispered, "Maggie?"

"Yes, Sir?"

"Isn't that so?"

She said nothing.

"Isn't that so?" Patie repeated.

"Yes, Sir," she breathed softly.

"Maggie, I believe God is giving you an opportunity to minister to your husband—to help make up for what you have done. And, on top of that, to be a positive Godly influence in your husband's life—and—it doesn't stop there—to help develop a Godly marriage and home."

"Can you guarantee all of that, Brother Corbin?" Maggie's voice was pleading, hopeful not confrontational.

"No, I can't, Maggie. Mills is a free moral agent— "

"Sir?" Maggie interrupted. A free–oh—moral?"

"A free moral agent," Patie repeated. Some people say 'free will,' that Mills has a 'free will.' He may respond positively to you or negatively, we cannot say. But we can say this. Even if he responds negatively, two things will occur in you. You will know you have done what God says is right—that you have done your best. And, God will bless you with inner joy and peace with which to get you through whatever Mills does. That is what God's Word does promise and the Scriptures cannot be broken."

"Then, what do I do, Brother Corbin?" Maggie's voice was soft, tearful. The preacher believed she was as sincere as a broken, but hopeful heart could be. The words were music to his ears.

At 4 o'clock that afternoon, Jamie and Sissy's door bell rang. From their master bathroom, Bettye Jo's daughter called out with a broken voice to her husband. "Jamie, can you get that?"

"Yes," Jamie responded, walking out of the closet where he had been looking for a dark tie. "Got it."

As Jamie made his way through the now deserted living room toward the door, he speculated that someone else was bringing food. The young, transplanted "Cajun" husband and business executive smiled through misty eyes as he considered that–Southerners expressing their love and compassion at a time of death through gifts of food. He had often seen people do that, where he grew up in Houma, Louisiana. Glancing into the dining room, he wondered if anything else could be placed on the already laden table. And, he was still thinking about it when he opened his front door. Fred and Ronnie Ogden stood there, hand in hand, reticent reserved smiles upon their faces, which seemed to Jamie to reflect a measure of doubt and worry.

The grieving husband and father, as had Sissy, expected Fred and Ronnie to visit the funeral home or attend the funeral, or perhaps both, but they had not expected them to visit their home. "Fred, Ronnie," the surprised man greeted. "How are you?" he asked, extending his right hand to each of them.

"Fine," Ronnie replied quickly. "We're so, so sorry, Jamie. Is Sissy here? Did we catch you at a bad time?" Fred smiled weakly and nodded his agreement with his impulsive wife.

"No, no, not at all. Won't you come in?" Jamie invited, moving out of the doorway.

"Thank you," Ronnie responded, walking into the room, her husband following. "Is Sissy here?" she asked again.

"Yes, she's in the bedroom, dressing. We plan to get to the funeral home at 5:00 o'clock."

The Ogdens did not answer.

"Let me go tell her you are here. I don't know how close to being

45

ready she is. Please sit down and make yourselves at home. Can I get you anything to drink?"

Both visitors shook their heads. Fred answered, "No, thank you."

With that, Jamie turned and walked briskly out of the living room, down the hall and into the bedroom. Sissy heard him come in and before he had a chance to say anything, she stuck her head out of the bathroom, "Who was that, Honey?"

"You won't believe it, Sissy. It's the Ogdens."

Sissy stiffened, and stood straight up. She took a quick step out of the bathroom, her face, already streaked a little with her tears, was wrenched. The word exploded from her throat. "WHO?"

"The Ogdens."

"What are they doing *here*? I knew they were coming to the funeral but why would they come *here*? Did they say? I mean—I guess they are trying to be respectful, but—" Sissy's voice trailed off. She stood before her husband in her housecoat, the little makeup upon her face failing to cover the tear stains, her shoulders drooped in discomposure. She quickly fought the anger which she felt, but her disconcertion was very evident. Jamie, too, was very displeased. He resented the effect it *would* have and *was* having on his wife and the lack of grace it evidenced in the visiting couple.

"I don't know for certain why they came by here, Honey. I would like to believe it was out of concern for you. A show of love and respect, maybe. But I confess, I'm not sure I really believe that."

"I'm not sure I do, either, Honey," Sissy agreed. She knew her husband. She could see the wheels turning. "Then why?"

Jamie took his wife's hand and led her to the bed. Sitting down beside her, he turned toward her. "Sweetheart, I hope I'm wrong, but I wonder if they came by here to talk to us alone—maybe try to find out what we know. I'm hoping I'm wrong," he repeated, but—"

Sissy interrupted him. "I think you are right, Jamie," a dark expression enveloping her face, her eyes narrowing, her heart beating rapidly, the veins on her forehead suddenly pulsating. "I'm not going to come out and talk to them."

"What do you want me to do?"

Sissy shook her head. "I *cannot*—I mean, I *cannot believe* they would have the gall to—how could they—at a time like this?" her mind moving beyond Jamie's question.

"I may be wrong, Sweetheart."

Sissy shook her head again. "No, I don't think so. That's what they want. They want to feel us out. They realize they can't really get a reading on what we know at the funeral home or at the church or cemetery tomorrow. That's what they want. Jamie," she whispered, tears of sorrow *and* anger rolling down her cheeks. "Will you handle them for me?"

"Of course, I will, Sweetheart. What do you want me to do?"

"What I want you to do, I can't ask you to do," Sissy admitted, the muscles in her face relaxing slightly.

Jamie smiled.

"Would you go back out there and tell them we know everything? That I'm not prepared to talk to them right now?" Sissy hesitated. Jamie waited. "And, Jamie, would you tell them that we're Christians? And that we're trying with all of our hearts to forgive Daddy and both of them? And that we know Mom is in Heaven with Jesus right now?"

Jamie twisted toward his wife, and gently placed both arms around her neck. He drew her tenderly closer, not noticing nor caring that the tears and moist makeup was staining his white shirt. "Sissy, I've been proud of you many times in my life but never more than right now. God has given you a Christ-like strength that I'm not certain I would be able to exhibit in these same circumstances."

Muffled upon his chest, the grieving wife whispered, "Yes, you would."

A minute later the faithful husband walked back into his living room. Fred stood. Ronnie stared at him, conscious of the necessity of maintaining a soft expression upon her face. When Jamie sat down, so did

Fred.

Neither of the visitors spoke. They both waited for Jamie. They were not forced to wait long. Whether it was his Cajun upbringing or his commitment to the Lord and his wife, he wasted no time opening the conversation.

"Fred, Ronnie, Sissy wanted me to tell you that she and I know everything: what the four of you were doing; that Mom decided to stop; we know she met Patie Corbin and prayed to receive Christ and how Dad and you were, as it turned out, violently opposed to her stopping the relationship."

When Jamie reached that point in the conversation, he hesitated and noticed the facial expressions and body language of his two visitors. Both looked as though they were actually sick.

Jamie continued. "She also wanted me to tell you that we know Mom is in Heaven today with our Lord Jesus Christ and that—"

With that statement, Ronnie suddenly leaned forward and blurted out, "Well, of course she is, Jamie."

Jamie stared at Ronnie. Her face was flushed now, and her eyes narrowed. The son-in-law knew he could not allow that comment to go unchallenged.

"Mrs. Ogden," he whispered formally, "I mean we *know* Mom is in Heaven right now. It's not a glib concept nor an opiate for a suffering daughter and son-in-law. We *know* Mom is forgiven for the sin which she was committing with you and Dad and is in Heaven. We *know* that, we don't just hope it."

Ronnie leaned back again. Her face was still flushed. Anger flashed through her eyes.

"Sissy and I want you to know something else, too. We are Christians and we are trying with all our hearts to forgive Dad and the two of you."

Then Jamie added something which Sissy had not asked him to say. "We know soon God will give us the ability to forgive you just as God

48

for Christ's sake has forgiven us. And just as God loves us, we will be able to love you."

As though sitting on springs which had suddenly been released, Ronnie stood. Fred said nothing but Ronnie seemed unable to remain silent. "Well, that's nice Jamie. We love you, too. We'll see y'all at the funeral home." Her words were proper but the tone of voice was very caustic.

CHAPTER FIVE

A PRESSURE OF A DIFFERENT KIND

"Finally," Patie breathed out loud, "the four lane." He had left his house an hour before and drove to Federal Highway78, a four lane road from Memphis to Birmingham. The two lane road from Tishrock through Belmont to 78 was narrow and curvy, which had afforded him little time to think about much more than driving. But now, on the four lane, his mind traveled back to his two visits with Maggie, one in his office and the one on the phone a few hours earlier. Had he left anything out?

Patie mentally listed everything he had said to her: make a commitment every day to view yourself *first* as a minister of the Gospel, not a hurt wife and Mills as a ministry, not a husband; speak the truth in love to Mills; do not argue or try to drive him into being a good husband; if he hurts you tell him the truth that he's hurting you; and if you shed a tear or two, that's okay, Jesus wept; then say "I forgive you." Don't be suspicious but be prepared for the possibility of two things—finding out he hasn't broken the relationship with the other woman completely off, and for him leaving again; spend some time alone in Bible study and prayer each day; and keep a relationship diary each day for me to see at our next appointment.

The preacher-counselor knew there was much more to be dealt with and ministered to than that which he had given Maggie so far, but these things would begin to construct a foundation upon which a good marriage might be built. Oh, yes, Patie suddenly remembered, he had stressed

51

to Maggie several times. "Don't blame yourself for what Mills did. And don't allow him to blame you." An adulterous man will often try to do that, as he points out to his wife her flaws. "Refuse to argue in defense of yourself, Maggie," Corbin had told her. "Just look him squarely in the eyes and softly say something like, "Mills, I will no more take the guilt for *your* adultery than I would ask you to take the guilt of mine, if I do it."

Satisfied now that he had counseled Maggie to do enough to last until their next appointment, and, perhaps more importantly, he had not counseled her to do anything which would damage the situation, the driver redirected his attention to the road. According to the signs, he was passing through Jasper, Alabama, and Birmingham was about 70 miles away.

All of Dimples' attention was focused upon the items in her bottom desk drawer. She was sitting in her chair with her head pointing almost straight down, looking for a red-leaded pencil—or pen, which ought to have been in her top drawer, but wasn't

"Dimples!"

The voice shocked and astonished the secretary. She jumped, jerked her body upward and bumped her head on the corner of her desk. "WHAT!"

"Oh, Dimples, I keep forgetting you spook easily. I'm sorry." It was Ann Chester. She was standing just inside Dimples' office.

"Hi, Ann," Dimples responded, rubbing her head, having by then raised completely up—without the pencil. "Yeah, I've done that all my life. Got it from my mother, I think. She was always— aw, I've told you that story before. Come on in."

Ann sat down quickly in one of the chairs fronting Dimples' desk. "Patie gone?"

"Umh hunh. Left a couple of hours ago. Y'all have a nice visit last night?"

"Yeah," Ann replied solemnly. "I would have called you last night when I got home but I figured you were already asleep. I knew I would see you today. Did he seem upset to you this morning?"

"Kinda'. He wasn't quite as chipper as he usually is. How did he seem to you last night?"

"About the same as you saw him," Ann surmised. "Kind of— well— introspective, I guess I would describe it–but not bad. He may have been a little more depressed than he appeared to be. You know how men are—gotta' be tough."

"Do I ever," Dimples grinned. "Jack would never go to the doctor if I didn't make him and he would never admit he was worried about anything. But *you* look a little worried."

Ann, whose shoulders were slightly slumped and whose eyes had dropped while her friend was talking, pulled her head up sharply and smiled. "No, not really. I was just thinking how difficult it was probably going to be for Patie over there. I mean, not only is he going to a funeral but it's a funeral where a husband killed a wife whom he had just led to the Lord—and the husband killed her in part because of it."

By the time Ann finished talking, Dimples had formed a wide smile on her face and was staring at her long time friend. But she said nothing.

"What?" Ann blurted out.

"You're worried about Patie," Dimples grinned.

"Well, yeah, a little, I guess. Anybody would be, aren't you?"

"You're worried about Patie," Dimples repeated, still grinning, ignoring Ann's question. "You're really worried about him!"

Ann looked at Dimples for a moment, broke into a large grin herself, then laughed out loud, more because of the look on Dimples' face and the accusing tone of her voice than anything else. "Okay, okay, Miss Psychology, I admit it," she confessed, leaning forward in the chair and looking her friend in the eye. "But he is a friend and a great addition to our town and— "

"Someone you enjoy being with," Dimples quickly inserted.

"Well, yeah, but mostly I don't want him getting discouraged and deciding to leave Tishrock. I have a feeling he's going to add a lot to our town."

"What that boy is gonna' need when he gets back is a party," the secretary suddenly asserted. Her abrupt change didn't surprise the lady editor. But it did amuse her.

"I think so, too," Ann agreed. "When is he coming back?"

"Thursday afternoon, tomorrow. The funeral is in the morning."

"Want to do it tomorrow night?"

Dimples thought for a moment, then declared. "I don't think he could come. Seems like—wait." With those words she sprang from her chair and dashed into the preacher's office. His calendar was lying open on top of his desk. "No," she called back. "He speaks at a Rotary banquet in Iuka tomorrow night. We couldn't plan it by then anyway," she surmised as she walked back into her office. "Not enough time."

"Friday night, then?" Ann asked, then answered her own question. "No, we have a football game here Friday night."

"And Patie is saying the prayer before the game," Dimples remembered.

"Saturday night, then," Ann avowed.

"Saturday night it is!"

"We need to plan it," Ann considered.

"Meet at my house after prayer meeting tonight?"

"Sounds good, Miss Morgan," Ann stated in mock seriousness, as she rose from her chair and walked smartly toward the door. "See you then."

Ann's body language had modified from sadness almost to elation.

The four lane highway 78 *was* four lane alright, but it wasn't interstate. When it got to within fifteen miles of Birmingham, Patie started running into traffic and traffic lights. He glanced at the car clock. It was almost 6:30, which was okay. Visitation started at 6:00 and he would be a little late. But being there the entire time wasn't necessary.

The preacher had already learned to think ahead, to try to mentally picture the situation into which he would be entering, especially if that situation was a new one. And this would definitely be a new situation for him—not attending a funeral—but attending it as a minister of the Gospel. People would be at visitation who might remember his football days. And, of course, he wanted to be a blessing and used of the Lord to comfort Sissy and Jamie as much as possible. Then there were the Ogdens, Ronnie and Fred. He would definitely need to prepare for them, that is, if they came to visitation. Maybe they will decide to come only to the funeral. No, that's not fair, Corbin counseled himself. Maybe they need to come to the visitation! Maybe their hearts will be broken over what Phil did to Bettye Jo, not angered at me. Maybe, if they are there, God has brought them in order for him to share Christ with them. "Lord, if they *are* there," Patie whispered, "please give me the grace and the wisdom to minister to them. And please, Lord, help me get my flesh out of the way—"

"Oh, there it is," Patie blurted out loud, almost a continuation of his prayer. "I-59 and 20." The preacher was upon the intersection so quickly he almost missed the entrance to it. Quickly flipping his signal, he turned upon it, heading east, conscious of the fact that he had given the drivers behind him little notice. Oh, well, he thought, they'll see my Mississippi tag and understand.

Almost immediately after getting onto the freeway which punctured the heart of downtown Birmingham, he turned right onto Elton B. Stephens Expressway which wandered over the high hills to the east of the city and became Highway 280 to Sylacauga and then on to Auburn. That was knowledge which he had forgotten until he saw the signs.

Auburn! "Umh," he wheezed out loud, smiling. Boy, did we ever have some battles with them, he remembered, recalling his football-playing days at Ole Miss.

A minute later he saw it, immediately in front of him, a towering metal figure on top of a very high hill looking down upon its "adopted" city. Vulcan–the Greek name for the god of the forge.

As hard as the old redeemed football player tried he could not keep his mind from darting back to the past. He hated doing that, finding his mind going back to those things which his spirit did not want to remember but which his flesh yearned for. He had prayed Philippians 3:13 and 14 many times, "Forgetting those things which are behind, and reaching forth unto those things which are before, I press toward the mark for the prize of the high calling of God in Christ Jesus." Since becoming a Christian almost four years before, those verses had become very precious to Patie, as had Paul's cry in Romans 7:15 through 25. He understood the import of them, primarily because they were the words of God but also because Paul battled every day. Satan working through the flesh, or old nature of mankind, seeks to control the mind. God the Holy Spirit, of course, does the same thing. In the battle between the flesh and the spirit, the mind becomes the high ground. And as in literal warfare, whoever controls the high ground has a marked advantage and would most likely temporarily win the permanent battle.

The picture in Patie's mind was as clear as the statue before him. While still married at the end of his professional football career, he had brought an Ole Miss coed to Birmingham for the weekend. They had eaten at the restaurant and bar in the Vulcan.

The preacher knew before he made this trip, upon realizing the funeral home and the church were located near the statue, that it would invoke old and sinful memories. "I know both are forgiven and I thank you for that," he prayed out loud as he drove past the statue, looking for the exit to Montevallo Road, the street which would take him to the funeral home. It wasn't true, of course, but it just seemed like praying out loud and hearing the sounds might better help move his mind back under the control of the Holy Spirit.

Patie stood in the lobby of the large funeral home directly in front of the bulletin board which announced the visitation room of each deceased person. The third name down read Mrs. Bettye Jo Appleby, Room 103. He shook his head slightly as he considered the consequences of the last few days. Burning inside his soul lay a mixture of joy and sorrow, tainted with a little anger. Phil had killed Bettye Jo because she would not participate in evil, moral depravity, with the Ogdens and him any more. And she wouldn't participate any longer because she had trusted the Lord Jesus Christ and had become a child of God. And he, an old sinner saved by grace, had experienced the blessing of leading her to the Lord. Phil had no right to do what he did. He could have walked away from his wife, but he didn't. Satan still attacking God's children! That was the source of Patie's anger. Phil had no right to touch God's child, Patie's sister in the Lord.

Corbin was still standing in front of the bulletin board thinking about the anger and experiencing a little guilt for having it, when he remembered what one of his seminary professors had said about that kind of anger. "It's one of the few things which wasn't totally corrupted in the fall of man—anger because of man's cruelty to man, righteous indignation, left over from before the fall." When the professor was asked by a student to further elaborate, the professor explained. "Even when a lost man sees a grown man sexually abuse a child, it produces anger in him. That's a left-over characteristic which God placed in man before the fall." In a later class, the same professor declared, "When a culture sears its collective conscience to a point where anger toward that child abuser is no longer present, that culture would probably do well to prepare itself for the judgement of God."

Patie gently nodded at the memory of the professor's words and walked down the hall to Room 103.

The room was crowded. He stood outside the doorway for a second, noticed the book for visitors to sign, signed it, and eased into the room.

The open casket lay against the far wall of the spacious room. It was surrounded by several large flower arrangements. Only then did he realize he had, in the midst of all the activity, not thought about flowers or a gift, or anything else through which to honor Bettye Jo.

The room itself was partially filled with chairs. People sat in about half of them, other visitors stood in an open area between the chairs and the casket. Some of the people were quietly talking; some sat in chairs saying nothing; some were smiling; not a few were gently crying, handkerchiefs held at the ready in their hands.

Patie needed to meet Sissy and Jamie, of course, and he would do that soon. But he wanted to see Bettye Jo first. When a couple moved away from the casket, and a slight opening developed, he eased into it, standing adjacent to the lovely woman's head. He looked down at her from two feet away, remembering how completely she seemed to have given herself to the Lord, just three days ago, that early morning at the end of the swinging bridge. The longer the preacher stood there looking down at Bettye Jo, the more certain he was he saw it—peace—and a very soft, slight smile, emanating from it.

He had read a book about death which Mom had given to him years before he became a Christian. It was written by a mortician who was a committed believer. In the book, the author insisted he could discern, ninety percent of the time, whether a deceased person whom he attended was a Christian. He went on to explain. "The view the Lord gives them of Himself just before the soul leaves the body places a slight smile upon their faces." Apologetically almost, he went on to describe the look of horror left upon the faces of many who had never expressed or exhibited an interest in God.

Bettye Jo reflected a beautiful peaceful expression.

As the preacher looked down upon the body, a distinctive burning began to occur in his nasal passages, indicating to him that tears might not be far behind. He was thinking about that and Bettye Jo's peaceful expression when a soft female voice to his left gathered his attention.

"Brother Corbin?"

Patie wheeled toward the young woman. He would have known her anywhere. She was almost an exact replica of Bettye Jo, as her mother must have looked twenty years ago. "Yes."

"Brother Corbin, I'm Sissy."

"Sissy," Patie exclaimed, immediately thrusting his right hand toward the young woman. "I would have known you. You are the—"

"Thank you," Sissy interrupted, and ignoring his outstretched hand, gently leaned toward him, placing her cheek against his. "Mother was beautiful. Thank you for the compliment," she smiled, slight streaks on her cheeks indicating her continuing sorrow and heart-brokenness.

Patie saw clearly, in the midst of Sissy's hurt, a strength. Taking both of her hands in his, the preacher looked directly into her eyes, one lone single tear now sliding down the tough old athlete's face. "I am so sorry, Sissy."

"Thank you, Brother Corbin." Then, holding onto one of his hands, Sissy led him away from the crowd of people to a place against the wall near the head of the casket where no one stood. With Patie against the wall and Sissy's back to the crowd, she spoke in barely more than a whisper. "Brother Corbin. I love my mother. But given the opportunity to have her back in sin or see her as she is now, I will take her as she is now."

Patie smiled and nodded. He sensed she wasn't through talking so he said nothing.

"I wanted you to know that, just in case anyone said anything to you. I wanted you to know how grateful Jamie and I are for you allowing the Lord to use you in Mother's life."

"You mean the Ogdens? That they might say something to me?"

Sissy nodded. "Yes, but not only them. Some of Dad's relatives are here, too. Most of them are respectful and educated people but, as much as I love them, many of them have no relationship with the Lord, or church, or anything spiritual. Dad's father and brother have already shown a little—oh—attitude, I guess, about Mother changing and *that* driving Dad away. They kind of blame Mother for what happened."

"Surely not for her death!"

"No, not directly, but I think they *would* blame her openly if she were alive. Now, they blame you for Dad being in jail, charged with killing Mother."

"I'm sorry about that, Sissy, for your sake. I'm sorry your relatives feel as though they need to blame your mother. Please don't worry about them blaming me, okay? Please."

Sissy nodded.

"You promise?"

She smiled. "I promise."

"Two other things, Brother Corbin. I wanted you to know all this now. They are here and they may try to confront you tonight."

"Thank you, Sissy. I know it's hard for you to tell me this. Thank you so much. I'll try to be prepared for it, but I'll sure be praying it won't happen. You said there were two things," Patie asked.

Sissy nodded again. "The Ogdens will be here tonight."

The moment Sissy whispered that discomfiting fact to the preacher, she turned and looked toward a young man nearby, who was holding the hands of a little boy and a slightly older little girl. They immediately started moving through the crowd. When they arrived, Sissy smiled and said, "Now, Brother Corbin, I would like for you to meet my family. This is Jamie, and this is Alexandra, our daughter, and this—this young man—is Caney, our son.

Patie smiled and shook each of their hands. "I am really glad to meet you both—beautiful young lady and I imagine a very lively young man."

"Too lively," Sissy smiled. "We wanted them to come see their grandmother and to meet you. A friend is taking them to his house now."

Leaning over the children, the mother gently directed, "Say goodbye to Brother Corbin."

Alexandra looked up at the minister, smiled and said, "Goodbye, Brother Corbin." Caney said nothing and pulled on his father's hand. A few seconds later they had disappeared through the throng of visitors.

Turning toward Sissy, Patie commented. "Caney is sort of an unusual name. Family name?"

Sissy daubed the tears from her eyes and smiled again. "Kind of. Jamie is from Houma, Louisiana. His family grew sugar cane and everyone called him Caney when he was growing up. We named Caney for him."

"Is Jamie's dad still alive?"

"No," Sissy answered quietly. "He was killed in a hurricane several years ago. He was a fine man. Loved the Lord."

"That's great," Patie said. "He must have had a great influence on Jamie."

"Yes. And on me. We loved him very much."

Changing the subject, Corbin reflected, "Sissy, I know you need to visit with everyone. Don't worry about me, okay?"

Sissy nodded. "You have a room?"

"Yes, near here. I have one reserved."

"We'll take care of that," she whispered.

"Don't you worry about that, either, okay?"

Sissy smiled and turned away but said nothing. Suddenly she wheeled back toward Patie. Her voice was quiet but her eyes were a little wider and her face was slightly darkened in a flush. "There they are, Brother Corbin. I cannot believe they have the gall to come here tonight, but there they are—the Ogdens."

Patie looked through the crowd and spotted the couple. He did not believe Ronnie and Fred had yet seen him but he was certain they would before long. He would not run from them. As Sissy walked away, he turned his face partly toward the wall and prayed, "Lord, please give me a gentle loving spirit and please turn this confrontation into a quiet ministry of love, for your glory." When he turned back around, they were no more than ten feet away and walking toward him.

CHAPTER SIX

A CASKET AND A CONFRONTATION

As Sissy and Jamie slowly drifted through the mass of people, they saw the Ogdens moving toward Patie. Sissy leaned over to her husband and asked, "You see that?"

Jamie nodded.

"What do you think we ought to do, Honey?"

Shaking his head, Jamie quietly reflected. "Nothing. I think it will be alright, Sweetheart. I don't believe things will get out of control in here. You visit with people on the other side of the room. I'll be back in a few minutes."

Patie turned around to look directly into the faces of two people whom he *assumed* would be adversarial but whom he prayed would *not* be. He had already decided on his reactions if they verbally challenged him. First, he would force a pleasant expression onto his face. He would not exhibit fear nor resentment. And he would allow them to greet him first. If they approached him and did not greet him, only then would he extend his hand and greet them by name.

From four feet away, the pair broke through the assembly of visiting mourners and stood immediately in front of the new pastor. Neither was smiling. Nor did either extend a hand.

Neither did Patie. It took a measure of discipline for him. His nature was to smile at old friends or even old acquaintances, and extend a warm handshake. And even now, under this most unusual circumstance, even extraordinarily unusual, his nature compelled him to do it. He resisted, looked Fred directly in the eye, then Ronnie, then Fred again—and waited.

A moment later, Fred spoke. His voice was very hoarse, indicating to Patie either deep anger, which, because of the surroundings, would be suppressed, or nervousness. "Patie." He did not extend his right hand. Neither did Ronnie, who said nothing, but continued to glare at him.

"Fred," Patie replied. Turning to his old college girlfriend, he held his eyes on her for a couple of seconds and greeted her with a medium-loud and very firm voice. "Ronnie."

The hostile woman did not reply. Neither did she remove her hardened gaze from Patie's face.

"We want to talk to you." Fred's voice wasn't overly assertive, but it wasn't broken, either. His eyes were squinting and there seemed to be a very fine line of perspiration across his upper lip.

Patie noticed all of that and he almost smiled. At that point he realized Fred and Ronnie had probably rehearsed this meeting, just as he had.

"I would like to talk to both of you, too. Would you like to—" Patie was about to ask them if they would like to find a quiet place in another room.

Fred interrupted him. "This looks like a good place."

Patie considered Fred's proposal. Why would he want to talk about anything serious, and apparently the conversation would be serious, in the middle of a crowd of people in these circumstances. Ah, the preacher reasoned, he probably knows I won't argue with him in here—I'll just listen.

Corbin shook his head a couple of times before he answered. "No, I don't think so, Fred. This may or may not be the time but it definitely isn't the place."

Fred said nothing but Patie was fairly certain that he and Ronnie would follow him out of the room.

"Tell you what," the preacher proposed, "give me a minute to tell Sissy and Jamie what I'm doing and I'll meet you in the lobby."

"Why do you want to tell them that?" Ronnie asked, her voice a little too loud. It was loaded with contempt.

"Because I'm certain they have seen us talking and will see us leave, Ronnie," Patie replied with authority. "And besides," he softened the tone of his voice, "we're going to talk about Sissy's mom, aren't we?"

"Probably," Ronnie answered sharply.

"Then I think she has a right to know that. I'll meet you in the lobby."

With that declaration, Corbin eased past the couple and made his way slowly through the people. A moment later, he explained to Sissy what was about to happen. He had turned to leave her, when she touched his arm. "Brother Corbin?"

Patie turned back toward her. Accompanying the tears was an expression of concern.

"Do you want to do this?" the grieving daughter asked.

"Not really, Sissy, but it's part of ministry" he smiled, hoping that would assuage her worry.

Sissy nodded. "As soon as you come back in, I want you to meet our pastor."

"I'm looking forward to that, Sissy. We'll need to talk about the service tomorrow. I'll be back in a few minutes."

Corbin hoped he was telling her the truth.

Abe Goodson, an Elder at Tishrock Community Church, walked slowly to the platform. People were filing into the sanctuary, some from the fellowship hall where they had eaten a good, old fashioned church supper together, some from outside. It was Wednesday night, it was Bible study and prayer service time, and it was the first Wednesday of Patie Corbin's tenure as pastor. He wasn't there.

"Let me have your attention, folks," Abe requested loudly, the microphone amplifying his voice even more. His announcement effected little change in the fellowshipping church members, who continued their boisterous visiting, totally unthreatened by Abe's entreaty. Suddenly from the rear of the auditorium, sounded a loud "AMEN, BROTHER ABE, WHAT'CHE GOT FER US T'NITE?" It was Lester Junkin, the large "clown prince" of the SINO Sunday School class and the recognized best church "Amener" in Tishomingo County.

Abe grinned. He and Lester had known each other all their lives, grown up together, gone to school together. To Abe, and just about everyone else in town, if not the county, Lester was a funny man, though not because he tried to be, which, of course, made him even funnier.

Lester's question spoken with such volume began the process of silencing the crowd. A minute later the sanctuary was quiet.

"Folks," Abe began explaining, "Brother Corbin called me this morning and asked me to lead the prayer time tonight. He apologized to me and asked me to apologize to you."

The crowd grew exceedingly quiet. Tishrock Community Church wasn't a legalistic church, but for the preacher to miss his very first Wednesday prayer meeting was highly unusual.

"And," the elder continued, "he asked me to explain to you why he's not here and also he asked us to pray for him."

Abe hesitated for a moment. He *seemed* to have everyone's attention. "Some of you may have already heard," he announced, smiling slightly and looking away from Dimples, who was sitting to his right at the far end of the third pew with her husband, Jack. "But some of you probably haven't. Sunday night after service, Brother Corbin met two couples who were staying out at the park. Monday morning he experienced the joy of leading one of the ladies to Christ. She and her husband were from Birmingham. Yesterday the husband apparently shot and killed his wife."

Those words seemed to send a shock wave across the assembly of people, some emitting a quiet "Oh, no." Some saying nothing. Some immediately lowering their heads.

"Brother Corbin," Abe continued, "was asked to speak at the funeral service in the morning. Because of the irregular situation, he believed he should meet with the family and their preacher tonight at visitation. There are a few items we need to discuss tonight and several things we need to pray about, but before we do, I think we might have a special time of prayer for Brother Corbin and the family, so—"

"Abe, I'd like to ask something before you pray."

Abe turned toward the sound of the voice . He knew the source of the question before he saw the face. It was Chest Hudson.

Chest Hudson was a deacon. He was a lifelong member of the church, a short, stocky man who made a living from a small farm eight miles out of town and from working for one of the supervisors, grading gravel roads. He was clean-cut, a handsome man in the face, married to an attractive lady, and the father of six children. He was known for "bein' agin'" almost everything the other people in the church were "for." Although some church members were almost too doubtful about his commitment to Christ, no one questioned his commitment to the church. That was "his" church and he supported it by "giving and attending." He voted against Patie Corbin coming as pastor.

"Of course, Chest," Abe welcomed, more outwardly than inwardly. He suspected the question might be negative.

The members of the church grew even quieter, if that were possible. They suspected the same thing Abe did. Martha Sue, Chest's wife, sitting next to him, dropped her head, as she had done many times through the years.

"Are we gonna' have Bible study tonite'?"

Abe did not answer quickly. He wanted to be in total control of the way he answered. "No, not tonight, Chest. We're just going to pray tonight."

"Abe, I come to Wednesday nite' services primarily for Bible study. My family and me, we pray at home. We all favor studyin' the Bible on Wednesday nites'."

Abe didn't respond to Chest's comment. He only nodded in understanding. Then the Elder asked if anyone wanted to pray for the pastor and the situation in Birmingham. One by one, many church members stood and prayed until, it seemed, half the congregation had done so.

Ronnie and Fred reached the lobby before Patie did. They were standing ten feet to one side of the hallway when Patie walked up the hall and into the lobby, spotting the two immediately. With an authoritative voice, he said, "Fred, I'll try to get us an office."

Across the lobby, the preacher saw a sign which read "Office." An older woman sat behind a desk, a pleasant smile on her face. When Patie introduced himself as one of the preachers conducting Mrs. Appleby's service and asked for a private office, she led him to a nearby room.

Patie turned and motioned to Fred, who had been watching. A moment later, the three of them were alone in the office. Patie sat behind a large ornate desk. The Ogdens sat in front of him in two chairs. Fred unbuttoned his jacket and rested upright and stiffly in his chair, a stern expression continuing to darken his handsome face. Ronnie abruptly crossed her legs, a look of complete disgust governing her face.

Fred started to speak. Patie held his hand up, a motion which the man understood. He stopped. His eyes narrowed even more. Ronnie quietly sneered.

"Before we talk," Patie explained, "I'd like to pray." He almost added, if that's alright with you, but he didn't. He wanted to pray and he did not want to give them the option of preventing it. When the pastor closed his eyes and dropped his head, Fred and Ronnie were staring at him. When he said "amen," opened his eyes and raised his head, they were still staring. Their expressions had not changed. The old sinner, saved by the marvelous grace of God, almost smiled. Six years ago, his attitude would probably have been much the same as theirs.

"Now," Patie calmly asked, "what did you want to talk to me about?"

Ronnie spoke first. "You know you killed Bettye Jo, don't you?"

Amazing how God's Spirit brings wisdom and understanding to Christians. If Ronnie had asked him that question, which really wasn't a question but an accusation, ten minutes after he heard about Bettye Jo's death, he might have been inclined to agree with her. No one can assume the moral guilt for another adult's sins. Not even Christ, who assumed and accepted the *legal* guilt for mankind's sins, accepted our *moral* guilt. He paid the legal debt, but His perfect nature was not contaminated. He possessed no sin nature, no moral guilt.

Patie looked Ronnie firmly in the eyes. "No, I don't Ronnie. Would you explain to me just how I did that?"

"I don't need to explain how you did that! You already know how you did it!" Her voice was sharp, filled with anger and resentment. Her face was contorted, her beauty now lost in a twisted mass of human flesh.

"No, actually, I don't Ronnie," the preacher responded, very conscious of fashioning softness into his voice, something the flesh of the old competitor did not want to do. Again, he found himself experiencing the words of Paul, "The flesh wars against the Spirit and the Spirit against the flesh."

"Then you're stupid, Patie," Ronnie blurted out, "There's no need of trying to talk to you." She glanced over at her husband, looking for support, perhaps, or maybe a signal to leave.

Fred said nothing. He continued to glare at Patie.

"Ronnie, you and Fred approached *me* and you asked to talk to *me*.

69

Is that all you want to talk about—that one accusation that in your opinion, I killed Bettye Jo? I guess we could have had this conversation in there by Bettye Jo's casket, if that's all you have to say."

"You're a smart—, aren't you, Corbin?" Fred cursed, the words literally exploding from his mouth, like built up water through a broken dam.

Patie, still leaning back in the large office chair behind the desk, his arms resting on the arm rests, did not physically flinch at those words. But he imagined his heart fluttered an extra time or two. He hoped his face wasn't flushed. "Well, Fred, I'd like to think I'm smart, or at least smarter, especially now that I'm a Christian." Then shifting his gaze to Ronnie, he added, "Although I do admit, I've done some stupid and evil things in the past."

Suddenly Ronnie sprang out of her chair and threw herself across the top of the desk, like an arrow shot from a bow, her right arm drawn back. She slapped the preacher on his left cheek, a blow exacerbated by the fact that Corbin simultaneously leaned forward in order to attempt to stand up. His face was moving toward Ronnie as her right hand moved toward his face. The slap was accurate and it was loud. Patie's face stung under its effect and he immediately sat back down in his chair.

When Ronnie launched herself from her chair, so did Fred and by the time Ronnie had landed her blow, Fred was moving around the desk toward Patie. When the preacher sat back down and saw Fred moving toward him, he thrust himself out of the chair. By the time Fred got to Patie, both of them were standing. Fred drew his right fist back, and swung.

Corbin jerked his head backward and Fred's fist whizzed an inch from the preacher's chin. But Fred's powerful swing rendered him off balance and he fell backward toward Patie.

The old athlete saw his opening and locked both his arms around the attacker from the rear. The move kept Fred from falling and it allowed Patie to control the angry man. Holding Fred in a vise-like grip from behind, Patie stole a brief look at Ronnie. She was standing at the front side of the desk, her eyes wide, a satanic snarl written on her face. At least, the minister thought, she isn't entering into the fray.

Fred struggled to free himself from Patie's hold, to no avail. Patie, however, knew he had to let him go. He wanted to let him go! And so— he spoke quietly to the squirming man, "Fred, stop trying to get loose and promise me—"

"Go to —," the restrained man cursed again.

Knowing he was in control of the situation, at least physically, Patie decided he would, by his words impute a touch of gentleness if not humor into the situation. "No, Fred, I'm not going there. I *was* going there but I got saved. I'm not going there anymore."

"Got saved?" Ronnie snapped. "Saved from what? You ———— ————-, you let Fred go."

"I will, Ronnie, Patie answered, "as soon as he promises he will sit back down and talk. That's what you both came in here to do isn't it, talk?"

Somewhere in the confrontation, Patie realized that Fred and Ronnie had not come to talk. They came to incite him, to control him, to pull him down off his pedestal. They wanted to disprove and discredit the "so-called" preacher and everything he stood for.

Neither said anything, but gradually Fred stopped struggling.

"Fred," Patie spoke quietly in the man's ear from behind, "You promise?"

Fred said nothing.

"Fred?" Corbin asked.

Still he said nothing.

"Fred?" Perhaps ten seconds passed. Reservedly, Fred nodded.

"You promising, Fred?"

"I said 'yes,' didn't I?"

"I think so—I hope so. Just wanted to make sure."

Patie turned Fred loose.

The assailant pushed Patie's relaxing arms away, straightened his coat, and flopped back down into his chair. He did not look at Patie nor did he offer an apology.

Patie looked at Ronnie again. She, too, had sat back down.

The preacher also eased back into his chair. He wanted to make no sudden moves, which might register as anger in Fred's and Ronnie's minds. After sitting down, he waited a few seconds before he spoke. And when finally he did, his voice was gentle.

"Fred, Ronnie, before we go any farther, I want to say one thing about what just happened. Ronnie," he said directing his comment to the woman, "You knew me 'back when.'" Then shifting his gaze to Fred, he continued, "and Fred, you knew about me. If the two of you had done to me six or seven years ago what you did to me a minute ago, one, maybe two of us, would be lying on the floor bleeding by now—maybe dead. And you know that's true. But about four years ago, I got really sick of my life. I was almost killed several times and I ended up in a wonderful preacher's office in Eagle Pass, Texas."

Patie had been looking at both of them as he spoke, shifting his gaze from one to the other. Neither looked back at him until he mentioned almost being killed. Ronnie looked up. Most of the contempt seemed to be gone from her face.

"The preacher's name was Jess," Patie continued. "He opened the Bible and explained who Christ was and is and what He had accomplished on the Cross for every person who will accept it. When I realized what He had done for me—and for you— it broke my heart. That day I turned from my old life and gave myself to God. God gave His Holy Spirit to me. Fred, Ronnie, I'm not perfect, but I asked the Perfect God to save me and live inside of me, and—"

"I don't want to hear this," exclaimed Ronnie. "I didn't come here to be preached at." Her voice, though not compassionate, was not as caustic as before. Fred said nothing. Nor did he look up.

"Ronnie, I'm not preaching *at* you nor at Fred. As one friend to another, I'm simply telling the truth about what happened to me. May I say two other things? And then we'll talk about what you want to talk about."

Ronnie looked over at Fred. Fred said nothing.

"Go ahead," the wife invited, a little exasperation now coloring the tone of her voice.

"Thank you, Ronnie. I'll be brief. First, after I prayed to receive Christ, a strange thing started happening inside of me. I started loving people instead of using them—and that ability didn't come from me. It was given to me by the God who lives in me now and who loves you and me.

"Second, I want to give you these." Patie held up two little booklets which he had taken from his coat pocket without either Fred or Ronnie noticing. He slid them across the desk. "And I'm asking you to read this tonight—at least before the funeral tomorrow."

Ronnie ignored the two booklets, but Fred raised his head and looked at them. Glancing at Ronnie, he took one of them and placed it in his shirt pocket.

"Now," Patie offered, "I'm gonna' shut up and let you talk for awhile, if you would still like to—"

The anger on Fred's face was replaced now with a measure of worry. And when he spoke, the concern filtered into his voice, moving it from aggressive to "modified appeal."

"Phil said Bettye Jo told you what we were doing!" Fred waited for an answer before he continued.

Patie nodded. "Yes, she did, Fred."

"Well, I guess that means you will broadcast it everywhere—to everybody."

"What do you mean?" the preacher asked.

"I mean, I guess you will tell everyone."

Patie was puzzled. He did not understand who the "everyone" might be about whom Fred was talking, so he asked. "Fred, by everyone, you mean Sissy and her family?"

"Yes—and everyone else you talk to. The members of your church."

"Oh, Fred," Corbin explained in genuine surprise, "I'm not going to tell my church members about that. And I'm not going to tell anyone else about it, either. I had never thought of doing such a—" he hesitated in the middle of the sentence. "Fred, I can't spread that kind of information. Scripture prohibits it. But as far as Sissy and Jamie are concerned, they already know about it. They knew about it before Bettye Jo talked to me. That was one of the things bothering Bettye Jo so much."

Changing the subject, Patie questioned, "Fred, do you and Ronnie have children?"

Fred looked at his wife then back at Patie. "Why do you want to know?"

Patie ignored Fred's question. "Do they know about it?"

"NO!" Ronnie instantly exclaimed, "and you'd better not —"

"I'm not going to tell them," Patie quickly promised. "But you need to ask yourselves some questions, like, would it bother you if they found out?"

"Of course, it would bother us," Fred admitted.

"Well, then, try to understand Bettye Jo's agony. Her only child *did* know. Phil may have acted like it didn't bother *him*, that Sissy knew, but it bothered Bettye Jo. And by the way, I personally believe it bothers Phil, too, although right now *that* bother may be secondary to what he did to her."

"Phil didn't mean to kill her, Patie." Fred's voice had softened considerably.

Patie was aware that up until then, neither of them had referred to him by his name. Doing it now had more than a little significance to the man trained in human behavior by Scripture and experience.

"What do you mean?" Corbin had not talked to anyone about the details of the killing.

Fred explained. "He pulled the trigger, alright, but he wasn't trying to kill Bettye Jo. He was trying to scare her into continuing—you know—what we were—"

"I understand, Fred. What happened?"

74

"He put the pistol to his own head to shock her, make her see how continuing on—how important it was to him. Bettye Jo grabbed his wrist with all her weight, pulling on it. They fell to the floor and the gun went off. The pressure of her pulling on his hand pulled his trigger finger."

Patie slowly shook his head but for a moment and said nothing, attempting to picture in his mind's eye how it could have happened. It made sense to him, but then he was forced to admit he certainly wasn't an expert in such things. Beyond that, someone could be lying.

Turning back toward Fred's wife, Patie quietly asked, "A few minutes ago you accused me of killing Bettye Jo, Ronnie. Do you really believe that?"

"Yes," she quickly answered, "Both of us do. If you hadn't talked to her, she would still be alive today."

"That's probably true, Ronnie. But Bettye Jo could not continue committing that sin with you all. Don't you understand that? She *could not* continue. She's in the presence of the Lord right now and she's already forgiven Phil."

"And YOU saved her, or whatever you call it."

"No, Ronnie. Almighty God saved her. I only told her about Him."

For a brief moment no one said anything. Finally, Fred spoke. "Patie, when you are called to testify at the trial, are you going to tell them what Bettye Jo and Phil and Ronnie and I were doing?"

The question shocked Patie and the surprise registered upon his face. He dropped his chin upon his chest suddenly and breathed out loud, "Oh, my God and Savior, I hadn't even thought about that."

CHAPTER SEVEN
BEYOND THE METAL SCREEN

Patie had no good answer for Fred's question, for he had not had time to consider it before being asked. Only after Ronnie and Fred had left the borrowed office did the preacher reflect deeply upon that which had been inquired of him. If called to testify in the trial, which most assuredly he would be, he would be under oath. But somewhere back in the inner recesses of his memory, perhaps in seminary counseling class, had he not been taught that information given to a preacher in a counseling session was privileged? Whether or not it is, is certainly important but it isn't as important as God's will. If he refused to testify, he pondered, it would not be in order to help free a murderer. It would be a refusal to talk about the sin of Bettye Jo, in order to protect, not only her name, but the emotional state of relatives.

The preacher leaned back in the desk chair, folded his arms behind his head and began to swing his legs upon the corner of the desk when he realized that wasn't *his* desk. "Humh," he breathed out loud. "I can see another phone call to Jess."

Patie's thoughts were interrupted by a man's voice coming from a head leaning into the doorway, looking into the office. "Brother Corbin."

"Yes," Patie answered, jerking his head up toward the sound.

"I'm Dan Devonshire," the voice continued as the man stepped fully into the doorway.

"Oh, Dr. Devonshire," Patie exclaimed, rising quickly from his seat. "Please come in."

Dan Devonshire, Sissy's Baptist pastor, was not a large man. Standing a trim five feet, ten inches tall, perhaps, he had a very pleasant face. His eyes were brown and widely spaced, with a twinkle which reminded Corbin of Dimples'. His nose was straight and his mouth pulled wide by a large smile, exhibiting two rows of large white teeth. His brown hair was relatively short and parted on the right side. He wore a dark green coat, a grey shirt, grey and green tie and grey trousers. He held a Bible in his hand.

Dr. Devonshire walked quickly toward Patie, his hand outstretched. "Brother Corbin, it's really good to meet you."

"It's good to meet you, My Brother. Won't you sit down?" Patie motioned toward one of the chairs, grinning. " I'm acting like this is my office. I don't think anyone would mind us using it a little longer, do you?"

"No, they don't mind," Brother Devonshire related. "I asked them about it. They're members of my church. It was offered to us as long as we need it."

"Great," Patie exclaimed.

"Everything go okay in here, Brother Corbin?"

"You mean with the couple I just talked to? Dr. Devonshire, do you know Fred and Ronnie?"

"Yes. I met them out in the hall, when they came out of here. Attractive couple. I did not know them before."

Patie nodded. "Do you know the situation?"

"Yes," Dan answered, his voice low, nodding his head. "A tragic thing." He hesitated a moment, started to speak again, then stopped, a serious expression replacing his smile. "Brother Corbin, would you—"

Patie interrupted the pastor. "Dr. Devonshire, you might as well call me Patie. Everyone else does—if you don't mind."

The doctor smiled–a slight smile, not as big as the one he fashioned a few moments ago. "I don't, Patie. Thank you. Please call me Dan, too, if you will."

Patie nodded in agreement.

"Patie," Dan spoke quietly, "Bettye Jo came to me just as you asked her to do. She told me just about everything, I suppose. My, my, I can't imagine she left anything out of *that* story."

"We humans commit some sordid sins, don't we, Brother?" Patie observed.

"Indeed we do," Dan agreed. "Would you—do you mind—" the pastor was stammering a little.

Patie could see that Dan wanted to ask him a question. He waited.

"Patie, if you have peace about doing it—if you don't, now," he injected "—please don't—but if you feel free to do it, will you tell me about Bettye Jo receiving Christ. I would love to hear about it, but if you don't —"

"I would like to tell you about it, Dan. I think Bettye Jo would rejoice with us as we tell the story." So beginning with the party in the cabin at Tishomingo State Park, Patie related all that had happened to Dan Devonshire, the pastor who would have helped Bettye grow into spiritual maturity had she lived.

Dimples and Jack walked briskly into their house, which was only three blocks from the church, depositing their Bibles and her purse on the round breakfast table which sat in the kitchen by the window. The secretary immediately started making coffee. Over her shoulder she called, "Jack."

Jack was half-way between the kitchen and the den. He stopped but said nothing.

"Jack!" Dimples yelled again.

That time Jack answered, though not enthusiastically. "Yes!"

"Jack, don't go to the television set yet. Ann's coming over here in a few minutes. I need you to do something for me."

Without moving, Jack asked, "What?"

"Come in here and I'll tell you."

Jack slowly turned and started back into the kitchen, silently positioning himself about three feet behind his wife.

Dimples yelled again, this time a little louder, "JACK!"

Jack, a grin on his face, answered with the same volume. "WHAT?"

Dimples jumped and wheeled around, drawing her hand back like she was going to hit him. "Jack, you know I don't like it when you do that." She was not smiling but most of the twinkle was still in her eyes. "One of these days—! Look in the refrigerator and get the cheese, the grapes and the raw vegetables out. Then look in the freezer and—"

By the time Dimples had commanded Jack to look in the refrigerator, he already had the door open and was bending over looking. The sooner he finished, he figured, the sooner he could get to the Western Channel and Randolph Scott. "Where are they, Dimples?"

"In the refrigerator."

"I don't see them."

"They're in there," she declared, a touch of frustration in her voice.

"What are they in?"

"The cheese is in the cheese compartment on the door and the grapes and vegetables are in plastic containers."

Jack reached over to the door and extracted the cheese from its compartment, slamming it a touch too loudly on the counter without straightening up. "Everything in here is in plastic containers. What color are they?"

Over the years, the man and woman had gone through this same exercise a thousand times. The wife turned disgustedly away from the coffee pot. She swatted her husband on the back side, barking out a new command. "Move over," which Jack did gratefully and without hesitation.

Dimples reached into the refrigerator and withdrew two large plastic containers which she dropped onto the counter next to the cheese. "For the life of me, I cannot understand why men cannot find anything in the re-frigerator!! One of these days I'm gonna' make an appointment with Dr. Levitch in Memphis and see if he can explain it to me." She had turned back to the coffee pot.

"Who's Dr. Levitch?"

"A Christian psychiatrist."

"A Christian named Levitch?" Jack quizzed.

"Completed Jew," Dimples explained, her eyes fixed on what she was doing. "A great psychiatrist."

Jack was shuffling sideways six inches at a time out of the kitchen.

"I betcha' Randolph Scott never had to get anything out of the re-frigerator for his wife," Jack speculated, raising his voice so Dimples could-n't tell he was easing out of the kitchen.

"I 'spect not!" Dimples giggled.

"Need me to do anything else, Honey?"

"No, thank you. You've done enough. Be sure to give my love to Randolph."

Jack didn't hear her. He was already in the den, scrolling up to the Western Channel. He wouldn't have understood anyway—not about Ran-dolph Scott.

Ann pulled her Mercedes up to the side of the Morgans' home and stopped in the driveway behind Dimples' car and Jack's pickup. She looked at the old house and marveled again. It had been in Jack's family since the Civil War, a large pale yellow columned wood house, purely Southern, with manicured front and back yards resting under at least ten large oak trees. It wasn't a large home, as old homes go, but it certainly wasn't small.

The newspaper editor grabbed a notebook from the passenger's seat and bounded up to the carport door. Knocking, she opened it slightly and heard Dimples yell, "Come on in, Ann."

An hour later Dimples and Ann had planned the party, the place, the food, the drinks, and the party list. It would be at Ann's house and a list of twenty-four couples made who would be invited—only after Dimples talked to Patie on the phone tomorrow after the funeral.

When Patie finished telling Dan the story of Bettye Jo's conversion, the Birmingham pastor shook his head and then smiled. Looking at the other preacher, he uttered in a low but very strong voice, "God is so good, Patie. It's not hard to see His sovereignty in that marvelous story. I'm just so grateful you were there and that you were used of God."

"So am I, Dan. I have to admit I was a little hesitant about being on that trail early in the morning with a man's wife. I suppose our Lord circumvented my ignorance."

Dan chuckled. "He has certainly circumvented mine plenty of times, to Him be the glory."

"Amen," agreed the Tishrock preacher, "Amen."

For the next fifteen minutes the two preachers, using Sissy's and Jamie's requests, planned the service, the songs, the eulogy and the sermon. Dan, because he was very familiar with the family, would speak the eulogy. Patie would preach the sermon, an honor and a blessing which he did not anticipate. He came to Birmingham assuming he would perhaps lead in prayer, or, at the most, present a short eulogy about Bettye Jo's salvation. Dan would handle the gravesite.

At the end of the session, Dan prayed beautifully and meaningfully that God would be honored through the service the next day and that it would remind all of us about the temporalness of life on this earth, especially those who may never have before trusted the Lord Jesus Christ.

Patie's phone rang at exactly 6:00 o'clock a. m. He twisted over, groped for it in the darkness and answered. A voice on the other end announced that it was 6:00 o'clock, the time which he had asked the desk to wake him. The old athlete thanked the voice, rolled onto his back, threw one arm across his forehead and grinned, remembering a funny story which a sports writer friend told about another sports writer who worked at a paper in Nashville, Tennessee. It was one of the few funny stories which becoming a Christian did not eliminate from nor even diminish from his consciousness. It was still as funny now to the old halfback as it had been when he first heard it. Patie's grin widened as he recalled it.

It seems the sports writer, Tony, was in Atlanta covering a sports event. He was sitting in the lobby of his hotel early one morning near the front desk reading the newspaper and enjoying a cup of coffee. His attention was suddenly diverted by a commotion at the desk, only a few feet away.

"Young man," screamed a plump and very angry woman, "I'm Mrs. Johnson in Room 531. You were supposed to give me a wake up call at 6:30 this morning. YOU DID NOT and I'm going to be late for a very important business meeting. I'm telling you now," she screamed, "I want a call at 6:30 tomorrow morning and if I do not get it, you're going to be very, very sorry. DO YOU UNDERSTAND?"

"Yes, ma'am," the embarrassed young clerk quietly replied. "Yes, ma'am, I'm really sorry ma'am, yes, ma'am," he called out after the seething business woman as she scurried toward the front door of the hotel.

That night, Tony the sportswriter set his alarm clock for 6:00 a. m. When it went off, he quickly brushed his teeth, dressed and at 6:15 he dialed Room 531.

"Mrs. Johnson, this is the front desk. It's 6:30 and time you got your fat bottom out of bed!"

The mischievous troublemaker then hustled down to the lobby, bought a newspaper behind which he partially hid, and waited. A minute or two later, a robed, frizzy-haired, enraged Mrs. Johnson burst from the elevator and headed for the innocent, unsuspecting, and soon-to-be attacked young man behind the counter.

From his "50 yard-line" seat, Tony beheld the battle.

Corbin chuckled out loud at the story—again. "Lord, I don't know if my remembering it offends you. If it does, please convict me of it," he whispered. Then slipping to his knees beside the bed he prayed once more for the services about four hours away. Ten minutes later, the ex-football player was riding a stationary bicycle in the motel workout room, reading his Bible at the same time.

A few miles away from Patie's motel, a disconsolate prisoner sat in his jail cell, his head down. Phil Appleby stayed in that position fully twenty minutes before slowly lifting his eyes and looking through the bars at the wall clock. Six-thirty. *In three and a half hours my wife's funeral will be held and I won't even be there,* he grieved. *How could I have been so stupid, how could I have been so stupid?* he thought over and over and over again. *How could I have done that,* he silently wondered as he had done ten thousand times since it happened.

Had he been given a mirror to look into, he would have seen a middle-aged man who now looked far beyond his years. His greying hair was unkempt. His eyes were bloodshot and bleary. His face was covered with a three day growth of hair and lines of worry had begun to appear where just a few days ago, there were none. The thick striped canvas prison clothes hung loose upon his thin body, a body made weaker because he could not eat. And he smelled bad, a mixture of sweat and bodily secretions which he could not–nor did he care to—wash off.

The man's mind bounced from his wife to his daughter and son-in-law, to his grandchildren, to the event which ended Bettye Jo's life, and back to her again, reproducing the cycle over and over. He had not meant to kill her, the despondent man believed. He had once *known* he had not meant to kill her, the day it happened, the day they locked him up in here. But in the midst of overwhelming guilt, and the unbearable shame which accompanied his deed and his incarceration, the once successful business-man had begun to doubt that which he had once known to be true.

Sissy had not been to visit him. But he knew she would come—after the funeral. She would be forced to—by her love, her desire to hear him recount the death of her mother and by her nature. And he would tell her that it had been an accident.

The imprisoned man looked at the clock again. It had been an hour since he last looked at it. But only five minutes had passed.

The chapel at the funeral home was packed, attesting to the good name which the family obviously held in the area. During the service, the relatives, as is the custom in many areas of the country, were segregated in an ante-room, where they could see the casket and raised stage area but could not be seen by the visitors. The singer and the two preachers sat on the platform.

Patie did not search the crowd for Fred and Ronnie, not so anyone could tell, at least, but in his periodic glances he *did* spot them. They sat on the back row. He was too far away from them to inspect their expressions. He could only imagine what they were thinking.

When Dan finished presenting the eulogy, he introduced Patie, including his football career, his position presently at Tishrock and the fact that he had prayed with Bettye Jo to receive Christ.

At the end of the introduction, the Mississippi preacher walked slowly to the podium which was only eight feet away. His emotions were myriad: joy at believing Bettye Jo was with the Lord; sadness at the occasion; sympathy for Sissy and her family; a desire to honor the Lord in all he said; and, to his dismay, a touch of anger toward the Ogdens for even being here, anger which produced in him an accompanying touch of guilt. The middle-aged man and new pastor believed in the sovereignty of God—that Fred and Ronnie were here for a purpose. So he would share the gospel before the service ended but he disliked doing it for people who viewed him with contempt. Well, at least Ronnie does, he thought, as he opened his Bible on the speaker's stand. Perhaps not Fred. Based upon what Sissy said, apparently Bettye Jo's and Phil's sins had not been made public, not yet.

The preacher verbally recognized the family then the visitors. He read the Scripture and he spoke—quietly—reverently—but with power which he clearly recognized as coming from the very Spirit of God. He spoke on the temporalness of human life; that which happens when the soul departs the body; he taught the definition of the soul; and he remembered to everyone the prayer which Bettye Jo had prayed. He recalled the peace which Bettye Jo exhibited after her prayer and her prayer and her determination to walk with Christ. He ended the twenty minute talk by stressing the love which the mother and grandmother had for her family. Finally, he shared the Gospel of the Lord Jesus Christ, quickly covering man's sin plight, Christ's vicarious atonement and man's invitation to receive what the Savior had done for us. When he finished, he looked at Fred and Ronnie. The man's head was bowed. Ronnie glared directly at him. Patie prayed and turned the service back over to Dan

By habit, Patie Corbin, upon Phil Appleby entering the room on the opposite side of the screen, stood. A few years ago, he either would not have stood, or if he inadvertently did, upon reflection, he would have felt

like a fool. No, that's not right, he thought, a few years ago I wouldn't even have been here.

"Phil," the preacher greeted reservedly.

Phil nodded, said nothing and sat down, his head bowed, his face grotesquely contorted.

If Patie had ever seen a man in abject misery it was right now, in the man who slouched on a stool beyond the metal screen. The preacher's heart emptied and left was nothing but pity and compassion. God would judge Phil. Patie found, much to his surprise, that somehow in the realization of his own forgiveness of guilt, he possessed no condemnation for Phil Appleby. Romans 8:1 flashed through the Mississippian's mind: "There is therefore now no condemnation in them who are in Christ Jesus." The preacher discovered another dimension to that verse. With no condemnation in him, he had none with which to condemn the murderer in front of him.

"Phil, I'm really glad you agreed to see me. I know it wasn't easy for you to walk out here and face me. It took as much courage and strength as anything I've ever seen." Corbin wasn't certain that statement was absolutely true but he wasn't certain it wasn't, either. He needed to say something which allowed Phil to hear the love and compassion in the tone of his voice and that *something* needed to reflect positively upon the prisoner.

Phil lifted his head toward the screened opening which separated the two men. Tears had plowed light furrows down his sweat and salt-covered face. Death had dimmed his eyes. Touches of saliva rested in the corners of his mouth and on his chin. "Why *did* you come, Patie? To taunt me?" The hopelessness in his voice had neutralized any anger the killer might have had for the preacher.

"No, Phil, I didn't come to taunt you." Patie hesitated just a moment, making certain of his next words. The falter gave opportunity to Phil to ask another question.

"What then, to save me?" His voice offered no threat.

"Phil, I can't save you. Only Almighty God has the power to do

87

that. Salvation is in Him and no other. But, yes, I would like to see you come to Jesus, and I did come to tell you how you can do that, if you will allow me."

Phil's chin had dropped again to his chest. Through the screen, the preacher could see drops of tears fall from the man's reddened eyes.

"I came to tell you something else. I came to tell you I love you."

With those words, the prisoner jerked, as severely and as clearly as if he had been stuck with a sharp knife. When he spoke, his voice was hoarse and halting. "No—man—has—no man has ever told—me—that—not—even my—my father."

Patie responded–perhaps a little too quickly, he immediately thought. "Well, I love you, Phil, as a Christian. The love comes from God to me and I pass it on to you. Phil," the pastor declared, "would you do something for me?"

Phil looked up at Corbin, a question etched upon his face. "What?" he asked, as if to say what can *I* do for *you*? "What you're doing now. Looking at me. I want to look you in the eyes when I say this, Phil. I want to help you. I want to see you have peace and forgiveness in your heart and I want to know what happened, so I'll know how to try to help you."

"You want to help me?"

The pastor nodded. "Yes, but I need to know exactly what happened."

"You're not a lawyer, are you?" Phil whispered brokenly through the screen.

"No, no, I didn't mean to imply that. But I know some good attorneys. Will you tell me *exactly* what happened?"

Phil looked sternly at his visitor. He started to speak, hesitated, and then asked, "The law send you in here?"

Corbin wasn't prepared for that question. The "NO" exploded from his mouth. "No, Phil, I promise you. That thought never entered my—" he stopped in the middle of the sentence. "Phil, if you believe that, please don't tell me anything. But I promise you, I did not come here for that purpose."

The imprisoned man studied Patie's face—for a full thirty seconds. Then he nodded, and looking the preacher directly in the eyes, told him the story. He had gone to see Bettye Jo and had taken a pistol. Knowing Bettye Jo would never believe he would kill *her*, therefore possessing no leverage by threatening to do that, he held the pistol to his own head, with no intention of killing himself. Bettye Jo grabbed the pistol with both of her hands, pulling it away from his head. But in doing that, she pulled the barrel of the gun toward herself—AND—pulled the weapon against his trigger finger.

By the time he finished telling the story, he was sobbing. "I swear by God Almighty, I didn't mean to do it, Patie. It was an accident. I didn't mean to–do–it!"

Patie had been waiting for that—for Phil to call his name—"Patie"—with a non-threatening tone. And on top of that, he received a bonus. The prisoner had verbalized God's name.

"Phil?"

The convict looked at him again.

"I believe you."

"You believe me?"

"Yes," the pastor nodded.

"You believe me?" Phil asked again, unbelievingly.

"Yes, I do, Phil. I believe you."

"Thank you, Patie, thank you, thank you."

"Phil, in telling me the story, do you realize you mentioned God by name?"

The man didn't answer. He simply looked at his visitor, but he looked with newly softened eyes.

"Will you let me tell you about that God and His Son and what they have done for you?"

Ten minutes later, exactly as his wife had done a few days earlier, Phil Appleby prayed to receive the Lord Jesus Christ. The moment he finished the prayer, with new tears and an expression of far more internal peace upon his face, the new child of God thrust his two open palms against the screen.

With a great smile upon his face, the preacher placed his two open palms upon the screen opposite Phil's.

An hour after leaving the Justice Complex, Patie finally reached Highway 72, the road to Iuka. Easing his vehicle up to 65 miles per hour, he blurted out loud, "Well, Lord we buried one of your children but we saw another one raised. Thank you, Lord." Then the man silently recounted all that he did, wondering if he had left anything out. He told Phil how to study the Word and taught him how to pray. He promised him he would tell Sissy, Dr. Devonshire, and officer Morgan that he prayed to receive Christ. He gave Phil the name of the Ashton Law firm in Farese, Alabama, one of the South's great law firms, friends with whom he had gone to Ole Miss. And he promised to stay in touch. Then he ended the visit with a simple declaration to the new Christian. "Phil, the greatest thing about spending eternity in Heaven is that Jesus will be there. But so will Bettye Jo." As Patie had stood to leave, Phil stood, too. His face still reflected sadness, but there was new life in his eyes. "I love you, Brother," the pastor called over his shoulder.

Corbin wasn't certain but he thought he might have heard, "I love you, too, Patie." Maybe it was his hungry imagination. Maybe not.

CHAPTER EIGHT
Two Invitations of a Worrying Kind

Patie drove up to the front of the church, stopped, grabbed his Bible and walked quickly to the front door. Like the Union Captain who moved to Tishrock after the Civil War, he rubbed his hand over the five bullet holes. It wasn't an act of superstition. It was a commitment to the wonderful and mysterious sovereignty, and perhaps, Decree, of God. Those five holes, placed there by a drunk Union soldier one hundred and fifty-five years ago, led to the conversion of the captain. And the conversion of Betty Jo Appleby followed by her death at the hand of her husband led to his conversion. The preacher moved his hand over the five holes for a few moments and prayed for Phil Appleby.

"Good mornin', Dimples," Patie called out, walking toward his desk. The door between his office and Dimples' was open. The preacher couldn't see her, but as usual he heard her bumping around.

"Mornin', Brother—oh—Patie. I'm havin' a hard time gettin' used to calling you Patie."

"What are you doing in here? You need some help?"

"What do you mean?"

"Well," Patie explained, "you're producing a lot of noise. All that cries out for help. What are you doin'?"

"Movin' a file cabinet."

"Moving a file cabinet? Wait a minute. I'll help you," the preacher who was just about to sit down, exploded. He hustled into Dimples' office.

"Too late. Got it now," she retorted, brushing her hands on her shirt. "Thing was dusty on top."

"You ought to clean up in here sometimes."

The secretary turned and glared at her pastor.

"Don't look at me like that, Dimples. I was just kidding!"

"Was your steak good last night?"

"What?" Corbin asked, surprised.

"Was your steak—" Dimples said, her eyes glittering.

"Dimples," Patie interrupted.

"Sir!"

"How in the world did you know I ate steak last night? And don't answer that by saying this is Tishrock. I ate steak in Iuka. At the Rotary banquet—which reminds me," Patie considered, "you don't usually get steak at a Rotary meeting, nor any other civic club meeting. How did you know?"

"Was it good?"

"My steak?"

"Yes, Sir. Was it good?"

"Yes, it was—very good. Cooked just like I like it—medium rare. How did you know, Dimples?"

"Well, Iuka is still Tishomingo County and besides, my cousin cooked 'em," Dimples replied, looking into one of the file drawers.

"Your cousin? Who was your cousin?" Patie had moved around to the side of the file cabinet so he could see Dimples' face.

"Pinky."

"Pinky? Pinky—oh—" Patie repeated, trying to remember meeting a Pinky. "What was his last name?"

"Abraham. He's a Jew."

92

"Pinky Abraham! Dimples, I don't remember meeting him."

"Probably not. He and Goldie had to leave early." Dimples was still looking in the drawer. Patie was leaning on the cabinet.

"I'm not even going to ask why they had to leave early." Corbin chortled. "But I am going to ask you this. Do you have Jewish blood in you?"

"Would it matter to you?" Dimples did not look up from the drawer.

"Of course not. God's not through with Israel nor the Jew yet. I wold love to know you are a "Completed" Jew."

"I'm first cousin to Goldie. She married Pinky."

"Has he received Christ?"

"No, not yet. Goldie's hopin'. It's harder livin' with him than she thought it was going to be, what with her bein' saved an all, an' him not."

"Yeah, I imagine it would be. That's why God tells us not to be un-evenly yoked togeth—well, I know it is hard." Patie caught himself, he hoped, in time not to get embroiled in another lengthy doctrinal discussion.

"Why do you call him Pinky, Dimples?"

"That's his name," the secretary answered, raising up from the drawer and looking at her boss. "'Course it's a nickname."

"Why do folks call him that?" Patie asked again, changing the question slightly.

"Color of his skin, I reckon. It's sort of a bronze, coppertone color. Reminds you of pink."

"Humh," the preacher breathed, turning to walk back into his of-fice. He didn't want *that* conversation to proceed any farther.

"I need to talk to you, Patie. Messages from yesterday. Can I do it now? And besides, I want to hear about the funeral," the secretary pro-fessed, following him into his office.

Patie stood up from his desk and stretched. Glancing at his watch, he said, "Well, I reckon the mail is up. Think I'll go to Holie Preacher's Club this morning, Dimples . Is there anything else you need to tell me?'

"Yes, sir, a couple of things."

Patie waited a few moments before he spoke, thinking Dimples would identify the "couple of things."

"Okay," he responded, stretching out "Okay" so that it sounded like it had three or four "o's." "You want to do it now?"

"Yes, Sir."

Patie waited again. Dimples seemed to be having a hard time starting. The preacher began to experience a little concern. "Dimples."

"We planned a party for you."

"You—ah—you planned—a—party? For me?"

Dimples was looking down at the floor. "Yes, sir."

"You planned a party for me!" the pastor repeated, his voice trailing down. "For me! You planned a party!"

"Yes, Sir."

"Well, Dimples, just by some wild chance that I have been granted by someone the unreasonable right to do so, may I ask you a few questions about this party. I mean, I don't want to violate any Tishrock principles or—"

"Yes, Sir, you may ask." Dimples was still staring at the floor.

Patie couldn't see Dimples' eyes but he imagined they were shining at *this* conversation. She appeared to be a little disconsolate but she certainly wasn't discomposed. The preacher wasn't amused by her behavior but he certainly wasn't offended and he wasn't even surprised by it. But he admitted to himself that he enjoyed teasing her, perhaps a little *too* much. He had to exhibit a little resistance to her tendency to plan his life, though, which he had already discovered she seemed inclined to do. "HUMH," he grunted a good bit louder than normal. "Would you like to give me all the information about this PARTY or would you have me ask the questions?"

"You ask," she blurted out quickly.

"All-right," Corbin obeyed, stretching out the first syllable. "First, when exactly is this party?"

"Saturday night."

"What time."

"Six-thirty."

"Where?"

"Well, at first we planned to have it at Ann's house—"

"Ann?" Patie interrupted. "Ann—oh—Ann? Do I know this Ann?"

Dimples jerked her head up. "Ann Chester, you know who—" she shrieked, stopping in mid-sentence. "Oh, Patie, you're pulling my leg."

"No, I'm not," the preacher quickly teased, "don't you go out of here telling people that."

Dimples glared at her pastor, her eyes still sparkling but no smile her face. She thought he was teasing but she wasn't quite sure. "No—I— oh—I meant you're joking with me."

Patie smiled. "So, you and Ann Chester planned the party and it was to be at her house, but you moved it?"

"Yes, Sir."

"Where to?"

"The Fromptons. You remember! Anselm and Myrtle."

"I remember. Now, I have one more question for you. Why?"

"Well, we knew yesterday had to be pretty hard on you, Patie, and we thought you might need to laugh some, so we decided to have a party."

"We?" Patie asked.

"Umh hunh. Ann and Jack and I."

Patie sat back down. He didn't want to appear to be hovering over his secretary. "Thank you, Dimples."

Dimples smiled. "You really mean that?"

The preacher grinned. "I really mean that. And you're probably right. Also, I need to meet some more people. Many folks coming?"

"About forty. About half from our church. Jack and I will pick you and Ann up."

Patie frowned unconsciously. That wouldn't work. The four of them could not walk into that party together, absolutely not, without question. "Dimples, that won't work."

"Well, I thought you might say that, so I have a Plan B."

"Good. What is it?"

"Jack and I will pick Ann up and Josh and Mildred Addison will pick you up."

"That's good. Thank you, Dimples."

"You're welcome."

"Now, what's the other thing?"

"You said you wanted to talk to me about a couple of things. That's two. We've talked about one."

"Oh, yeah," Dimples remembered, "tell Cricket hello for me."

The preacher really looked forward to meeting with the other preachers this morning. The week had been a tough one and he wanted to ask the other ministers to pray for Phil Appleby, as he had promised the new Christian. As Dimples had taught him to do, he stuck his head in all the businesses between the church and the post office, wishing them a good day; Homer's Shoes, Rufus' Café, Peggy's Dress Haven, Motors An' Sech, the Minnow Seine, Horace's Machine shop, Nelda's Family Hairloom Shop and a few others.

At Horace's Machine Shop, which was little more than a large shed, a covered area, walls on three sides but completely open on the front, Patie heard his name called even before he had a chance to speak, or before he saw anyone. "Brother Corbin!"

The preacher looked hard through a maze of equipment, large anvils, small grinding machines, motors with pulleys and belts and lots of other machines which he could not identify. Toward the back of the shop, in the midst of a noisy grinding sound and flying metal sparks, he saw a hand waving. He made his way slowly through all the impediments until he got to the two men, one sharpening a tool and the other one watching. The man watching was the man who waved. The "waver" looked familiar and the preacher believed him to be a member of Tishrock Community Church.

"Howdy, Preacher," the large man smiled. He was wearing overalls, which many of the locals, Patie had already discovered, called "overhauls," with a short- sleeved pink shirt underneath them. High work boots protruded from beneath the overall legs and upon his head sat a sweat and grease covered Atlanta Braves baseball cap, cocked at a weird angle. "I know you cain't' 'member everythang' whut' with you graduatin' from Ole Miss an' all. I met cha' Sundee' at church. Name's Harkum Hector."

"I remember, Harkum. 'Cept you didn't have that cap on Sunday. I hardly recognized you."

"I'd a' had it on if Tildi'd let me wer' it," he responded, sticking out his hand.

"Tildi. That your wife's name?"

"Yes, Sir. Wal', her name is Matilde but ever'body calls her Tildi."

The grinder had not looked up. With his back toward Harkum and Patie and through the noise of the grinding, the preacher wasn't sure he even knew he was there.

"How ye' been doin', Preach? Gittin' settled in?"

"Mostly, Harkum. Got a few more things to do around my little house yet."

"Good," the man said, through a pleasant expression, "Iffn' I can do you any hep', I'd be glad ." He glanced over at the grinding just a few feet away. "Gonna' ast' ye' a riddle. Whut's thet' man a' sharpenin' thar'?"

Corbin moved around to where he could see. He recognized the instrument immediately. "Harkum, when Sampson presented the Philistines with a riddle, he told them if they could figure it out, he would give them a bunch of new clothes. Exactly what do you propose to give me if I can figure it out?"

"Humh!", the farmer considered. "I'll give ye' 'zactly—naw', I cain't tell you thet'—thet'd' hep' ye' guess whut' it is. Tell ye' whut! You guess whut' it is an I'd invite ye' to the usin' of it," he grinned.

"Alright," Patie agreed, "I'd say that was a cane blade."

"Wal', I'd be a turkey gobbler," Harkum laughed, slapping himself on the thigh. "We got ourselves a country preacher. You couldn't a' knowed' 'at in New York. How'd ye' know 'at, Preacher?"

Patie couldn't help but laugh. Harkum's response tickled him but so did solving the riddle. "I grew up in Laurel but I had relatives down around Gloster. They grew sugar cane. I'd sometimes go down on Saturdays and help them cut cane."

"Wal', I declare," Harkum laughed. "So our preacher's cut cane. Never had a preacher come in heah' who ever cut cain' a'fore. Never as I recall."

"Cut it and raised it," Patie offered.

"You mean growed it?"

"No, Brother Harkum. Raised it!"

"Raisin' cane," Harkum breathed slowly, apparently trying to picture what that meant. Then he "got it." "Oh, heck, raisin' cane," he bellowed with great mirth. "Raisin' cane. You riddled me, Preacher shore. You did fer' a fact. You riddled me!"

Patie grinned as widely as did his church member. He decided, however, that he had better complete the story. "But, Harkum, I don't raise it any more. The Lord purged all of that out of me. You growin' Louisianne or P. O. J.?"

"Say whut'?" Harkum asked.

"Apparently you're growing sugar cane, what with getting your blade sharpened. I just wondered what kind."

"Ain't a'growin' sugar cane. Growin' sorghum. Whut' wuz' thet' ye called it? Louisianne and whut'?"

"P. O. J. Those were the two kinds of sugar cane grown around

Gloster. Louisianne and P. O. J. You were either a Louisianne man or a P. O. J. man and folks were adamant about which was best. I've seen folks almost come to blows over it and some of them were relatives."

"Shore' nuff'," Harkum considered. "Humh. Folks don't grow much sugar cane this far north. Some, I 'spect, but very little. We grow sorghum."

"Sorghum!" Corbin repeated. "How much you got?"

"'Bout two acres, givin' or takin' some."

"That the last one, Harkum?" The voice was that of the grinder. He turned around and saw Patie. "Harkum, why'n you tell me the preacher was standin' right behind me. I coulda' said somethin'!" He had a twinkle in his eyes.

"Brother Corbin, I wan'che' to meet a frien'—Wal' I thank' he's a frien'. I'll know when I check his sharpenin' out. This here is Cooter Ha-zlip."

"Cooter," Patie greeted, extending his right hand. That sounds like a nickname."

"It is," Cooter agreed, wiping his hands on his overalls and taking the preacher's hand. "Got it give to me 'cause I love to pull them big turtles outa' th' waterway. Love turtle meat."

Patie grinned. "Some folks in South Mississippi called turtles coot-ers, too, when I was growin' up."

Turning back toward Harkum, Patie asked, "What was it you said I would win if I guessed your riddle?"

"Said I'd invite 'ye out to a sorghum cuttin', strippin', toppin' an' a cookin', makin' 'em good surghum m'lasses. But now, Preach, I'se jesta joshin'. You don't really haf' to come do thet'."

"No, no, Harkum, I'll be there. When do you expect to be cut-tin'?"

"You shore, Preach? Hit' ain't easy work, if'n you remember."

"I remember. I'll be there. When you cuttin'?"

"Spect' next week. Or week after."

"Call me and let me know."

"Shore will, Brother Corbin, shore will. If'n you' shore, now."

"I'm shore, ah, sure. Call me. Lord bless you."

When the pastor reached the sidewalk, it would have been a close call to determine who held the most doubt about him cutting sorghum—him or the two smiling men he left at the rear of the shop.

A few minutes after leaving the machine shop, Corbin stood before the church's large post office box. He had opened it and was pulling the big bundle of mail from it when he heard a melodious female voice. "How're you, Brother Corbin."

For the life of him, the preacher could not locate the source of the sound. He reasoned it was probably Cricket but he could not find her.

"Lean over an' look in ye' box," the voice suggested.

The pastor obeyed. Cricket's attractive face was framed by the sides of his box. She was on the inside of the working area looking out.

"Hi, Cricket. How are you?"

"Jest' fine, thank ye'. How ye' ben' doin'?"

Before Patie had time to answer, Cricket continued, "Heard yo' cabin was a sight to behold, now thet' you've fixed it up an' all. Sure would powerfully lik' to see it sometimes."

Be careful, Corbin, Patie counseled himself. Gotta' say this just right. "I would love for you to, Cricket. Why don't you get a load of friends and y'all let me know what Saturday morning you're coming so I'll be there."

The message was subtle, Corbin realized. He hoped Cricket received it. She apparently did not.

"Gonna' take ye' up on thet' invitation, Brother Corbin." She smiled widely through the box.

Patie smiled back. He quickly closed the box door, practically slamming it in Cricket's face. He heard her say, "I'll call you, Brother Corbin," as he moved quickly toward the door. Three women and a man stood at the post office window. They were all looking at him. He spoke and they continued smiling.

"Brothers, y'all don't know how glad I am to see y'all today," Patie stressed, sitting at the table with the other preachers; Ralph Wellmon, First Baptist; Jerry Ferguson, First Methodist; Gerald Collins, First Presbyterian; Dave Smith, Church of Christ; and Stanley Ray, Assembly of God.

"We heard about the tragedy at Birmingham, Patie," Ralph Wellmon related. "It's a shame, but from what we heard, the lady had prayed with you to receive Christ."

"Yes," Patie confirmed. "Sure made the funeral easier, but I don't have to tell you ministers that. I just got into the pastorate. You've been there for years."

Gerald Collins agreed. "Just about the toughest part of my ministry is burying someone who may not know the Lord." The other preachers readily agreed.

"Can I get something for you, Brother Corbin?"

Patie jerked his head around. The lady who spoke to him was either Miss Minnie or Aunt Winnie, one of the twin owners. He did not know which. "Yes'm," he answered, looking at the other preacher's plates. Everyone was eating this morning. "I think I'll have a mug of coffee and a blueberry muffin."

"Butter?" the lady asked.

"No'm, not today, I don't believe."

"Brother Corbin," the lady inquired, "you know which one I am?"

"No'm," grinned the preacher. "How long do I have?"

The lady squinted her eyes and pretended to be angry. "One month."

"Come on, Miss Minnie," Ralph Wellmon beseeched, "he can't do it in a month. It took me a year."

"That's why he'll only need a month," Miss Minnie declared, turning quickly and sauntering back toward the counter. "I was measuring him agin' you."

Ralph and the other preachers guffawed. "Alright, Miss Minnie," the Baptist preacher called after her. "That did it. I"m going to cut my doughnuts down to two dozen a week."

Miss Minnie had disappeared into the kitchen before Ralph's words had cleared his mouth.

Patie told the preachers about his visit with Phil and the good news that the prisoner had prayed to receive Christ. That brought some huge smiles from the men and chorus of "amens" and "praise Gods." A few minutes later all of them had finished their snacks and having done so, entered their time of prayer . To a man, they asked God to authenticate and confirm Phil's conversion, not even knowing his last name—not even wanting to know it.

Patie had no sooner sat down at his desk than Dimples, who was out of the preacher's sight in the office, called loudly, "Doughnuts good this morning, Patie?"

"They looked good, Dimples, but I didn't eat any. Ate a blueberry muffin."

"I hear tell, though I don't know for certain it's true, that some of the other pastors take their staff doughnuts."

For a moment, this pastor found himself speechless. He had never thought to do that. "Dimples, I am really sorry. I will not go to Holie Preacher's Club ever again without bringing you some doughnuts—if you remind me. You aren't dealing with a young flexible brain here, you know."

"Cricket's coming out to visit you *this* Saturday?"

Patie's mouth dropped open. Momentarily, he considered asking

Dimples how she knew so quickly, but instead he just shook his head, leaned toward his desk and looked down at his small stack of messages. He hoped by not answering her question, she might think he had not heard it.

t Cokes, sweet tea, all kinda a' juice—oh yeah, an' Sprite and regular
ke an'—an' , whut' else, Mama?" he asked, turning toward Myrtle.

"Coffee."

"Oh yeah, an' coffee. Mildred?"

When the three had placed their drink orders with the wealthy busi-
sman and he turned to get them, Josh grabbed his friend by the arm.
ait, Anselm, tell me whut' Patie said about the Dawgs."

"Git' *him* to tell ye. I don't want to hear it again," the host grinned,
ving away from them and toward the drink table. "Y'all go fill ye'
es. I'll meet ye' at that table," he pointed.

"What did you tell him, Patie?" Josh asked.

"You serious, Josh? You really want to know?"

"Yeah. I might want to remind him every once in a while."

"The first time I came to Tishrock, Anselm and Myrtle picked me
at the airport in Memphis. I stayed with them and—"

"That was late last spring, wasn't it?" Josh interrupted.

"Right. Well, when we drove in between his two bulldogs, he cut
eyes over at me, grinned and said something like 'How did you like
sing between those two bulldogs.'"

"I told him it made me feel right at home because I ran unmolested
t through' em for four years when I was at Ole Miss. 'Course, that was
e. I never ran through any team unmolested, much less State. They
d to tear my head off, seemed like."

By the time **Patie** finished telling Josh and Mildred the story, the
e of them had moved closer to the food and the crowd. Others were
aking and waving to them, as they took plates and occupied their places
he end of the line. Patie had leaned over surveying the food down the
e when he felt a small gentle hand touch his left arm. He turned quickly
looked directly into the face of Miss Daisy Jo Crisp.

"How are you, Brother Corbin."

"Fine, Miss Daisy Jo. How are you," the preacher responded, tak-
her hand in his and leaning down for a brief hug.

CHAPTER NINE

WHAT IT WAS, WAS FOOTBALL

Patie walked into his bathroom, took a last glance at his hair, picked
up the hair brush and made one last swipe across the top of his head.
Then he picked up a can of hair spray and "glued" his hair down,
as he often referred to the practice. Grinning, he remembered his childhood. He never envisioned spraying his hair with hair spray like women
do, when he was growing up in South Mississippi. Greasing it down with
Vaseline hair oil or Vitalis, perhaps, but not spraying it down with hair
spray. Oh, how things change, the old converted playboy smiled to himself,
thinking how grateful to the Lord he was that *that* thought was true. A
minute later he pulled the plastic container of cappuccino mix which he
bought from a BP Service Center on the trip back from Birmingham, from
the cabinet and made himself a mug of it. Standing out on his front porch,
he acknowledged to himself the natural beauty of his environment again
and plopped down upon the swing, pushing himself and the swing backward as he did so, holding the mug carefully in both hands. The preacher's
mind rotated back to yesterday, as he waited for Josh and Mildred to pick
him up. It was Saturday afternoon, late.

Both Friday and Saturday mornings had been good days—no problems, few phone calls and only one of them sounded serious—an older man
who said he needed to see Patie. He agreed to come in Monday and fill out
the questionnaire, which, according to Dimples wasn't all that necessary.

"Why not?" the preacher had asked his secretary;

"I can already tell you why he's coming."

"Dimples, are you sure we can talk about this without it being gossip?"

"Is it gossip if everybody already knows?"

"Everybody already knows Mr.—oh–what's his name?"

"Purlis Breaker," Dimples answered. "Folks call him Otis."

"Yes, Purlis Breaker. Everyone already knows he's coming to see me?" Patie asked, missing the import of Purlis' nickname.

"Probably, but what I meant was that everybody knows why he *needs* to see you."

"And why would that be?"

"His drinking. He's an alcoholic."

"You know that for a fact, Dimples?"

"Yes, Sir, everybody in town, maybe even in the county, knows it. He walks around town drunk all the time."

"Umh," Patie grunted. "That's sad. I look forward to seeing him. Why do people call him Otis?"

"Mayberry. You know—Andy Griffith."

"Oh, of course," Patie acknowledged, surprised at his slowness of thought and a little ashamed that Dimples' personality and Purlis' nickname could be humorous to him.

The preacher was considering these things when his thoughts were shattered by the sound of a vehicle winding its way down his driveway. When the car stopped in front of his cabin, he recognized Josh Addison.

By the time Patie and the Addisons arrived, the grass along the driveway at the Fromptons home was covered with vehicles, meaning that they were among the last guests to get there. Josh parked his Buick at the end of the cars about fifty yards from the house. A few minutes later the

three walked into a noisy throng of people gathered arou[nd] pool behind the house. Anselm and Myrtle greeted the walked around the corner of the house. Mildred held food.

"Preacher, Josh, Mildred, y'all come on out he[re] man greeted. "We waitin' on y'all like two-week old be[s] the runt to nurse their mama."

"I can tell you are," Josh laughed, looking at the elers gathered around two long tables literally covered w[ith]

"Y'all 'bout to be late," Anselm grunted. "Gr[ab] plates each an' start fillin' 'em. I'll get ye' sompin' to [drink] want?"

"What you got?" Josh asked.

"Not everthang' I wanted to have," Anselm co[uld] know women. Myrtle wouldn't let me serve everthang' said lightenin' mite' strike or else the water in the swimm[in'] a'gurglin'."

Myrtle, who walked up to the three about the ti[me] sued his declaration, reached up and playfully twisted h[is] true," she corrected. "He was trying to shock y'all, espe[cially] Corbin." Then turning toward her grinning mate, she po[inted at] him and declared, "I'm gonna' have a talk with you, M[r.]

"Since he said it to us," Josh asked, "can we [?] do? I'd like to hear that."

"Me, too," injected Patie. "I'd *really* like to h[ear] that *and* making me ride in here between these two fin[e] again."

Anselm slanted his eyes and mockingly thre[w] "Don't you go a' talkin' 'bout my Dawgs again, Preache[r] ye' said 'bout 'em last time yu wuz' here."

"Made an impression, hunh, Anselm?"

"Shore did. 'Member it still. Now whut' do '[y

CHAPTER NINE
WHAT IT WAS, WAS FOOTBALL

Patie walked into his bathroom, took a last glance at his hair, picked up the hair brush and made one last swipe across the top of his head. Then he picked up a can of hair spray and "glued" his hair down, as he often referred to the practice. Grinning, he remembered his childhood. He never envisioned spraying his hair with hair spray like women do, when he was growing up in South Mississippi. Greasing it down with Vaseline hair oil or Vitalis, perhaps, but not spraying it down with hair spray. Oh, how things change, the old converted playboy smiled to himself, thinking how grateful to the Lord he was that *that* thought was true. A minute later he pulled the plastic container of cappuccino mix which he bought from a BP Service Center on the trip back from Birmingham, from the cabinet and made himself a mug of it. Standing out on his front porch, he acknowledged to himself the natural beauty of his environment again and plopped down upon the swing, pushing himself and the swing backward as he did so, holding the mug carefully in both hands. The preacher's mind rotated back to yesterday, as he waited for Josh and Mildred to pick him up. It was Saturday afternoon, late.

Both Friday and Saturday mornings had been good days—no problems, few phone calls and only one of them sounded serious—an older man who said he needed to see Patie. He agreed to come in Monday and fill out the questionnaire, which, according to Dimples wasn't all that necessary.

"Why not?" the preacher had asked his secretary;

"I can already tell you why he's coming."

"Dimples, are you sure we can talk about this without it being gossip?"

"Is it gossip if everybody already knows?"

"Everybody already knows Mr.—oh–what's his name?"

"Purlis Breaker," Dimples answered. "Folks call him Otis."

"Yes, Purlis Breaker. Everyone already knows he's coming to see me?" Patie asked, missing the import of Purlis' nickname.

"Probably, but what I meant was that everybody knows why he *needs* to see you."

"And why would that be?"

"His drinking. He's an alcoholic."

"You know that for a fact, Dimples?"

"Yes, Sir, everybody in town, maybe even in the county, knows it. He walks around town drunk all the time."

"Umh," Patie grunted. "That's sad. I look forward to seeing him. Why do people call him Otis?"

"Mayberry. You know—Andy Griffith."

"Oh, of course," Patie acknowledged, surprised at his slowness of thought and a little ashamed that Dimples' personality and Purlis' nickname could be humorous to him.

The preacher was considering these things when his thoughts were shattered by the sound of a vehicle winding its way down his driveway. When the car stopped in front of his cabin, he recognized Josh Addison.

By the time Patie and the Addisons arrived, the grass along the driveway at the Fromptons home was covered with vehicles, meaning that they were among the last guests to get there. Josh parked his Buick at the end of the cars about fifty yards from the house. A few minutes later the three walked into a noisy throng of people gathered around the swimming pool behind the house. Anselm and Myrtle greeted the three just as they walked around the corner of the house. Mildred held a covered dish of food.

"Preacher, Josh, Mildred, y'all come on out here," the muscular man greeted. "We waitin' on y'all like two-week old beagles a' waitin' on the runt to nurse their mama."

"I can tell you are," Josh laughed, looking at the thirty or forty revelers gathered around two long tables literally covered with food and drink.

"Y'all 'bout to be late," Anselm grunted. "Grab ye' a couple a' plates each an' start fillin' 'em. I'll get ye' sompin' to drink. Whut' y'all want?"

"What you got?" Josh asked.

"Not everthang' I wanted to have," Anselm countered, "but you know women. Myrtle wouldn't let me serve everthang' I wanted to. She said lightenin' mite' strike or else the water in the swimmin' pool mite' start a'gurglin'."

Myrtle, who walked up to the three about the time her husband issued his declaration, reached up and playfully twisted his ear. "That's not true," she corrected. "He was trying to shock y'all, especially you, Brother Corbin." Then turning toward her grinning mate, she pointed her finger at him and declared, "I'm gonna' have a talk with you, Mr. Frompton."

"Since he said it to us," Josh asked, "can we be there when you do? I'd like to hear that."

"Me, too," injected Patie. "I'd *really* like to hear it, him saying that *and* making me ride in here between these two fine looking Bulldogs again."

Anselm slanted his eyes and mockingly threatened his pastor. "Don't you go a' talkin' 'bout my Dawgs again, Preacher. I 'member whut ye' said 'bout 'em last time yu wuz' here."

"Made an impression, hunh, Anselm?"

"Shore did. 'Member it still. Now whut' do 'ye want to drink—

Diet Cokes, sweet tea, all kinda a' juice—oh yeah, an' Sprite and regular Coke an'—an' , whut' else, Mama?" he asked, turning toward Myrtle.

"Coffee."

"Oh yeah, an' coffee. Mildred?"

When the three had placed their drink orders with the wealthy businessman and he turned to get them, Josh grabbed his friend by the arm. "Wait, Anselm, tell me whut' Patie said about the Dawgs."

"Git' *him* to tell ye. I don't want to hear it again," the host grinned, moving away from them and toward the drink table. "Y'all go fill ye' plates. I'll meet ye' at that table," he pointed.

"What did you tell him, Patie?" Josh asked.

"You serious, Josh? You really want to know?"

"Yeah. I might want to remind him every once in a while."

"The first time I came to Tishrock, Anselm and Myrtle picked me up at the airport in Memphis. I stayed with them and—"

"That was late last spring, wasn't it?" Josh interrupted.

"Right. Well, when we drove in between his two bulldogs, he cut his eyes over at me, grinned and said something like 'How did you like passing between those two bulldogs.'"

"I told him it made me feel right at home because I ran unmolested right through' em for four years when I was at Ole Miss. 'Course, that was a lie. I never ran through any team unmolested, much less State. They tried to tear my head off, seemed like."

By the time Patie finished telling Josh and Mildred the story, the three of them had moved closer to the food and the crowd. Others were speaking and waving to them, as they took plates and occupied their places at the end of the line. Patie had leaned over surveying the food down the table when he felt a small gentle hand touch his left arm. He turned quickly and looked directly into the face of Miss Daisy Jo Crisp.

"How are you, Brother Corbin."

"Fine, Miss Daisy Jo. How are you," the preacher responded, taking her hand in his and leaning down for a brief hug.

"Just checking you out," the older lady smiled.

"I told you I'd never forget you, Miss Daisy Jo. You placed an indelible print of yourself on my old feeble brain a few days ago."

"When you get down to the desserts, Brother Corbin, I want you to try some of my bread pudding. That's my only claim to fame."

"No, it isn't, Patie," Josh, who was listening to the exchange between the pastor and church member corrected. "Miss Daisy Jo is known for a lot more than her bread pudding, as good as it is."

By the time Josh finished making his comment, Miss Crisp had disappeared back into the crowd.

"Patie?"

The pastor turned and looked into the face of his neighbor. "Hi, Ann. How are you?"

"Fine, thank you. Come over and eat with us."

"Got room for the three of us?"

"Yeah. We've been kinda' saving you all a place. We have a big table."

"Good," the preacher replied with reservation which he hoped didn't show. Actually, he had rather sit with other people whom he did not know very well. "Where are you sitting?"

Ann pointed. "Right over there."

When Patie looked, Dimples was waving, her large sparkling eyes visible even at that distance.

"Let me make my way down the rest of the table and we'll be right on over, or at least, I will." Then, turning to Josh, he asked, "That alright with y'all?" He knew they had heard the conversation.

"Fine," Mildred answered. Josh was busy digging chicken pie from a large dish. He didn't respond.

It was only after Patie, Mildred and Josh had sat down that the preacher noticed carefully the decor. The seven or eight tables at which the people ate were covered with blue and maroon cloths, and scented insect-repellent candles burned on each of them. Four large square floor fans moved the muggy late afternoon air, much to the pleasure of the crowd, all of whom seemed to have dressed for the occasion—short sleeved shirts, blue jeans, khakis, and a few in shorts. Soft Christian music floated through the air, provided by an outside speaker system. The area was illuminated by underwater lights in the swimming pool and soft spotlights from the eaves of the pool house and the home itself.

"Thank y'all for putting all this together," the preacher declared, appearing to be more grateful than he actually was, raising his voice slightly in order to be heard over the din of the crowd. "I know it was a fair amount of trouble for two working girls."

"Not really," Dimples retorted. "We had lots of help. All the ladies brought the food, four or five men set up the tables, and Amselm and Myrtle furnished the home and decorated."

"Humh," Patie grunted. "Exactly what did you and Ann do, then?"

"We organized," the secretary declared.

"And called everyone," Ann added. "We Tishrock gals know how to distribute responsibility."

Patie chuckled. "I believe it. You all did a marvelous job. Thank you."

"LET ME HAVE YOUR ATTENTION," the booming voice of a large man standing at one edge of the patio bellowed. "Let me have your attention—quiet, please—quiet—quiet. Sally, would you hit that loud-mouthed husband of yours with a chicken leg or something?"

Everyone laughed.

Patie leaned over toward Josh. "I don't think I've met him yet. Who is he?"

"Thurm Willis," Josh whispered. "Runs the stone quarry. The town-appointed master-of-ceremonies. Chairman of the deacons of First Baptist."

Patie nodded and looked back at the man. He was in fact a large man, tall and pretty well built, although he appeared to be a little heavy, even for his height. He wore khaki trousers, and a beige shirt. His silver hair was parted on the left side and his large tanned face was lined with furrows, appearing to have been placed there by smiles. He had a large nose which might have been broken a time or two, and his bass voice attracted everyone's attention, finally.

"Thank you, folks, thank you. I hate to ask folks having so much fun to quieten down, but we need to get on with the program, such as it is."

"We got a program, Thurm? Suzy didn't tell me we were coming to hear you speak."

"Wal, what difference did *that* make. You'd a' come anyway when she told you we were gonna' eat."

The laughs of the people were perforated with "amens." Thurm gave them a minute to quiet down.

"Now," the big man continued, "we don't really have a program, but we are here to honor our newest citizen and to meet him, for those of us who haven't done that yet. And in a minute I'm going to ask Ann Chester to introduce him, but—"

ANN CHESTER ! Patie screamed inwardly. Ann Chester! Why in the world would Dimples and Ann decide that Ann should introduce me? Can't they understand what that might cause some people to think? A ministry is at stake here—my soul! The preacher's annoyance at the two women's lack of discernment almost caused his mind to miss Thurm's other comments.

"—but first, I want him to know," the large man continued.

Somehow Corbin managed to redirect his mind from his frustration back to the voice of the man who stood before him speaking.

"—just how honored we are to have him—to have you—in our community."

Patie looked up at the business man, smiled, and nodded.

"From what I hear," Thurm professed, "this man of God is really a Baptist parading around in Community Church clothes. I don't know how the Southern Baptist Convention missed him and how it missed sending him to one of our seminaries but regardless of that, Brother Corbin, we're really glad to have you in Tishrock."

Patie smiled and whispered, "Thank you."

"And now, here's Ann Chester to introduce him."

When Ann Chester stood, Patie Corbin's heart sank.

"Ladies and gentlemen," Ann spoke. Her voice was strong and confident. Obviously she had done this sort of thing before. "I, too, am honored to introduce Patie Corbin to you. I was surprised when Dimples asked me to do it, but when she realized that Patie and I are apparently the only two residents in town who hail from the Free State of Jones—That's Jones County, and Laurel for those of you who may not remember your history, she decided I should introduce him. Patie did not know me before he moved to town, but I certainly knew *of* him. His football and the family from which he came made him a bona fide hero in our part of the country."

Patie tried to look at Ann but he could not. Nor could he look into the faces of the other hearers. He dropped his eyes to the cement of the patio, gritted his teeth and waited.

At that point, Ann unfolded a roll of paper which she was holding in her hand. Three minutes later she had read most of his football exploits, his civic achievements and told a little about his family. Then she folded the paper and said, "But the greatest thing which ever happened to him occurred about four years ago in Eagle Pass, Texas, when he prayed to receive our Lord Jesus Christ. The second greatest thing was graduating from four years of seminary with a 4.0 grade average. But the THIRD greatest thing which ever happened to him was coming to Tishrock, Mississippi as a pastor. Friends, I present to you Patie Corbin."

By the time Ann finished the introduction, Patie had exercised a smile upon his face. He knew he was supposed to stand—and he did—but he did not know everyone expected him to speak. He discovered that truth after he thanked Ann, after he thanked everyone for coming, and after he sat back down. He discovered it through the ovation and calls of "speech—speech," emanating from the people.

Patie slowly stood up again. He looked over at Dimples and

frowned teasingly at her as though to say "I'll get you later." When he tuned back toward the people, Thurm was standing by his side, his right hand outstretched.

"Welcome to Tishrock, Patie."

"Thank you, Brother Thurm," the preacher smiled.

"Patie," Mr. Willis said, "we know God has given to you the wonderful gift of Pastor and from what we have heard from your church members, He has apparently blessed you with the spiritual gifts of preaching and teaching—"

The Baptist deacon was interrupted with a chorus of "amens."

"—but we have never had the opportunity, or at least most of us haven't, of hearing a pro-football player speak on the state of football today at all levels. Would it be asking too much to ask you to make a few comments abut that?"

Patie grinned. He had no choice. "No, it wouldn't, Brother Thurm. But please realize this," he advised, looking at the mass of people, "you will be listening to a has-been, I mean a real sure enough has-been. You sure you want to subject yourselves to that?"

Led by Thurm, who was still standing, the guests gave the ex-athlete another resounding ovation.

"Alright, then. You asked for it," Patie threatened. "Although I'm not certain you ladies are quite as enthusiastic as the men." Then locating Miss Crisp in the crowd, he asked, "Miss Daisy Jo, do you want me to do this?"

"No. I don't, but I am terribly outnumbered. I'll suffer through it and cleanse myself with some prayer and Bible study when I get home."

"Oh, me," Corbin groaned.

"Go ahead, Pastor. I was teasing you."

"Oh, thank you, Miss Daisy."

Turning to the people, Patie confessed, "I guess you can tell, I've already learned not to get crossways with Miss Daisy."

That comment relaxed the crowd a little and brought a smile to almost everyone's face. One man did not smile however and the pastor's eyes fell upon his face. He was sitting at a table to Patie's left. The preacher recognized the man as a member of his church, yet he could not, as hard as he tried, recall his name. It wasn't the lack of a smile upon the man's face which troubled the preacher, however. It was the fact that he could not imagine the man ever smiling. Somehow the features of his face and a smile seemed to be adversarial.

For the following twenty minutes or so, the old footballer examined the current states of high school, college and professional football and compared all three with the sport as it was played twenty-five years earlier. Then he summarized.

"I hope high school football can remain a sport rather than succumbing to the temptation to create out of itself a business. But in some places, I see it becoming just that—a business, with all the pressures of a business thrust upon the young men—boys actually—who play it. Of course, you understand I'm certainly not referring to Tishrock. Obviously, I haven't been here long enough to make that judgement. Perhaps because of the appeal of earning a college football scholarship and the big money of professional football later, some parents are tempted to become even another source of pressure upon their sons. When enough pressure is applied to young immature minds, all kinds of unfavorable attributes may be developed—and–the sport ceases to be fun. In addition, the lessons which might be learned on the football field like discipline and teamwork are lost, and —"

"Patie," a woman's voice called out from the back table, "I'm sorry to interrupt you, but may I ask you a question?"

"Yes, M'am. Where are you?"

The lady lifted her hand. "I see you. Certainly you may ask a question but just like the observation which all of you asked me to give, my answer to your question certainly has no more value than any of yours." Corbin could not see the woman clearly but from where he stood, she appeared to be about the right age to be the mother of a high school student.

Her question suggested it.

"Do you think some of us parents might push our children on the ball fields for reasons other than scholarships or money? Like for ego, wanting our children to be the best athletes or maybe even worse, wanting to relive our own youths? I've heard fathers scream at their eight year old sons right in the middle of a game in front of everyone. And mothers too."

The crowd, Patie noticed, grew extraordinarily quiet. The preacher guarded his words.

"M'am, understand, what I'm about to say doesn't apply to Tishrock as far as I am concerned because I've only been here a week and other than the football game last night, I haven't been to a single ball game."

Almost before Patie finished his sentence, a male voice bellowed, "What'd you think about our Chiefs last night, Preach? We whupped up on them Fulton boys pretty good, didn't we?"

Everybody laughed. Almost everyone. The unsmiling man was still unsmiling, Corbin noticed. "Sure did," he answered. "They looked pretty good in doing it, too, for the first game."

"M'am," Patie answered, looking back at the lady who asked the question. "I've seen that happen, unfortunately. "What that says to a young child, when a parent screams at him or her on the athletic field is, I accept you if you play ball well. I reject you if you don't. Other than physical or sexual abuse, little could be worse for a child."

Patie glanced at the lady. She was nodding. The man sitting next to her was looking downward. The preacher unconsciously imagined that this conversation would continue when the couple got home.

"Well, now let's summarize my amateur observations of college football," Corbin continued. "It is now a full-fledged business out of which all sport has been squeezed. At many colleges now, you have to pay the school for the *right* to buy athletic tickets. Then you have to pay for the tickets."

"AMEN!" Followed an agreeing voice.

"Is that a Rebel amen or a Bulldog amen?" Corbin asked.

"It could be either, probably," the voice answered, "but this is a Crimson Tide amen."

"Would you all like to hear my antediluvian opinion about what college football should do?"Corbin asked.

"Sure would, Pastor, as soon as you tell us what that word—anti-dell—or whatever it was means."

In the midst of all the laughter, Corbin replied, "Well, I don't rightly know, sir, but the seminary professors said we ought to use those words we learned every once in a while. Use it or lose it, you know? But as I recall it means something like old-fashioned or ancient. Maybe primitive."

"Go ahead, Preach," the voice ordered

Through his grin, Patie continued. "I think college football ought to return to one platoon—make the boys play offense and defense. The number of players could be reduced drastically, as well as the number of coaches. That could reduce expenses by perhaps as much as fifty percent. It would make practices harder which might cause the players to stay at home and study rather than be tempted to go out and get in trouble. And the "homes" they need to stay at ought to be dormitory rooms, in which an assistant coach lives."

The people to whom Patie was speaking grew strangely silent, except for one timid-sounding male voice. "You think that's ever goin' to happen?"

Corbin's answer was quick. "No."

That certain reply brought more laughter.

"Now, as far as pro football is concerned, I have an observation. First, in my antedil—ah— archaic view, I believe it's fundamentally wrong for a player to make more money that his coach. My second point I'll illustrate with a story. Several years ago at a Giants Old-Timers reunion, a sportswriter asked us a question. 'Would you have played pro football if the owners could not have paid you but got all of you jobs loading eighteen-wheelers at night after practice.' Out of a crowd of about fifty ex-players, all but two or three said 'yes,'"

"Thank y'all for taking me to the party tonight, Josh," Patie said, getting out of the Addison's car. "I had a great time."

"So did we, Patie, and you're welcome. We'll see you in the morning."

The preacher watched the tail lights of Josh's car disappear out his driveway. He was walking up his front steps when the headlights of another car splashed upon him and against his house. A moment later, a large pickup truck eased to a stop and Patie walked over to the driver's side of the vehicle. The man from the party who wasn't smiling lowered the car window. His wife sat stoically in the front seat next to him. He looked up at Corbin with that same stern expression. "Brother Corbin, I'd like to talk to you."

CHAPTER TEN

WHEN THE LIGHTS WENT OFF

"**P**lease get out and come in," Patie invited, looking first at the man, then at his wife, and then at the man again. "Both of you."

"No, thank you. We can talk from right here," the man who didn't smile decreed.

"I have a mighty good swing on my front porch and a couple of comfortable chairs. Sure would like for y'all to come in."

"No, thank you," the man declined again, looking obliquely at the preacher. "We can talk right here."

Corbin looked across the man to his wife. In the semi-darkness which gained only a little light from the fixture on Corbin's front porch, the lady looked pleasant enough, although she was not smiling either. The preacher had noticed earlier and could see now, she wore little makeup and her greying hair was pulled back into a tight ball on the back of her head. He could not see what she wore. The woman continued to stare out the front windshield and as far as the pastor could tell had not looked at him nor spoken a word since she and her husband arrived. For the life of him, Patie could not remember their names.

"Alright, if you insist. We'll talk right here. But before we start, I have to confess to you, I can't quite come up with your names. I am really sorry."

"We haven't met yet," the man snapped.

"Oh? Well, maybe that's the reason I can't remember," Corbin chuckled. "I know we didn't shake hands tonight but I thought we *may* have last Sunday or—"

"No," the man declared. "We haven't met yet."

"Well—then if it's alright with you, let's meet now," Patie invited, thrusting his right hand through the window of the truck. "I'm Patie Corbin."

The man who wouldn't smile shook hands with his pastor. "I'm Turk Burley. This is my wife Louise."

"Glad to meet you Turk, and glad to meet you, too, Louise," Patie responded, leaning over and again looking past the man to his wife.

Louise turned her head toward her pastor slightly and smiled, just for a second, a quick intriguing smile turning the corners of her mouth up only moderately and molding a deep dimple in her left cheek which dissolved as quickly as it had formed. Still, she did not speak.

"Turk!" Patie remarked. "Sounds like a nickname."

"'Tis. Real name's Clarence. I like Turk better."

"How'd you get it, if I might ask, Turk?"

Unsmiling, the man explained. "Grew up on a farm in Missouri, a turkey farm. Everybody started calling me Turkey and that finally got shortened to Turk."

"That's interesting. I thought I noticed a little mid-western sound to some of your words. We haven't corrupted your speech down here yet, it doesn't sound like."

Patie thought Turk was going to smile but he seemed to catch himself just in time. Unless the porch light was too dim to really tell, there seemed to be a sudden twinkle in his eyes.

"Brother Corbin, I—"

"I'm sorry, Turk, for interrupting you, but while we're talking about this, I'd like to ask about Louise. Are you from Missouri?"

"She's from here," Turk answered. "Born and raised right here in Tishomingo County."

"Is that right?" Patie was interested and wanted the couple to know it. "How did a Missouri boy and a Tishomingo girl get together?"

"Columbus Air Force Base. I was on active duty and Louise was working in the Officer's Club."

"That right! So you were an officer?"

"Yes. Got my twenty and got out."

"That's interesting, Turk, I'd love to talk to you about that sometime but I know you didn't come out here to talk about that tonight."

"That's right," Turk agreed. "Brother Corbin, I want you to know on the front end that Louise and I voted for the church not to call you as pastor." The man looked Patie directly in the eye when he issued his declaration. Louise dropped her head.

Turk continued. "But that's not what I want to talk to you about either. Can't do anything about that now, though to be honest with you we're kinda' looking for another church."

All Patie felt like doing was gently nodding his head in understanding. If the foundation is cracked, the building is going to crack. If, in Turk's mind, I shouldn't even be standing in the pulpit, then I can do very little to please him, the preacher thought. He certainly understood that.

"Now, Brother Corbin, here's what's bothering me. You've been appointed pastor of this church. First Wednesday night, you're out of town preaching a lady's funeral, who you led to pray to receive Christ at daylight out on the walkin' trail without her husband even knowing she was there. On top of that, word's gotten 'round town that you and Mrs. Chester are seeing a lot of one another and some say that a path's bein' worn between your house and hers. Then tonight, when you had a big crowd, you had a perfect opportunity to present the Gospel. Some of those people weren't saved. But what did you do? You talked FOOTBALL," the church member complained, stressing the word "Football" and holding the letter "f" between his upper front teeth and lower lip, creating a "fizzing" sound. Turk's contempt was very evident.

Patie said nothing at first, not for thirty or forty seconds. Finally, he nodded gently and peeped around Turk at his wife. She sat as she had the last time the preacher looked at her, with her head lowered, seeming to be gazing at her lap—or maybe praying. "Do you feel the same way, Louise?"

"Yes, she does," Turk answered.

"Turk, if you don't mind, I would really appreciate your *wife* telling me what she thinks."

Turk stiffened and when he spoke, he spoke sharply. "I speak for my wife. I'm the head of this family."

WOW! Patie thought. I have a far greater problem here than the other complaints Turk has with me. Give me grace, Lord. I don't want to say anything stupid and I *really* don't want to say anything divisive. Other thoughts were thundering in his head, too, thoughts which he could not even collect, thoughts which might nudge an already-negative man even farther away if they were verbalized. "Turk," Patie spoke slowly, lovingly and non-confrontationally, "I have to be honest with you just as you have been honest with me. Is that alright?"

The man nodded his head. "Of course." The tone of his voice indicated he felt no fear that he could be proven wrong. It even seemed to contain a particle of challenge, as though he might be hungering for a debate.

The pastor reminded himself that he must be very careful—careful to defend and teach truth while at the same time protecting the emotional state of a brother in Christ—or at least the emotions of a church member. It would not be easy. He would be forced to start the conversation at ground level, spiritually. "I need your permission to do something, Brother."

"What?"

"I need your permission to delay talking about the three problems you have with me until we settle the one I have with you."

"Why?"

"Because the difference is foundational to solving the other three, or so it seems to me."

Mr. Burley said nothing. Patie knew he was thinking. Finally, he answered. "Alright."

"Good. Thank you, my brother. Turk, do you believe every Christian has received the gift of the Holy Spirit?"

"Yes."

"Men and women?"

"Yes."

"Equally?" Patie inquired.

Turk's voice was still strong, and if not defiant, then certainly confident. He had probably experienced this debate before. "Yes."

"In all of His fullness?"

"What do you mean?'

"That Louise has been given all of the fullness of the Godhead, in the Person of the Holy Spirit, just as you have?'

"I believe that," Turk agreed. "Now, let me ask you a question, Preacher."

Good! That's good, Patie thought. He called me preacher. Maybe he's allowing this discussion to progress on a more level playing field. "Okay, of course you may ask me."

"Do you believe the Bible teaches submission?"

"Yes, of course I do," answered the pastor.

"Do you believe a wife is supposed to submit to her husband?"

"Of course, in relation to what she *does* in the family unit—not in relation to *who* she is, though."

"What do you mean by that?"

"Well," Patie began explaining, "she can't go out and buy a new house full of furniture without your permission. That has to do with what she *does*."

"Can I?" asked the husband.

"Yes, you can, my brother, but it wouldn't be very smart. God has given Louise to you as a help-meet, which means 'fitting helper.' To refuse to use God's helper is wrong, maybe sin."

123

Turk didn't answer. That, too, was good.

"Now," Patie continued, "in relation to *who* Louise *is*. Louise, as a Christian, which I'm assuming both of you are, is to submit to no one except Almighty God."

"Meaning?" Turk asked.

"Meaning, she doesn't need to get your permission to do anything which God, in His Word, commands all Christians to do. Studying the Word, for example, or praying or speaking the truth in love or exercising the fruit of the spirit, or even attending church services."

Turk grew strangely silent.

Patie continued. "In fact, Louise is to obey all Scripture except that which is given specifically to others."

"Could you give me an example of that?" the visitor's voice was softer.

"Of course. God said 'Husbands, love your wives as Christ loved the church and gave Himself for it,' Louise doesn't have to obey that verse," Patie chuckled.

The preacher stole another glance at the wife. She had lifted her head again and was looking out the windshield.

"Turk, we all have to submit to God and His word and to the government, as Romans 13:1 and 2, along with other passages teach, but when the government tries to force us to disobey Scripture, we have the right and privilege to obey God and disobey the government. Do you agree with that?"

For a moment, Turk said nothing. It was obvious he was thinking. Slowly he nodded.

"The same is true for wives. Louise has been purchased by the blood of Christ; she is a child of God; and she has been given the Holy Spirit. She belongs to Him and she must answer to Him for her life. That's what I believe with all my heart the Bible teaches, Turk." The preacher hesitated for a few seconds. He softened his voice and asked, "Do you find fault with that?"

Now it was the husband's turn to lower his head and Patie could almost see the "wheels turning." For the fourth time, the preacher looked beyond the husband to the wife. Her face was turned toward him and toward the porch light which shone behind him. A tear glistened in her eye and her lips formed two silent words which could not have been misread. "Thank you."

The sound of Turk's truck cranking caused the preacher to jump. "Wait, my Brother, we need to talk about the things which—"

"I'll call you, Preacher." Mr. Burley's voice was still firm but non-threatening. "And we'll see you tomorrow."

"Good," Patie replied. "And please, please, Turk, Call?"

"I'll call."

The weary preacher strolled into his bedroom and sat heavily down upon the bed, slipping his shoes and socks off as he did so. Changing into workout shorts and a tee shirt, he grabbed a Diet Coke from the refrigerator and a can of Yard Guard from the bathroom counter and ambled back onto his front porch, spraying a circle around himself as he plopped down upon the swing. "Lord," he prayed, "bless her heart, Louise is enslaved to a legalist, a Pharisee. She's a slave. Please free her and please touch his heart. He's just as enslaved as the Galatians were. Please free him." He glanced at his watch. It was 9:30. Usually by this time of night, he had begun to get a little sleepy. Not tonight. Speaking on football and facing legalism had opened the middle-aged preacher's eyes as wide open as if someone had propped them with toothpicks, temporarily, he silently hoped.

A rumbling in the southwest and flashes of lightening momentarily gathered Patie's attention, shaking his mind free, re-directing it to the weather. The native Mississippian had never been afraid of it, as was the nature of the majority of the people in the state—respectful of it—not fearful. Mississippi lay north and south and bad weather usually came across the state from the southwest traveling northeast. That meant, of course, when tornadoes developed, the chances of Mississippi, with its three hundred plus mile length stood relatively high chances of being struck. History had certainly proved that thesis to be true.

The preacher casually lifted himself from the swing and sauntered to the side of the porch which afforded him a better view. In the far distance, thunder rolled uninterrupted like the incessant beating of many drums in a boys' drum and bugle corps. Lightening flashed untiringly from a distance, splashing against the pastor's face like a battery of camera flashes at an after-game New York Giants interview. Patie stood there for a full two minutes, leaning against the corner post, his arms crossed, observing the distant disturbance in the southwest sky, and his mind, seemingly with a will unaffected by the rest of his being, propelled itself back through the misty years to a time when he was a little boy, growing up in Laurel with Mom. He was seven years old.

"Son, hurry, now. We need to go."

"Mommy, I can't find my football."

"You don't need your football, Patie," Mom cautioned, her voice raised slightly with concern. "You won't be able to play with it in the shelter. Make haste, now."

"Mommy, I don't want the tornado to get it."

The son-now-grown, smiled against the flashes of lightening and a lump formed in his throat. Mom had been disappointed with her son's lifestyle, his divorces, his *pursuit* of happiness which his mother knew would not provide it. He knew she was disappointed in him because the son knew his mother; and because, from time to time, she gently reminded him of the way she had reared him, of the Lord, of church, of providing a good name to leave to his children, his grandchildren, their children. But she never rejected him, nor even condemned him, even when he smiled, hugged her, and blurted out something stupid like, "I'll get it straightened out someday, Mom, I promise." She would squeeze him, playfully push him away and immediately change the subject. The son knew it would be about six months before she brought it up again.

"Lord," he whispered reverently, his eyes still squinting at the rapidly approaching disturbance in the sky across the ridge which enveloped his cabin and through the trees to the southwest, "I still don't know if this offends you or if it's permissible. If it is and if it doesn't offend you, please tell Mom I'm saved and preaching and please tell her I love her. Lord, if it offends you, please allow me to apologize. I know we're not to pray to the dead, but I'm praying to you, Lord, and you are alive. If somehow she already knows—thank you—thank you—thank you."

In his first year of seminary, Patie Corbin remembered, he had asked a professor of doctrine that question. "Do you think, Doctor, that the Lord tells your loved ones in Heaven what's happening down here on earth?"

"Possibly," the teacher thoughtfully answered "at least the good things. The Bible is silent on that subject, Patie, but I would like to think He does."

That question was the only one about God which seminary left unanswered, so far as he could remember.

The mind of the new resident of Tishrock's was jarred back to the present by the ringing of his telephone. His mad dash through his front door allowed him to reach it just before the recorder came on. "Hello."

"Hi, Patie, this is your neighbor. Have you looked at channel 9 tonight? The weather?"

"No, I haven't," Patie conceded. He recognized Ann's voice. "Channel 9? Is that Tupelo?"

"Yes. They have issued tornado warnings for almost all the counties in this part of Mississippi, including Tishomingo." Ann sounded calm, but she spoke a little more quickly, indicating to her neighbor *some* anxiety.

"Warnings or watches?"

"Warnings," Ann answered quickly. "That means one has been

127

spotted, doesn't it?"

"Yes. Did they say where?" Patie asked, moving to his television set and turning it on. "Hold on just a minute, Ann. I'm on Channel 9 now. Let's watch it."

Channel 9's regular programming had been interrupted. A large map of extreme northeast Mississippi was on the screen and an announcer was explaining the situation. A series of severe thunderstorms had developed along a line stretching southeast from Memphis to Hamilton, Alabama, generally down Highway 78 and moving northeast at twenty-five miles per hour. Tornadoes were "popping up," the man said, all along that line. One had been spotted near Blue Mountain; another one five miles north of New Albany; and another one near Mantachie, moving northeast. Everyone near those areas and northeast of them were advised to take cover "NOW." "This is a very, very dangerous system," the announcer stressed. "Other tornadoes are expected to—"

The screen went blank.

"Patie, did you lose Channel 9?" Ann asked.

"Yes. You did, too?"

"Yes. You on satellite?" Ann's voice was a little frantic.

"Yes."

"Direct?"

"Yes," he remembered though had *she* not mentioned "Direct," he probably would not have remembered what system he had.

"Switch to Channel 4. That's Columbus," Ann commanded.

Channel 4 was giving the same information. Both Ann and Patie stopped talking and watched. Another tornado had been spotted near Baldwyn at Brice's Crossroads Battle site and at Marietta, a small village immediately off the Natchez Trace Parkway. They, too, were moving northeast. Northeast of Marietta, lay Tishrock in Tishomingo County fifteen miles away. "Everyone in Tishomingo County needs to take cover "NOW!"

"Patie," Ann whimpered. "I really hate to ask you this, but I'm scared. Your cabin is where we always went when tornadoes— I'm sorry, Patie, I know you can't—it was like a shelter between those rocks—I know you can't— "

"Yes, I can. Come on. Do you have any candles? I imagine the electricity will probably go off."

"Yes."

"Bring them and some matches and come on. Don't forget your money and credit cards—and your valuables—don't forget them. Come on."

"Okay, okay," Ann whispered. "Thank you, Patie."

"Ann," Corbin hurriedly asked, "did anyone else come here during storms?"

"Yes, several families. Dimples and Jack and—"

"I'll call them. You come on."

Patie dialed his secretary. He could hear the uneasiness in Jack's voice. "Jack, this is Patie. Y'all want to come over here?"

"Yes, if it's alright. Dimples was just about to call you."

"Come on. I've already told Ann to come, but will y'all call everyone else who always comes here?"

"Yes. Thank you, Patie."

Corbin walked quickly back onto his front porch. The thundering had intensified and the lightening was continuous now, providing constant illumination. Both, which seemed distant ten minutes ago, were much closer now.

The preacher hustled down his steps and to his SUV. He pulled the vehicle to the far side of his house, making more room for the others who were coming. Then he retrieved his large flashlight from the SUV console and walked back into his house. Channel 4 was updating the information and several other tornadoes had been seen, one at Walnut, another close to Jumpertown, and one a few miles east of Red Bay, Alabama. The tornado which had passed through Marietta was moving up the Natchez Trace, aiming its angry power directly at Tishomingo Rock. Patie was standing in front of his television set, the remote in one hand, his flashlight in the other, when the power went off. At that same moment, a pounding sounded upon his front door. He flipped his flashlight on and moved briskly. Ann had just gotten onto Patie's front porch when the lights went off. He opened the door to discover the worried woman, a wry smile upon her face, altered a little by lines of concern at the corners of her eyes. She held two small canvas bags.

"Come in, Ann."

"Thank you, Patie. I'm glad you have a flashlight. I forgot mine," she declared, moving through the door. "Anyone else coming?"

"Jack and Dimples. Maybe others. Let me put the bags in my bedroom."

"This one," Ann explained, lifting one of the bags toward her host. "This one is full of candles and snacks."

"This heavy bag," Patie teased, "holds your two diamond rings?" As soon as Patie said that, he realized the out-of-place nature his humor must sound to a woman so worried.

Ann smiled. "That and my five bars of gold."

By the time Patie deposited the bag on his bed and got back to the living area, Ann had two candles burning, one on the kitchen counter and one on the "dead" television set. She was placing another one on a table and would soon have a total of six burning in the large room. Then she lit one in his bedroom and another in the bathroom.

Through the thunder, which now seemed to be directly overhead, Patie heard the sound of a radio before he knew anyone else was at his door. He opened it before Jack had an opportunity to knock upon it. Dimples and Jack stepped into the house, followed by another man, his wife, apparently, and three children ranging in age from about teen-aged to six or seven.

Jack lifted the radio up. "My battery-operated weather radio. Figured the electricity would go off," he offered, turning the sound of the radio down.

"Patie, I would like for you to meet friends. This is Jace Sunderlin, his wife Carey, and his children from oldest to youngest, Junie, Janice, and Jodie."

"Glad to meet you folks," Patie greeted, extending his hand to each of them. Ann, standing beside Patie, smiled and spoke.

"Patie," Jace said, "thank you so much for letting us come over here."

"You're very welcome. Glad to have you." Then turning to Jack, Patie asked, "Anyone else coming?"

"Not that we know of. We called some more but they didn't answer. Guess they hunkered down somewhere. Least I hope they did."

"Y'all make yourselves at home," the preacher invited, noticing that Carey and Dimples both held small bags. "Those bags holding valuables?"

Both women nodded.

"Want to put them in there?" Patie motioned.

"Thank you, Patie," Dimples smiled. Then taking Carey's bag, she took them to the bedroom.

Jack placed the radio on the kitchen counter and turned the volume back up.

Patie invited all the others to sit down. All did except the youngest Sunderlin girl, Jodie. She was crying. "Mister Patie?"

"Yes, Honey." Patie didn't remember her name. "Can I bring our puppy dog in?" Jodie asked, with red pleading eyes.

"NO, Jodie. We can't bring a puppy in Brother Corbin's house," the father emphatically declared.

"Wow!" Dimples exclaimed. "You hear that?"

Everyone stopped talking. The thunder and wind were almost deafening. The lightening was bright and unbroken.

Corbin looked back at Jodie. "You certainly can bring your puppy in here—if it's alright with Dad."

"It's a her," Jodie smiled through her tears. "Come on, Daddy."

"You sure?" Jace asked.

"More than sure. Y'all go get that puppy—or I will."

"Thank you, Patie. Come on, Jodie."

A few minutes later the two carrying the small puppy came back into the room. Jodie wrapped her small loving arms around the animal and drew it close to herself.

"What's her name?" the preacher asked.

"Lady Bug."

By that time everyone had sat down except Jack. He was standing by the counter, his head near the radio. "Folks," he asserted loudly, "it doesn't look good."

For a moment, no one said anything. Everyone was looking at Jack, nervously waiting for his explanation.

"The tornado is about two miles out of town. It's headed straight for us."

"Do any of you want to go into the closet or bathroom?" Patie offered, his voice hoarse with concern.

No one moved.

Jack explained. "This whole cabin is safe. One place in here is just about as safe as any other, we believe. But it might be good for all of us to move to the back of the house. It's farther back into the boulder."

With his advice everyone moved. Some sat on the dining chairs. The children, Carey, and Ann snuggled up to the back wall.

"Y'all, we need to pray," the preacher observed.

"Amen," Jack and Dimples agreed. Ann nodded. The Sunderlins said nothing, but both parents wrapped their arms around their children.

The preacher prayed. But before he finished, his voice could not be heard above the roar of the tornado.

CHAPTER ELEVEN
A Lesson in Faith

Patie Corbin had lived through the threat of tornadoes before, once in Laurel and another time near Gloster at his uncle's home. But neither of those had passed by quite as closely as this one.

From the time the roar of the storm had drowned the preacher's prayer out until it passed seemed like an eternity, although in reality it was only about seven or eight minutes. When finally it *did* pass, Jack was the first to speak.

"Folks, I believe it's gone."

Patie looked around. The Sunderlin family was embraced, the mother and father actually lying almost on top of their children forming what they hoped to be a protective canopy. Jack, Dimples, and Ann were sitting on the floor in the back corner of the living area of the cabin, their arms enfolding each other. Only the owner of the house had weathered the storm with no human physical contact. For a second or two, it had seemed strange to him.

"I think you're right, Jack," Jace agreed. "Is there a possibility that any more might be heading this way?"

Only then did Corbin's attention focus on the weather radio. It was still chattering, although the storm had rendered hearing it impossible. Still, so focused upon the tornado were the nine people who had endured the event together that even after it had thundered past, they weren't conscious of the radio's presence until Jace asked his question.

Jack lifted himself from the floor and turned the radio up. According to the announcer, the line of storms had moved north of Tishrock and were just now entering Tennessee and northwest Alabama. Apparently, they were safe.

"Is everyone okay?" Patie asked, looking from person to person through the dim light of two candles. For the first time he noticed all the other candles had gone out.

One by one, his guests affirmed their safety.

When Patie looked at Dimples, her eyes had widened and the sparkle, if dominant before, had intensified—partly from nervousness, he suspected. "Dimples, are you alright?"

Before the question had fully cleared Patie's mouth, the secretary blurted out "YES, SIR"—nervous shades of Barney Fife.

"You sure?"

"Yes, Sir," she repeated, though not quite as forcefully. "Can we pray?"

"We certainly can. Would you like to lead us?"

"You pray," she said quickly.

The preacher thanked God for their safety. When he said "amen," he glanced at Ann, who had not moved nor spoken since before the storm. She was holding Dimples' hand. Her head was lowered and she was crying.

"Ann, are you alright?"

Without lifting her head, she nodded and then said, "I'm afraid my house didn't make it, Patie."

"We don't know that, Ann," Jack counseled. "If everyone is okay, we'll go outside and see if we can locate the storm's path exactly. It was near us but it may not have reached over to your house."

Jace added, "I have a large flashlight and so do you, don't you Jack?"

Jack nodded.

"And I have one. Well, let's go look," Patie concluded wistfully, a little afraid of what they would discover outside. Yet it was time for them to know, he reluctantly realized.

"Oh, y'all," Patie continued, "I really dislike talking about this, but, if you will, conserve water. I have an electric pump in the spring and the electricity is off."

"What does that mean, Patie?" Ann asked. "Can we not use the toilet?"

Without getting any more specific, the preacher explained that the toilet might better not be flushed after every use.

"Just so we can use it," Ann retorted, a slight smile appearing through her worry. "You know, women usually have go when they're as afraid as we are."

Several of the people laughed. "Men, too," Jack admitted.

"Amen," the preacher confirmed. "Well, let's try to survey the damage."

Jack, Jace, and the preacher were shocked at what they saw, no more than twenty feet from the front porch. A large pine tree which stood beside the cabin had been blown down across two of the vehicles, Jack's and Jace's. Standing next to the destroyed cars, Patie shone his light up his driveway. The road was so covered with fallen trees that in the dark, it appeared one might walk all the way to the blacktop county road without ever touching Mother Earth. The ground where the three men stood was covered with small limbs and leaves. And the sky was dark—the night silent. There was no glow of lights from nearby Tishrock. Neither were there sounds of night insects nor tree frogs and a steady rain was falling. An eerie feeling crept up the back of the preacher and he turned to his companions, "Well, y'all, looks like it came right through here—between here and the blacktop."

The two men stood silent. They nodded their heads in agreement, though the owner of the house could not see them. "From the looks of the path," he continued, "if the storm came out of the southwest and was moving northeast, it ought to have missed town."

"And Ann's house," Jack surmised.

"Yes," Patie agreed, "and Ann's house."

"I'm really sorry about your place, though, Patie." Jack continued.

"I'm sorry about your cars, fellows," Patie countered. "I hope your insurance covers—"

"INSURANCE!" the pastor exclaimed loudly. "Fellows, you're standing by an ignorant preacher. This moment is the first time I have even thought about insurance. I cannot believe that!"

Patie sensed the other two men looking at him, but they said nothing.

"Anyway, I hope *you* both had insurance."

Both of them confirmed the fact that their cars were covered by insurance.

"Well, let's go back in," Patie suggested, "and tell the others the bad, and, I hope, the good news."

"I have a power saw, Patie. You're welcome to use it if you want it," Ann quietly offered.

"Thank you, Ann. We need to talk about that."

After the three men came back into the house, they, along with the women surveyed their situation. First, they all were blocked in by fallen trees, including the one which lay across the cars. Second, they had no communications with the outside. Even the cell phones were inoperative. The tower south of town, they speculated, was probably down. Third, they had no tap water but the critical nature of that problem was reduced by the fact that they could dip water in pans and boilers from the spring flowing under the house. Fifth, with the exception of Ann, the others were probably too far from their houses to walk home tonight. That meant sleeping arrangements must be made. Ann offered her house to the others if they wanted to walk the three hundred or so yards through the woods to get there. And finally, without electricity, they would have no air conditioning. Ann's house, it was decided, would probably be cooler due to the fact that she had many windows. She would be without electricity for certain, too, and she would probably have no water due to the fact that she got her water from a rural water system. That pump, like Patie's, ran on electricity. But she had no running spring to draw from.

When all these facts and a few others were examined, the entire group decided to stay at the preacher's house, at least until daylight. Then Ann remembered, "I have a tractor in my barn."

Everyone was silent for a moment, until the significance of what the editor had said permeated their fretting minds. Almost as one, the three adult men exclaimed, "Great."

"That means we can get to town—check on *it* and our houses," Jace reflected. "Good."

"Ann," Corbin quizzed, "you said you have a power saw? Is it in the barn ?"

"Yes! I haven't seen it lately but it's supposed to be there, gas, too. If the house and barn are still standing."

"Humm," Jack thought out loud. "We need to talk about this a little bit. Why don't one of us go with Ann to her house, check on her place, and get the tractor and power saw. One of us can then go to town on the tractor, if we can get there, and check on Jace's house and mine. The other two fellows can start clearing Patie's driveway."

"You want to do that tonight—or wait 'til morning?" Jace asked.

"What do y'all think? Wait 'til mornin' or start now?" Josh questioned, looking at everyone. "I don't think we're gonna' get much sleep tonight, not until we know about the damage."

"I agree with that," the preacher added. "I'd just as soon get started tonight."

"Alright. That okay with everybody?" Jack asked.

It was. All the adults were nodding their heads in agreement.

"Now let's see if I can get my raincoat out of that pancaked car," Jack breathed quietly.

The three men walked out onto the porch. Jack and Jace went to their cars, both of which seemed to be damaged beyond driving. Patie sat down in the swing, suddenly totally exhausted. A soft but steady rain was still falling, postscript to the fury which went before it. Tree frogs and night insects were beginning to chirp again, and in the distant north, toward Ann's house, a whippoorwill called. "A chip fell out of the white oak. A chip fell out of the white oak."

Patie was a little boy again, sitting in a swing with his dad out in the country near Picayune at his grandfather's house. "What is that, Daddy?"

"That's a bird, Son. It's a whippoorwill."

"What's it sayin', Daddy?"

The father smiled in the dim light which was shining through the living room window, pulled his son near him and whispered, "Listen and see if this might be what he's sayin', 'A chip fell out of the white oak!'"

The little boy listened, smiled and answered excitedly, "That *is* what he's sayin'! That's what he's sayin'!"

From across Bear Creek, the bass voice of a hoot owl and the two men walking back up the steps shook Patie from his thoughts. "Well, at least the hoot owls and whippoorwill have resumed their normal lives," Jack observed. "I hope we can resume ours that easily."

"Amen," the pastor agreed, standing up. "Find your raincoats?"

"Yep. But there's no way to drive these two cars," Jack announced again. "And we have you and Ann blocked in."

"Come listen to this," Dimples yelled from inside the cabin. The three men moved quickly back inside. The others were listening to the radio. Dimples turned the sound up.

From what the announcer said, the tornado skirted Tishrock, apparently passing between the town and Patie's cabin. Several people were known to have been killed and the damage was extensive but not as bad as it could have been, of course, had it struck the heart of the town. Electricity was off over a major portion of the county. No one knew when it might be back on.

"Y'all," the preacher softly stated, "this might be a good time for us to ask the Lord's power and strength be given to the families of those who've been killed or had great property loss." They all bowed their heads and Patie prayed.

When he finished, the preacher asked, "Ann, do you have a raincoat in your car?"

Ann nodded. "On the back seat."

"I'm going to get mine. I'll get yours. Jack, would you explain to the ladies what we're going to do ?"

The tractor cranked easily, one concern eliminated, and in a few minutes after arriving at Ann's barn, Jace disappeared toward town upon it down her driveway, which was not blocked. Finding the large power saw and gas can, Jack decided to crank it while yet in the barn, just in case it might need some adjustments, Ann having warned it hadn't been used lately. It was more difficult to start than the tractor, but after several pulls, a couple of slight adjustments and a squirt of quick-start in the carburetor, it, too, was running.

"Now," Patie suggested, "let's check on your house." A quick tour all the way around it indicated no problem other than thousands of leaves and tree limbs scattered across the veranda and yard.

"You want to go inside, Ann?" the preacher inquired of his relieved neighbor, "while we are here?"

"No, I don't think so. Everything looks okay."

Patie Corbin had never operated a power saw, or any other kind of saw for that matter, so Jack ran it for awhile. Patie, who had retrieved his double-bitted axe from under the house, began cutting the limbs from the trunks of the trees. The trunks, which Jack cut into six foot lengths, would be rolled out of the driveway.

The two men had been working for about an hour, when Corbin saw a light bouncing down the road toward them, going over, under and around fallen trees. It was Jace. He had driven the tractor as far into Patie's driveway as possible and walked the rest of the way.

When Jace climbed over the last fallen tree, Jack cut the power saw off. "Honey," he called loudly toward the house. " Jace is back!"

A few minutes later, the six adults were seated on the front porch focused upon the man who had been to town. "Well, first, the tornado missed the town and, of course, it missed our two houses. Other than no electricity, most of the town is alright."

"You have any trouble getting to town?" Jack asked.

"A little, right past Patie's driveway. Looks like the center of the storm passed over the highway fifty or sixty yards from where his driveway runs into it. There were a couple of trees partly across the road there, but I was able to go around them."

"Good, good," exclaimed Jack. "That's good. 'Bout how many homes were destroyed between here and town, you reckon?"

"Don't know for certain, it was so dark."

"Did you see lots of people?" Dimples asked. "I mean, in town."

"Folks everywhere, looking and checking their property out."

"Did you find out who died?" Carey asked.

"One family about three miles southwest of town, living in a house trailer. I didn't know 'em. Can't remember their names. And then, the Johnsons, everybody thinks. They found Helen's body near their house but—"

Dimples sobbed. "Oh, no, not Helen and Baxter. What about their children?"

"Don't know. A bunch of folks were out looking for 'em when I left to come back out here. It looks bad, though."

Those words left everyone silent. The knowledge of the names of those who had actually died seemed to drain the rest of the energy from Patie. Before long, the same thing seemed to be true for the others, too.

"I don't know about y'all," the preacher admitted, "but I think I have about had it for one night."

"Amen," chorused Jack. "I think I have had it, too. What do ya'll want to do?"

"Well, if I might suggest something?" Jace was asking, not declaring.

"Fine with me," Jack complied. The rest of the group agreed, with the exception of Ann. She said nothing.

"I thought about it coming back out here. If it's alright with y'all, why don't we go out to the blacktop and cut those two trees out of that road, so folks in cars can get to town. Then, Ann, if it's okay with you, I'll get us back to town on the tractor—have to make two trips—probably— that is, if you and Dimples want to go back, Jack."

"Honey?" Jack asked.

Before Dimples answered her husband, Ann whispered, "It's alright with me for you all to use the tractor, certainly."

"Thank you, Ann," Jack said. "Honey?"

"I don't want to leave Patie with all this mess," Dimples professed.

"There's nothing we can do about this tonight, Dimples," Patie assured. " It will still be here in the morning."

"Ooooh"—the preacher groaned as though he were struck with a sudden pain. "Y'all know what I just remembered?"

Patie looked at the faces of the people standing around him. All of those faces were blank, obviously not acknowledging what Corbin had just remembered.

"Tomorrow is Sunday!"

Under the trauma, no one else had remembered either.

"Jace," Patie continued, "did you happen to see or ask about the churches?"

"No, but I think they're alright. At least Community Church is, I reckon. It's on the other side of town.

"Jack, you and Dimples, we need to think about tomorrow. Ann, I know you are a member of First Baptist. I'm sorry, Jace, I'm not certain where y'all go. I've only been here for a week and—"

"We're members of Community."

"Oh, I'm so sorry for not knowing that, Jace. I haven't had time to learn all my members yet."

Jace nodded. Carey seemed embarrassed.

"Patie, we can't do anything about tomorrow, either, not right now," Jack concluded . "Why don't we go get those two trees off the black-top and think about it?"

Everyone nodded in agreement.

Then, turning toward the ladies, Jack instructed, "we'll be back in about forty-five minutes. Then we'll start transporting everyone home."

"Jack, what do you really believe? You think anyone will show up at church tomorrow?"

The three men had cut the trunks of the two trees at the shoulder of the road and rolled them into the ditch. They had gotten back to the cabin, satisfied their thirst from the spring, and washed their faces and hands. Everyone was standing on the front porch. Jace left with his family.

"Yeah, there will be people at church at 11:00 o'clock tomorrow morning, Pastor. At ours, and probably at all the others."

"I can promise you the Baptists will be there," declared Ann, smiling, "all who can possibly be there."

"Well, we can't let you Baptists get too far ahead of us," Jack grinned. "'Course we may not have on clean clothes, Preacher, or be freshly shaved or have our hair perfect," looking at Dimples, Jack avowed, "but I think most of us will be there."

In the same way the preacher had forgotten that tomorrow was Sunday, Dimples had forgotten she would probably have a real hair problem tomorrow. Unthinkable to the secretary was the prospect of going to church with less than perfect hair. A look of pain swept across Dimples' face, visible even through the dim light. Her eyes, though dulled a little by the current events, still reflected a little sparkle as she turned toward her spiritual mentor and boss, "Patie I may not be able to come to church tomorrow."

Corbin laughed. The others didn't. The preacher did not know Dimples was serious. The others did.

"Jack, can you drive that tractor?" the pastor asked.

Dimples' husband rolled his eyes toward his pastor in jest, though in the darkness of Patie's front porch, no one could see it. "Why, shore, Preach. I grew up on a tractor."

"Now, Honey," Dimples responded, "you grew up on a mule." Then turning toward her boss, she added, "But he can drive a tractor, Patie. He bush-hogs our pasture every once in a while, when his brother loans him his."

"Well, in the morning at 9:00 o'clock, I'll be waiting in my coat and tie out on the highway. Can you come pick me up?"

Jack hesitated before answering. His mind was trying to picture the preacher's arrival at church on Sunday morning in his coat and tie riding upon a tractor. "Well, Patie, I could, I guess, but I can do better than that.

I can get someone to come get you in a truck—or car."

Patie laughed. "Don't want your preacher to arrive on a tractor? No offense, Ann, since that tractor is yours."

"No offense taken, Patie," the neighbor grinned. The other three could not see her grin.

"What if the other churches heard that our preacher had to come to church on a tractor," the secretary declared.

"What do *you* mean "if," Patie asked.

"What do you mean "what if," Dimples asked back.

"This is Tishrock," the preacher answered quickly.

"Oh," the secretary giggled. "They *will* hear about it, won't they?"

"I won't tell anyone," Ann promised.

"Wait, wait," Jack interrupted. "Preacher, we'll pick you up either on a tractor or in a vehicle in the morning at 9:00 o'clock at your driveway. Agreed?"

"Agreed," Patie snickered, pleased that he had been granted the opportunity to tell Dimples, "'This is Tishrock.'"

"Well, Jack continued, "Jace ought to be back out there by now. Dimples, you and Ann ready?"

"Yes," both women answered, almost simultaneously.

Then, turning toward her neighbor, Ann whispered softly, "Patie, if it's alright with you I may come back over here in the morning with a couple of buckets for water. I *would* get it out of Bear Creek, but the creek will probably be muddy after all this rain—if the electricity isn't back on by then."

"Of course, Ann. Come kinda' early and I'll carry the water back for you."

The newspaper editor said nothing. The pastor could not see the appreciative smile upon her attractive face. Neither could he see the slight frown behind the smile, placed there by anxiety at the prospect of being alone in her house the rest of the night.

CHAPTER TWELVE
WHY DO THANGS' LIKE THIS HAP'EN, PREACH?

Patie watched the light bounce, jiggle, point alternately down at the ground and up into the sky, as his three friends made their way carefully up his debris-covered driveway. Finally, the light disappeared and the sounds of their voices faded away. He turned to walk back into his cabin and was suddenly gripped by the engulfing quiet and loneliness. Walking slowly back into his now deserted cabin the preacher sauntered over to his silent electricity-deprived refrigerator and extracted a can of still cold Diet Coke. A minute or two later, he was thoughtfully pushing himself back and forth in his swing, his mind racing, perhaps unlike it had raced since becoming a Christian. It was racing toward his family.

More than five years had passed since the converted reprobate had walked out of his house in Germantown, Tennessee. He had left more than his wife and home and every personal thing. He walked away with little more than his clothes; three scrapbooks covering his athletic life in high school, college, and with the New York Giants; a few pictures of his two children, and , when he left, three grandchildren, now numbering four. He slowly shook his head in disbelief that he had so casually discarded everything which had at one time meant so much to him. Not until the middle of his first year in seminary was the redeemed man, father and grandfather finally able to forgive himself for what he had so callously done, no small task for the relatively new convert.

Becoming a Christian had awakened his dead spirit and sensitized his seared conscience. Within a week after praying to receive Christ in Jess Gingrich's office, the guilt had descended upon him like a giant crane lowering a locomotive upon a set of railroad tracks.

Jess explained the fact to Patie that the guilt which he was experiencing was natural, but that it no longer belonged to him—that Christ had graciously bought it with the price of His blood. The old sinner found *some* relief in knowing the truth about Christ's vicarious atonement and how it applied to him, but from a practical standpoint, he still staggered under the knowledge of what he had done. He contacted every person whom he had offended, either in person, by telephone, or letter and asked forgiveness, especially Mattie, his wife, his children and grandchildren. The members of his family and many of the others had forgiven him and for a while, the pain of what he had done seemed to lessen some, but as time passed, it gradually returned. The problem was finally gloriously resolved one day in a Dallas Seminary professor's office.

Sitting in the darkness of a storm-shattered night on the front porch of his new cabin near a little town in northeast Mississippi, the newly appointed pastor of a small church smiled as he remembered that day.

The sign on the professor's desk said, "Dr. Dwight Jones—Biblical Doctrine." Patie knocked.

Dwight Jones and Patie had become good friends in the student's first year at Dallas. They were about the same age and during the years Patie had played football at Ole Miss, Dwight, a Louisianan by birth, had played football on partial scholarship for Mississippi College, a small Baptist liberal arts school in Clinton, Mississippi. Although Corbin had never heard of Dwight, Dwight had followed Patie's career.

When the Baptist student graduated from Mississippi College, he enrolled in seminary where he earned his bachelor's degree and his doctorate. After ten years as a missionary in the jungles of Brazil, he returned to the states and accepted a teaching position at Dallas Seminary, teaching Biblical doctrine.

146

Patie and the professor had become such good friends that they often ate meals together, "argued" football and teased each other about "your deteriorated athletic prowess."

"Come in," Dr. Jones had invited.

Dwight Jones was a stockily-built man, five feet ten inches tall, a solid, muscular frame. His hair was thinning and grey around the edges. His face seemed always to sport a pleasant expression and the perpetual twinkle in his eyes expressed the nature of his soul. His knowledge of the doctrines of the Word of God extended far beyond that of many teachers, a fact his personality tended to conceal. There seemed to be no ego in him, and apart from his incessant jesting with Patie, no foolishness, especially concerning the Lord and His Word. He taught his classes in a long-sleeved shirt with tie, the neck unbuttoned. That was his dress when Patie first walked into his office.

"Patie! Come on in!"

"You have a minute or two, Doctor?"

"Sure do, unless you came in to bombard me with some more of that Ole Miss Rebel heresy."

"Not today," Corbin grinned, "although who could deny that it would do you some good."

"Well, it's a proven fact that I need more good, that is, human good," Dwight laughed, "although I'm not certain I can get it from Oxford."

"Probably not," Patie relented. "I need to talk to you about something else, if you have time."

"Shoot.'

"Dwight, I'm just sick about what I did before I was saved, especially to my family. I know I'm forgiven and I'm so grateful for that, but here I sit forgiven and they're still hurting. It seems—"

"Seems like you need to pay the piper for it, doesn't it?" Dr. Jones interrupted.

"Yeah, and I'm really hurting over it. I can barely stand myself

147

knowing what I've done to my family. I get sick at my stomach thinking about what I've put them through—and am *still* putting them through. Plus, I need to know something. How can God ever use me after what I've done? How can God use *me* while my family and other people are still hurting so badly?"

"Well," Dwight Jones deliberately and carefully replied, "Let's handle the two issues separately, shall we?" The professor looked at his student and waited for agreement. Patie looked across the desk at his friend, brother in Christ and professor—and nodded, confirmation to the teacher that he was to continue.

"Could it be, Patie, that you *are* paying the piper?"

"Sir?"

"You're hurting. You're certainly paying a price for your sins."

"Should I be? I mean, if Jesus took my sins upon Himself and cast them as far away from me as the east is from the west, where is the pain coming from? On top of that, I can hardly bear knowing that my family is still hurting so badly. How can we help—ah—how can I—get some relief to them?" the new Christian asked, his voice low and shaky, his eyes beginning to moisten.

"Patie, sin hurts–it pollutes–it destroys. Through you, Satan brought destruction and pain into your family. But I know for a fact that you have asked your family and everyone else whom you have ever hurt to forgive you, haven't you?"

Corbin nodded.

"Patie, those who have forgiven you in Christ aren't hurting nearly as badly right now as you are. That includes your ex-wife and children who are Christians and have forgiven you, doesn't it?"

Again, the student nodded.

"Well, then let's realize *that* and let's thank Christ for *that* because apart from Him and that which he accomplished on the Cross, it would not be true. You agree?"

"Yes, I certainly do," Patie quickly responded, understanding the principle.

"Don't ever think, my old football-playing buddy, that the evil which you perpetrated upon others is beyond Christ's comfort. You haven't taken First and Second Corinthians yet, have you?" Dwight asked, abruptly changing the subject.

Patie slowly shook his head. "No."

Dr. Jones opened his Bible to II Corinthians 1:3 and read through verse 11. When he finished reading, he explained the passage: that suffering and pain were the "forerunners" of comfort; that affliction brought the comfort of God in order that we may be able to comfort those who are in any affliction with the comfort with which we are comforted; and that God is the source of all comfort.

"Now, my brother," Dwight Jones commanded, "you look me directly in the eye and tell me that you are so arrogant you think your sins are so great God cannot bring comfort to those who have forgiven you. You still have enough old football all-American fleshly pride to think that?"

Patie looked at his teacher and friend. The professor wasn't smiling. "Well, ah, I don't think *that*—I don't think!"

"Not only is your tongue tied, my friend, but so is your mind. But don't you think that?"

Dwight's voice was firm and sure but Patie easily recognized a slight tone of love and compassion in it. It made him smile. "You know I can't say 'yes' to your question!"

"No, you can't and neither should you live 'yes.' Forgive yourself, Patie, and let the fact that your gracious God has brought comfort to those upon whom you brought pain and affliction satisfy you. Let there develop within you a deep, deep, deep reservoir of gratefulness for what our Lord has done for you, so deep it will always overflow into those to whom you minister. You understand?"

"Yes, I think I do," Patie answered.

"Good. And, by the way, the same principle applies to the other issue about God using you. Just as God's comfort is greater than your ability to impose pain and affliction, God's grace is greater than your sins. For you to say your sins, which, of course, have been forgiven, render you unusable by God, is to say your sins are greater than God's grace. THAT, my beloved brother, smacks rather close to heresy."

"Umh!" Corbin grunted.

"A good response, Patie! 'Umh!' I hope you don't write that down for an answer on your next test."

Patie laughed. Dwight smiled.

"You ready to pray and apologize to God for your arrogance?"

Patie stared at his teacher. He wasn't smiling. "Yes, I am."

After the prayer, Dr. Dwight Jones finally smiled across the desk at his pupil. "I don't expect you ever to have the problem again, Patie, but as added protection I want you to read something." He reached into his bookshelf behind his desk and extracted his faded maroon copy of Louis Chaffer's book simply entitled <u>Grace</u>, and handed it to Patie. " This is a very rare book, Patie, almost one hundred years old and out of print. I'm going to loan it to you with two restrictions," Dr. Jones said, thrusting it toward his friend but continuing to hold onto it.

"What are they?" Patie asked.

"First, you have to read it over the weekend and have it back on my desk by Monday morning."

"And—"

"And," Jones continued, "if you find yourself in a situation where, in order to protect this book, you must die, then you protect this book."

"That means I die?"

"That's right."

When the seminary student turned to leave Dr. Jones' office, he glanced back at his friend. His head was down and he was writing. Corbin could not see if there was a smile on his face, but he wanted to think there was.

Tonight, though, a slight touch of that old problem had seeped back into the preacher's heart and mind, a deep sickening as he remembered

150

again what he had done to his family and to all the other people whom he had hurt. Maybe it was the tornado. It had brought him face to face with possible death—thrusting him into a mental state to which he was unaccustomed. Families needed to be together in times like these, when death might be only a breath away. He had learned at Dallas Seminary and learned well. His age and his insatiable hunger for God's Word had driven him deeply into his studies. Had he somehow eagerly grasped the "letter of the law" and missed its spirit? The pastor was immersed in those thoughts when he was jarred from them by the "putt-putt" noise of some kind of motor coming from the direction of Ann Chester's house. It sounded like—what are they called? Four wheelers? Yes, four wheelers. The sound was growing louder. Obviously the vehicle was coming nearer.

About a hundred or a hundred and fifty yards from his cabin, the noise stopped—at about the old fence, Corbin speculated. He grabbed his flashlight and scampered, as quickly as possible, up and around to the back of his cabin. No sooner had he gotten there than he saw a light bobbing through the trees toward him. He turned his light off and waited.

When the light had reached a point forty or fifty yards from the cabin, a woman called out his name. "Patie—Patie—can you hear me?" It was Ann.

"I hear you, Ann," Corbin yelled, turning his light on and waving it back and forth in her direction. "What's wrong?" Even from that distance, the preacher heard a clanging, like pieces of metal banging together.

"Nothing's wrong. Give me a minute, I'll explain when I get there," Ann called back as she made her way slowly through the dense forest, which was thick with trees, but not so much underbrush. The clanging grew louder.

"Finally!" Ann breathed, standing before her neighbor, a flashlight in one hand, two aluminum or tin buckets in the other hand, one slipped down into the other. A large glass jar rolled around inside the buckets. "I knew I wasn't going to be able to sleep, so—"

"I thought you would probably go home with Dimples for the

night," Patie interrupted.

"Well, I considered it. They asked me to, but I wanted to be home tonight. I don't know—I–I guess with the tornados and all, I just kinda' wanted to be home." Her voice sounded sober, melancholy, maybe a little sad.

"Well, I can tell you came for water," Patie surmised, turning toward his cabin. "You want to get it now?"

"If you don't mind. I was going to wait until tomorrow morning, but I needed water tonight. I hope I'm not too much bother."

"Of course not. I was swinging in my swing, mired down in deep thought when I heard you coming. What was that, a four-wheeler?"

"Yeah, my son's. Deep thought, huh?"

"Yep! Deep thought with a touch of self pity which I shouldn't have been wallowing in. Thanks for shaking me out of it," he said, as the two of them approached the steep rocky bank beside the cabin. "Better give me your hand. Bank's pretty slippery after all the rain." A few moments later the two stood beside the running water flowing from beneath the cabin. Ann gently removed her hand from the preacher's and then whispered, "From His innermost being there will flow rivers of living water."

Corbin laughed. "I had never thought of my spring in relation to that verse of Scripture. I wondered why it fascinated me so much!"

"Where is that verse of Scripture?" Ann asked, setting the two buckets on the ground beside the flowing water.

"John 7, about the middle of the chapter, around verse 30 or 40, I think, somewhere right along there."

"Great verse. It popped into my mind while I was making my way over here through my muddy pasture. Well, let me get my water and get going. Give you a little time to get rested up before tomorrow," Ann offered, bending over and separating the two buckets and the quart jar. "It won't be enough to take a full bath in, but I can at least take a "spit bath," brush my teeth and make morning coffee."

"You came over here for bathing water?"

Ann nodded, her head barely visible in the dim and refracted light coming from the two flashlights. "Um humh."

The thought burst immediately into the preacher's mind. And following that, a question. Did it come from the flesh backed by evil intent? Or did it come from the Holy Spirit, through a heart of Christian hospitality, like that found in Lydia in Acts, Chapter 16? And then—the shocking words of Turk Burley earlier. "Word's gotten around town that you and Mrs. Chester are seeing a lot of one another and some say a path's bein' worn between your house and hers."

"Ann," the pastor stammered, "I'm not necessarily suggesting this and please, please don't read anything into it, but—ah—but you are certainly welcome to bathe in the spring under the house here. I mean if you —"

"Thank you, Patie, but I didn't bring soap or a towel. It's nice of you to offer it, though," she interrupted, touching the preacher lightly on the arm. Then dropping to one knee, the attractive woman filled one bucket with cool clear water.

Making his voice stronger so he would not sound guilty, Corbin continued, "Ann, I'm not pushing you to do it, but I have soap and a towel. You're welcome to them."

Ann said nothing. Momentarily, on one knee, she considered what her neighbor offered—how it would look—whether or not it was a proper thing to do. She was certainly not accustomed to bathing outside the house and certainly not under a man's cabin. But it was night and she did trust him and she needed a bath, even though she would be forced to redress in her "dirty" clothes in order to get back home. Her answer did not come quickly nor easily, but it came. "You sure you don't mind and it's alright?"

Patie was sitting on the couch, a candle burning on the end table furnishing just enough light to convince the pastor he needed his flashlight in order to read. Having remembered Lydia and her hospitality, he was looking at her salvation experience again from Acts 16. "What a heart Lydia had," he whispered out loud. "A hungry heart, to know truth; a hearing heart to receive truth; and a hospitable heart. 'Come into my house and stay,' she begged those who led her to Christ, Paul, Silas, Luke, and others. I might preach on Lydia tomorrow."

"Patie!" It was Ann, calling from the front yard.

"Yes," Corbin answered, springing up from the couch and walking quickly out onto the front porch.

"I'm bathed and dressed. Thank you so much for the soap and the towel and the wonderful running water."

"Feel better?"

"Much better. Much, much better. I put your soap and towel on the steps here," she replied, pointing her light toward them. "I'm going home now."

"Wait, Ann. I'm gonna' help you carry your water back to your four-wheeler," Patie offered, walking quickly down the steps to where she was standing.

"I can manage, really, they aren't very heavy."

"No," the preacher firmly inserted. "I'm gonna' help you. You take the quart jar. I'll take the two buckets, at least to your four wheeler. My Mama taught me to be *that* much of a gentleman."

Patie had been standing at the entrance to his driveway about five minutes, dressed in a sports coat and tie, his Bible in his hand, when he saw a pickup truck approaching from the direction of town. When it began slowing down, he imagined it had come to pick him up. When it stopped and he saw the driver, he knew it had come to for him.

The driver was Lester Junkin, the large "crown prince" of the

SINO Sunday School Class. He stopped his truck even with the preacher and leaned over, glaring out the passenger side window, which was rolled down.

"How ye' doin', Preach? Ye' look a little lonely ah' standin' ou' cheer' on this road. Ye' need a ride somewhur'?"

"The worst way, Lester," Patie responded, leaning over and looking back at him through the open window. "You know where I might find one?"

That question gave the big amiable man pause. He wasn't certain whether or not Patie was joking.

"Wal,' mebbe'. Git' in. Jack sent me out here to git' che'. He figgured' ge' didn't wanna' walk all th' way to church."

"I appreciate that, Lester," Patie grinned as he climbed into Lester's truck. "Thank you for coming after me."

"Yo're welcome, Preach. I didn't wanta' hafta' do th' preachin' this mornin'. At' storm tore up jack rite' along here last nite', didn't it?"

Beneath the serious expression on Patie's face and Lester's mention of the storm, Patie smiled. He had not heard that phrase, "tore up jack," in a very long time. Had he not been born and reared in Mississippi, he probably would not have known what it meant. "Sure did, Lester. I imagine there are at least ten trees still lying across my driveway. Have you heard whether any more people in the county were killed, other than the Johnson family and that other family who lived in a trailer a few miles southwest of town?"

"The Megason's?"

"Was that their name—Megason?"

"Yeah, shore' was. Storm killed thet' whole family—the man, his wife and two children. Really sad."

"It sure is, Lester. Really sad."

"Um humh. All of em' wuz' within ah' hunnert' feet of the trailer. Why do thangs' like this hap'en, Preacher? Does the Bible say?" Lester asked as he turned his truck around and headed back toward town. He didn't wait for an answer. "So far as I know, though, them two famlies' is the only ones killed. Hits' really sad. Whut' about it, Preach? Does the Bible say?"

Lester really wanted to know. Patie could see it in his face.

CHAPTER THIRTEEN
A DOG NAMED JAKE

The chain saw lay at the feet of the preacher like a squatting armadillo, a symbol of a labor into which the Southerner had never plunged. Horizontal trees lay across his driveway, a tangled tunnel of blockade, needing to be removed, and done so by that afternoon, else the four vehicles, two still "healthy" and two very "sick" beneath the "infection" generated by the twisting storm of last night, could not be liberated.

Patie looked hard at the twisted mess. "Y'all sure we can get all these trees cleared off my driveway today?"

"Not iffen' we don't get at it," Lester Junkin blurted out. "'Sides, I want to see a preacher on the end of a chain saw. Oughta' have brung' my camera."

"Well, Lester," Patie retorted, "hang with me and you'll sure see it, that is if you trust me with yo' chain saw."

Lester grinned, "I trust you with *it*, Preach, but I may not trust it with *you*. That's a powerful ornery chain saw. Takes some babyin' mostly, but ever now an' again', ye' hafta' kick it, kinda lik' my ol' daddy's bird dog."

Anselm Frompton, who was standing on the far side of Lester, laughed. "I remember that bird dog. Name was Jake, wudn't it?"

"Shore' wuz', Anselm," Lester answered, twisting around and looking at his friend. "How n' th' world did you remember thet? 'Hits been thirty year since ol' Jake died, I reckon."

"Used to bird hunt with yo' dad some. One time I saw him down three birds with one shot, I 'spect over 'ol Jake. He claimed he waited a' purpose 'til they crossed 'fore he pulled the trigger. Don't ritely' know if I b'leve that!"

Lester laughed. "My daddy could spin a tale or two, I 'member thet' shot, him a' talkin' 'bout it. Never did know iffen it wuz' true."

Patie walked over to one of the fallen trees and sat down upon it, curious about ol' Jake and wanting to hear the story before they started clearing his driveway. He was just before asking Lester about Jake when Lester pointed his long forefinger and asked, "You 'tard already, Preach?"

Corbin chuckled, partly at the way Lester asked the question and partly simply because he asked it. He had already anticipated the big amiable church member commenting on his sitting down. "No, but I want to hear about Ol' Jake before we get started. Besides, we don't want to go off and leave the other fellows, do we?"

"Naw', recken' not," Lester agreed. "'Cept they mite' be smartern' us. They mite' a' decided not to come. You know anything' 'bout bird huntin', Preach?"

"A little. I used to hunt with my two uncles in South Mississippi, back when there were lots of quail. They are about played out down there now, though."

"Up here, too," Anselm explained. "Folks say the fire ants and armadillos got 'em."

"Plus the coyotes," offered Lester.

"Yeah, coyotes, too," agreed Anselm. For a minute neither Lester nor Anselm said anything as though their minds were preoccupied with the reason that quail in Mississippi seemed to be almost extinct. Finally, Patie, glaring at Lester, asked again, "What about Ol' Jake?"

"Wal', Ol' Jake was a pointer and—"

"Dang good 'un, too," Anselm surmised.

"Yeah, a dang good 'un. Wal', ye' know, when a pointer gits' on a trail of birds, or a' windin' 'em either, he stiffens thet' tail and gits' low to th' ground and slips along 'til he gits' close to 'em, then he stops in a pointin' position. Then th' dog and th' people ease forward 'til the birds git' up."

Lester glanced at Patie to see if he looked like he was understanding. He did. Lester continued.

"Wal', one day Ol' Jake got to actin' funny. He would go out a' site' over a ridge or in the woods to whur' Daddy couldn't see him, then after a while he would come a' slippin' an' a' slidin' half on his belly an' get' rite' behind Daddy, an' quit a huntin'"

"That's weird," Patie observed, saying that partly because he *did* recognize *that* as unusual behavior and partly because he wanted Lester to *know* he recognized it.

"Yeah! Wal', at first Daddy didn't know how to make "Ol Jake git' out from behind him and git' back to huntin', much less why he was doin' it in the first place. So, one day, Daddy turned around to Ol' Jake, reached down and twisted his ear and said, 'Jake, git' to huntin.' Wal', wouldn't ye' know, Ol' Jake yelped an' sprung out from behind Daddy an' started a' huntin' agin'. So from then on, when Ol' Jake would quit huntin' and come git' rite' behind Daddy, Daddy would twist his ear an' Ol Jake would start huntin' agin."

Patie looked at Lester, who seemed to be finished with the story, and then at Anselm. Anselm was grinning, apparently remembering the tale. Patie looked back at Lester. "Did your Dad ever find out what was making Old Jake do that?"

"Yeah, he shore' did. One day Daddy an' me an' somebody else—may 'ave been you, Anselm—wuz' standin' on a ridge. Jake wuz' a'trailin' birds—"

"Naw', wasn't me, Lester. Mite' ave' been Coonie Phelps. Coonie hunted with y'all a good bit, didn't he?"

"Yeah, he shore did. Good shot, too. 'Bout as good as Daddy."

Corbin didn't want to stop Lester's story, but he was curious. "Coonie? Where did he get *that* name?"

"Coonie?" Lester repeated. "I don't know. You know Anselm?"

"'Reckon I do, Lester. He's a rite' smart good coon hunter. Had some of th' best coon dogs in th' country. Folks come from all over to hunt coons with 'im jest' like they come from all over to hunt birds with yo' Daddy."

"You were about to say, Lester, that Jake was trailing birds with y'all looking from up on a ridge," the preacher reminded his friend.

"Yeah, wal' we wuz' watchin' Ol' Jake trail birds from —oh—I recken' 'bout seventy-five or a one hunard' yards away a'lookin' down rite' on 'em, Ol' Jake, when Ol' Jake run a big covey o' birds up. You know he wuz' supposed to point 'em and wait for us to git' thar'," Lester explained, looking at his preacher.

Patie nodded.

"Wal', when Ol' Jake run thet' covey of quail up, he hit th' ground jest' like somebody had a' shot 'im. Then he crouched an' slunk a wide circle 'round an' come an' got right behind Daddy."

"Well, I declare," Patie proclaimed. "Jake had been running birds up. That's why he came and got behind your Dad. I wonder why he did that, though? I mean, I would have thought he would have run *away* from your Dad rather than *to* him."

"Yeah, you'd a' thought. Daddy reckoned he come to 'im to pay for his sins. When Daddy twisted his ear hard 'nough to make 'im hurt a little, he'd yelp an' then go on an' hunt."

"WOW!" Patie exclaimed. "What a lesson that is! Is that a true story, Lester?"

"It's a true story, Patie," Anselm injected. " Wade Junkin told me with his own mouth."

Lester nodded in accordance.

"Wow! The preacher repeated. "You know, fellows, I could preach a sermon on that. We humans sin and we know we deserve to be punished just like Ol' Jake. But instead, we do penitence and a bunch of good deeds hoping at our deaths, our good deeds will outweigh our sins and somehow that will please God. Ol' Jake just took his punishment and that freed him to hunt again. Christ took our punishment and that frees us to hunt—to serve Him—to please Him–again."

All three men were reflecting on the compelling Jake story and the lesson contained in it, when the sound of tires against the blacktop road a quarter of a mile away moved them from their thoughts. A moment later Anselm observed, "Wal' thar' comes th' rest of our hep'."

Patie stumbled, literally, over to his front steps and unceremoniously plopped down upon the third one from the bottom. His tee shirt was soaking wet, as were his jogging shorts. Sweat sloshed in his Nikes. The preacher, his wet elbows resting upon his wet knees, twisted his head and looked up his driveway. It was completely open now, a yawning outlet, flushed out by seven men, three power saws, four axes and a copious measure of perspiration shed over an arduous six hour period of back-breaking labor. With sweat dripping from his entire body, the preacher called to the other six men. "Y'all come on and rest for a spell. We'll get the trees off the cars in just a few minutes."

One by one the "lumberjacks" complied. They were as hot and tired as the pastor.

"Now, let me get you something else to drink. Spring water is good but after a while, a body needs a little more kick than water."

"KICK?" Josh Addison yelled from fifteen yards away. "What kind of kick you got in your house, Preacher?"

Patie's grin was decidedly weakened by his physical state. "Not that kind, Josh, but I have a few things stronger than water—Diet Cokes, Diet Sprite, orange juice and apple juice, I think."

The preacher took their orders and pushed himself up from his sitting position. He was turning to walk up the steps and into his cabin when

Lester exclaimed, "Preach, I ken' see whur' ye' been a' sittin'. You left a mighty big print o' yo' backside on thet' third step."

Patie turned and looked back at where he had been sitting. Left there was a clear, wet outline. "You should have seen the print of my bottom seven hours ago, Lester. It was probably twice that big." He walked on in the cabin midst chuckles and laughs A few minutes later, every man held a cool drink, and was reclining restfully somewhere on the steps or on the porch, mostly in a state of quiet. Abe Goodson, one of the leaders of the church was the first to speak. "Wal', Patie, I want you to know how much I appreciated the sermon yesterday, wal'? I think ever'body else did, too. Not often is a town allowed to witness the evil of a tornado and whut' it can do to God's people an' why, wal'. Sure helped me understand, wal'."

Several other men agreed by the nodding of heads and "amens."

"Thank you, Abe, and thank y'all, all of you. I was gonna' preach that sermon eventually, anyway. The Lord allowed it to be speeded up a little, maybe because I need to reflect upon it as much or maybe more than you all. I imagine every preacher in the county preached on it yesterday, don't you reckon?'

"I know Brother Ralph preached on it at first Baptist," Josh stated emphatically. "Mike Thomas told me he did."

A few of the other men nodded.

"Well, Jack, you ready to get trees off your car and off Jace's?"

"Yep, I'm ready. I was hoping Jace would have been here by now. I 'spect he'll be on a little later. I told him we'd cut the tree off his car if he wasn't here by the time we got to it, if he wanted us to!"

Even though the two trees which had crushed the automobiles had been cut into six-foot lengths, the strength of all six men was still required to lift them off the cars. Neither vehicle was drivable. However, arrangements had already been made for wreckers to come after them—as soon as the driveway had been cleared.

The workers were gathering their tools to leave when Lester turned to his pastor. "Preach, what you doing Friday and Saturday?"

Patie thought for a second, arranged his calendar in his mind—or tried to—and confessed, "Just normal stuff, Lester, unless Dimples has scheduled me appointments today. Why?"

"Wal', ye' agree ye' owe me a days' work?"

The other men were listening and watching, already suspecting Lester's question.

"I agree," Patie complied, "maybe more than a day. Maybe two days."

"Glad to hear ye' say thet', Preach. You ever cut sorghum?"

"Cut sorghum?" Patie asked, surprised at the question.

"Yeah, cut sorghum. You ever cut it?"

Patie slowly shook his head and answered Lester's question even more slowly. "Nooo, I don't believe I have, Lester. Cut some cane before, a little. What do you have in mind?"

Had Patie looked at the other men, he would have seen interesting expressions on their faces.

"Cuttin' sorghum, Preach. I'm cuttin', strippin', toppin', an' cookin' sorghum Friday and Saturday. We gon' to have us a real sorghum party. Yore' invited."

Suspicious now, Patie looked at the other men. They were grinning. "You any kin to Harkum Hector? Or somebody named Cooter?"

"Naw, I know 'em, but we ain't no kin. Why ye' ast'?"

"'Cause they asked me to—oh—doesn't matter. I'll be there. Where and when?"

"I'll call ye' Thursday and give you directions to my house."

Patie could hear the laughter as the men walked up his driveway to their vehicles which were parked on the blacktop road. He could not know precisely what they found humorous but the pastor suspected it had something to do with sorghum.

"Dimples, do I have any messages?"

"A few. You want me to give 'em to you over the phone or wait 'til you come in, in the morning?" the secretary said.

"Are they urgent?"

"According to my thinking or yours? You get any work out of Jack today?"

Patie stood quickly from the steps where he was sitting, still sweating profusely. He was astonished at Dimples' ability to throw a totally different question into their discussions, a question which to a man seemed completely divorced from the subject. "Did I get any work out of—what does that have to do with my messages, Dimples?" Patie quizzed, trying again to make sense out of his secretary's comment.

"It's kind of simple."

"It is? Well, explain it to this ol' dumb preacher."

"Well, I want Jack to do some work around the house this afternoon."

Patie waited for Dimples to complete the thought. She said nothing else.

"And?"

"And what?" the secretary asked.

"Well, what does that have to do with my messages?"

"I need to get home to show him what I want him to do."

"So?"

"Patie, you being ugly to me?"

"NO!" Corbin almost shouted, baffled totally now by Dimples oblique commentary. "Sorry, Dimples, I didn't mean to sound short with you. I'm trying really hard to understand. Explain what getting home to show Jack what to do has to do with my messages."

Dimples did not reply immediately. Patie waited, a little less than fully patient. Finally she spoke.

"Well, if I give you your messages now, it's going to take a while, and I need to get home —"

"To show Jack what to do—I know–I understand," Patie interrupted, "but if I'm willing to wait, you can give me the messages tomorrow."

"Tomorrow!"

"Yes, tomorrow," the preacher concluded, satisfied that his mind and that of his secretary were finally working together. "Go on home, Dimples, I can wait until tomorrow, I think."

"You may not want to wait 'til tomorrow to get one of them."

"Which one is that?"

"The one from Pearl Sue."

"Pearl Sue?" the minister asked. He was certain he was supposed to remember Pearl Sue but for the life of him, he couldn't.

"Yes, Sir. You know. Pearl Sue Scroggins. Fern Whetstone's big sister."

"Oh, of course, Pearl Sue. I should have remembered. What did she want?"

"Wanted to bring Fern and Millaree in to see you in the morning."

"What did you tell her? Wait—I thought they were coming in later in the week."

"They were," Dimples agreed

"So, they want to change their appointment to tomorrow."

"Eight o'clock in the morning. Did you work Jack hard today?"

Corbin shook his head, quickly and violently, a symbolic gesture of dislodging the cobwebs of confusion. He was glad Dimples could not see him. "What did you tell her—oh—what did you tell Pearl Sue?"

"I told her you would see them."

"Okay—oh—okay. I will. And yes!!" Patie thought he would try

165

to turn the conversational tables on his secretary by combining the answer to two situations. But what he said apparently made perfect sense to *her*. "Well, I'm gonna' go home and see if I can get him to do them anyway."

As they both hung up, Patie wasn't certain he knew what his secretary was going to do. That conversation made him wonder if the fact that the telephone people had repaired the tower damage was a good thing or bad.

Across Tishrock, on the other side of the town from where the tornado had carved its ugly trail thorough Tishomingo County, a small man wearing a western hat and dressed in khaki trousers and a short-sleeved khaki shirt, parked his ten-year old Chevy pickup in his carport, got out, slammed the door and walked authoritatively into his house. Chest Hudson's work clothes were, like the pastor's, saturated with perspiration. The deacon at Community Church had been working in the sun all day. A scowl, which occupied his face most of the time, seemed especially contorted. The angry man slammed his hat down on the clothes dryer as he passed by it on his way from the carport into the kitchen. "Well, you want to know what Dr. Christian did today?" he demanded of his wife, who stood ironing clothes just inside the kitchen.

Martha Sue Hudson was a tall, slim, attractive lady, well-liked in the community and heavily involved in Tishrock Community Church. She and Chest had grown up in Tishrock and had known each other from birth. They married two days after they graduated from high school, neither having ever dated anyone else. They were two natures apart, total opposites. She assumed good in everyone until she was shown the bad. He believed bad until he was shown the good, and even then, he had trouble accepting the good.

Martha Sue looked up at her husband of thirty-two years and the father of their four grown children. "Hi, Honey."

"Hi. You know what OUR PREACHER did all day today?" Chest asked his wife, contempt for Patie very evident.

Martha Sue gently shook her head.

"He never went to the church today! Can you believe that? He worked at his house all day."

The wife glanced back down then up again, her hand and iron continuing to move smoothly across the white dress shirt spread out on the ironing board. "I think Brother Corbin and some other men cleared the trees off his driveway." Her voice was soft, non-challenging and non-provocative—she hoped. She had been through this many times in their years of marriage. Chest would make a negative comment about someone and expect her to answer in kind. When she assumed the opposite position—either attempting to explain the other person's reason for doing what he did—or outright arguing with Chest—his negativism would often intensify, which led to verbal fights. Chest had never hit her, but he had come very close. After a few years, she learned to say nothing. But that, too, eventually grew old—not for her husband–but for her, creating circumstances which required more discipline than fighting. Time had forced upon her a creative alternative–a response but a non-threatening response. One which allowed her to say *something* but in the process did not challenge her husband's negativism. It worked—most of the time.

"I know THAT, Martha Sue! Ever'body in town knows THAT! WHAT he did wasn't the issue. A preacher is supposed to be around the church house on Monday morning—a REAL preacher always is. He coulda' hired somebody to clear his driveway."

Martha Sue nodded in understanding of what he said, not necessarily in agreement. "Well, maybe he decided to move his day off to today. Maybe he'll work on his normal day off."

"When is his normal day off?" Chest's voice was softer, his demeanor less confrontational.

"I'm not sure," the wife answered, looking up at her husband. "I think Dimples listed it as Friday in the bulletin, but I heard someone say he said he wasn't taking a certain day off."

"Wal', you know why he said that," the irate man quickly responded, pointing his finger generally in the direction of the church. "Keeps things confused. That way he can come and go as he pleases. Nobody can keep up with 'em. That's why he said *that.*"

"Honey, I don't know for certain he said it. Somebody told me he did. It may not be true."

"Sounds like 'em. I still can't believe we hired a playboy football player for our preacher. We need to put a' elder or deacon on that path he's already wore to Ann Chester's house ever' night. What Patie Corbin oughta' be doin' right now is sitting on a bar stool somewhere in New York City. That's where he belongs!"

Martha Sue smiled, her face turned downward, deliberately looking long at her ironing so her husband could not see her expression. With a touch of boldness, she whispered just loud enough for him to hear. "Or, New Orleans, they have lots of bar stools there."

"Yeah, in New Orleans, they've got lots—" Chest, who had turned toward the refrigerator, growled. Stopping in mid-sentence, the antagonistic man turned back to look at his wife. He could not see her face nor the smile which was on it. But he wondered if she was reminding him he got drunk and fell off a bar stool in New Orleans on their honeymoon.

She was.

"Well, I'll tell you one thing," Chest yelled back at her as he pulled a Coke from the refrigerator, "I'm gonna' go talk to him real soon now—and not just about that. He needs to answer for some other things, too."

The refrigerator door was closed gently, which Martha Sue was pleased to hear.

CHAPTER FOURTEEN

A Man Unknown

"**M**ornin', Pastor—oh—Patie."

"Mornin', Dimples. You get any work out of Jack last night?"

"Not much. He didn't get home 'til 5:00 o'clock."

"Five o'clock's the quitting time for Jack's body, huh?"

The preacher was standing in the middle of his office, holding his Bible, looking through the separating doorway into Dimples' office. Dimples was looking into her file cabinet.

"And his mind. Especially his mind."

"Wonder why 5:00 o'clock necessarily?" Patie questioned.

"Goes back to his childhood. He sacked groceries an Saturday at the Pig. Got off at 5:00 o'clock. Somehow 5:00 o'clock got notched in his brain. Everything shuts down 'bout then."

"Humm," Corbin considered. "All my messages on my desk?"

"All 'cept one."

"Oh?" Patie exclaimed, thumbing through the stack which Dimples had placed carefully on his desk. "Where is that one?"

"In my head."

"Oh, oh, lost forever," the preacher teased, thinking maybe his disjointed conversation with his secretary yesterday afternoon had earned him the right.

Dimples wheeled around toward the open doorway, her hands planted firmly on her hips, her eyes now beaded, though not enough to extinguish all the twinkle. "Jack told you to say that, didn't he?"

"No, I thought of that all on my own—but I was jest-a-joshin'," he confessed quickly. "Why? Does Jack say that to you?"

"All the time."

"Well," Patie teased, "you tell that boy he needs to come counsel with me about that."

"I'd like to sit in on that counsel session, seeing as how you are as guilty as him—oh—as he. You want the message?"

"Sure do—if you're still willing to give it to me."

"It was from Chest Hudson and—"

"Did you say 'Chest'?"

"Um Hunh, Chest, like my—ah—like your chest," the secretary explained, touching her chest just below her chin. Her face was flushed.

Patie decided quickly and wisely to ignore her embarrassment. "Wonder how he got that name? Do you know?"

"Yes, Sir," she answered, turning back to her file cabinet.

"Well?"

"Sir?" she asked, wheeling back toward him. "Oh! His full name is Chesteen Lynn Hudson. He didn't want to be called Chesteen or Lynn so everyone just calls him Chest."

"That makes sense. What did he want?"

"Wal', Patie he's not one of your biggest fans."

"He's not?" Patie asked, Dimples statement surprising him a little. "Down South, 'not one of your biggest fans' always translates into, 'He doesn't like you at all,' and maybe even worse, 'He hates your guts.'" He couldn't imagine what he had done to create that kind of animosity in a man he could not even remember meeting. "Is he a member here?"

"Um humh, a deacon."

"He's a deacon?"

"Um humh."

"Come on in here, Dimples, please if you don't mind. I need to talk to you about this."

Dimples swished into the preacher's office and sat down in one of the chairs across the desk from Patie, a slight frown announcing the unpleasantness of the coming conversation. Before Patie spoke, she did. "But I wouldn't worry too much about it, Patie. Everybody knows how negative Chest is 'bout everything."

The pastor knew not *every* church member would agree with *everything* he did—common sense and Jess Gingrich telling him that. But he couldn't imagine how he had already made that great an enemy—apparently. "You said Chest wasn't a fan of mine. You weren't perhaps speaking athletically, were you, Dimples?" Corbin asked, wistfully.

"No, sir, I don't guess. I don't know 'bout that."

"What then, Dimples. What have I done to make him an enemy?"

"Wal', now, Patie, I didn't say he was an enemy, I said—"

"I know—sorry, Dimples, I didn't mean to misrepresent what you said." Patie's statement had clearly bothered the secretary. "What have I done to cause him to have a problem with me?"

Before Dimples could answer, a loud knock sounded on the secretary's outer office door. She looked at her watch, then at Patie. "That's the Whetstones, probably. What do you want to do ?" she asked, standing up.

"Tell them to come on in. But I really want to talk to you about this after they are gone."

Dimples nodded as she turned toward her office, a little concerned that she might have been part of a problem.

Fern was a tall very slender man. He had removed his grease-stained felt hat with several holes in it and was holding it in his hands, when he and Millaree walked guardedly into Patie's office. He was a kindly-expressioned man, a several day's growth of beard on his face. He entered

171

the office a few feet in front of his wife and was wearing overalls, a khaki shirt, and thick-soled work boots.

Millaree was a short woman, appearing even shorter today than she had last week when Patie visited their home. Rather plump, she wore a long loose-fitting dress with large flowers of various kinds imprinted upon it, blue tennis shoes and white socks. Her stringy dark hair hung half-way down her back. Her eyes were widely spaced and Patie surmised that in her earlier years she was probably a very attractive young woman.

"Won't y'all come in an' have a seat?" the preacher invited, pointing at the two chairs in front of his desk.

Neither said anything, but both took their seats just as Corbin had directed, Fern looking sightly uncomfortable, Millaree flashing a big toothy smile.

"How have y'all been?"

Fern said nothing. Millaree answered, "Middlin'."

Patie nodded and was careful to look Fern and Millaree directly in the eye. "Did y'all remember not to do what I asked you not to do?"

"Ye' mean 'bout not talkin' 'bout me goin' to Memphis?"

At these words, Fern shook his head belligerently, but remained silent, neither looking at his wife nor Patie, his eyes wide and focused straight ahead past Patie's right shoulder to the wall beyond.

"Yes, about you going to Memphis at Thanksgiving, Millaree. Have either of you talked about it?"

"Naw, Sir," the woman responded. Fern said nothing but continued to shake his head, though less violently now.

"So, Millaree, Fern was a man of his word like Pearl Sue said?"

"Yas', Sir. Now, Fern's a man o' his word alrite', shore is, always has been. He shore is," the wife nodded.

Fern stopped shaking his head. "Well," the pastor asked as gently as he could, "Millaree, are you still planning on going?"

"Yas', Sir," she nodded.

Fern started shaking his head intensely again and Patie knew he had to somehow bring Fern into the conversation for several obvious reasons, but also in order to stop him from twisting his neck so violently.

"Fern, would it be safe to say that you are not in favor of Millaree going to Memphis?" The preacher wasn't trying to be funny but he knew anyone standing outside his door listening might find it thus—under the circumstances.

Fern said nothing, but he stopped shaking his head.

"Fern?"

The husband nodded his head, slowly, carefully.

"Fern, may I ask you to do something for me?"

The man didn't answer. He stopped nodding.

"Fern, you gotta' talk to me. Y'all are wasting your time coming to see me if you won't talk to me. Will you do that, talk to me?"

Still the counselee said nothing, his eyes now fastened on the floor at his feet.

Patie turned to the man's wife. "Millaree, why won't he talk to me? Do you know?"

"Yas', Sir."

"Why, then?"

"Brother Corbin, I'd druther' him tell ye'."

Patie looked back at the obstinate man sitting before him. "Will you talk to me, Fern? I'm asking you as preacher but more than that—I'm asking you as a friend so we can solve this problem. Will you talk to me and tell me why you don't want Millaree to go to Memphis?"

Fern shook his head again, though less fiercely this time, apparently refusing to talk rather than displaying his displeasure at the prospect of his wife visiting Memphis.

"Fern, if you won't talk to me, is it alright with you if Millaree tells me why you won't?"

The troubled man lifted his head and for the first time in two visits, looked Patie directly in the eye—and spoke. His bass voice was deep and melodious—and his grammar and diction were of a fairly educated man.

The preacher had already imagined how the farmer might sound. But when he spoke, the preacher was shocked, and very little shocked him.

"Brother Corbin, I don't mind if Millaree tells you the story, if you believe, and I reckon you do, that you need to know it. But I don't want to hear it," Fern declared, standing. "I'll walk around outside until y'all finish an' you come get me."

Fern stood to leave, and Patie stood, too. With a voice subdued by the unexampled nature of the occasion, he muttered, "Thank you, Fern. I'll come get you when Millaree finishes."

When Fern reached the door, he stopped and turned back, facing the preacher. "This story hasn't been told in thirty years and I'm not in favor of it being told now, but under the circumstances, I seem to possess no choice. Millaree, tell it truthfully, please." With that, request, the lanky man disappeared through the door.

Patie looked at Millaree. "Please honor Fern's request, Millaree. Please tell me exactly what happened."

Millaree nodded. "Yas', Sir, I will, I promise. Wal', hit' wuz' a' long time ago, 'bout thirty-five year' ago, I 'spect, when Fern's Mama and Daddy bought th' farm rite' on the other side o' Bear Creek from whur' we wuz' a' livin', and—"

"We?" Patie interrupted.

"Unh hunh. My Daddy and Mama an' my brothers an' sisters. Anyhow, Fern an' his family moved 'cross Bear Creek from us but when they moved thar', Fern wuz' in the army in Viet Nam in some powerful bad stuff."

"By bad stuff you mean combat?"

"Yas', Sir, he killed lots o' them people over thar'. An when he come back, he went to college so's he could—"

"He went to college? Where?"

"Up at some school in Virginny' somewhur'. Anyhow, he grad'eated an' come here to his Mama and Daddy's house hopin' to git' a job teachin' in a school 'round here somewhur."   .

"So he got a degree in education?" Patie asked.

"Yas' Sir, I recken' if thet's whut' it takes to teach. Wal', when he come back here, I caught him one day swimmin' in Bear Creek without no clothes on. Hit' kinely' embar'ased him but I wouldn't leave, jest' a teasin' —him. Finely', though, he hollowed, 'I'm a gittin' outa' this water. You better leave.' I didn't though. Him an' me, we started meetin' down there at the creek an' we started—ah–we started–I know 'hit wuz' wrong, Preacher. 'Hit wuz' sin." Millaree dropped her head.

"Yes, it was, Millaree, but if you are a Christian, it's forgiven sin. You understand that don't you?"

The woman nodded, "Yas', sir."

"Is that when you two got married?"

"No, Sir, not rite' yet. My Pappy caught us."

"Unh!" the pastor breathed. "What happened?"

"Wal', hit' wuz' bad. We 'uz in a'swimmin' with no clothes on when Pappy walked up an' he wuz' powerful mad, on account o' whut' we 'uz a doin', but on account a' Fern's age, too."

"Ya'll weren't about the same age?"

"Naw, Sir. He's rite' smart older'n me. I 'uz seventeen . Fern wuz twenty-four."

"Umh!" the preacher wheezed again. "What happened then?"

"Wal', him and Pappy, they got into a powerful bad fite'. But Pappy couldn't hold a lite' to Fern a' fitin', Fern bein' young an' a soldier an' all. Fern hit Pappy and he fell an' his head hit a rock . "Hit' par'lized 'im."

"Your dad?"

"Yas' Sir, he shore wuz', rite' thur'. 'Hit wuz' a' acccident. I seen it all. Fern didn't mean to do 'hit. But them lawyer people didn't 'blieve hit'. They took Fern to Parchman 'fer two year. 'Course he got out in a year an' a half."

The preacher shook his head in disbelief and amazement. He could never have imagined he would be hearing a story this incredible when Fern and Millaree walked into his office this morning. "When did y'all get married?"

"When Fern got out o' Parchman. My Mama and my brothers an' sisters wuz' agin' it, but I'us grown by then. I sold 'em my part of the farm an' me an' Fern bought the place where you come last Sundy'. We started a' farmin' hit'. Done purty' good, too, hit' a' bein' bottom land an' all."

"Millaree, did y'all have any children?"

"Naw' sir. Hit' wuz' sumpin' wrong with me or Fern one. We tried hard."

Patie nodded in understanding, but he still didn't know why the trip to Memphis was so abhorrent to Fern nor why Fern was so closed-mouthed about it. "Millaree, explain to me why Fern is so against you going to Memphis, will you?"

Millaree nodded, "Yas, Sir. 'Wal, when I gradea'ted high school, Fern wuz' still at Parchman. I hired out me a job in the glove factory down nar' at Fulton an' moved down nar' cause I didn't have no car to git' back an' forth. Got me a bedroom in a boardin' house. I wuz' makin' purty' good, to. I saved me 'bout twenty-five dollars evr' month," the wife declared, her voice gradually trailing off into silence. Patie waited a minute or two for her to continue but she didn't.

"What happended then, Millaree?"

"Wal', this here's the bad part. I don't ritely' 'ker 'bout talkin' 'bout hit'."

"Does it have anything to do with you going to Memphis?"

"More'n likly'."

"Well, we need to talk about it. Do you drink coffee?"

"Yas, sir, shore' do," she responded quickly. "Why?"

"Does Fern?"

"Yas', Sir."

"How do you drink it?"

"We both lik' hit' purely black."

"Tell you what," Patie suggested. "You think about this. I'll take

Fern a mug of coffee and bring you and me one back. You decide whether or not you want to tell me about it, okay? While I'm gone. Okay?"

Millaree hesitated as though she were thinking. Finally, though, she agreed, "Yas, Sir."

The coffee pot was in Dimples office, but Dimples wasn't. A very large, older flushed-faced man sat at her desk writing. When Patie walked into the room, the man struggled to get to his feet.

"No, no, don't get up," Patie exhorted. "Please keep your seat."

The man sat clumsily back down.

"I'm Patie Corbin." the preacher introduced, extending his right hand toward the man, who, as the pastor could now see, was filling out a counselee's questionnaire.

The man, who was wearing khaki trousers and a loose fitting soiled white tee shirt, took Patie's hand. His own hand was large but his grip was weak. "Brother Corbin, I'm Purlis Breaker. Folks here about call me Otis."

"What would like for me to call you?"

"Purlis," the man spoke—without hesitation.

"Purlis, it's good to meet you. I see you're filling out the question-naire."

"Yes, Sir."

"Well, give me as much information as you can. I'd rather have too much than too little," Patie counseled, pouring the mug of coffee for Fern. "Would you like some coffee?"

"Dimples poured me some before she left. Oh, Dimples said to tell you, if you came in here, that she'd be back by nine. Something 'bout so Cricket could give you the mail and you could get to Preacher's Club."

"Thank you, Purlis," Patie said, narrowing his eyes, and glancing back at his visitor to see if he were smiling. He was.

177

"She also told me to tell you she was just kidding and that you would know it."

Patie, standing by now at the door with a full mug of coffee for Fern, asserted, "You and Dimples must know each other real well."

"From birth," Purlis explained. "Brother Corbin, Dimples told me you used to drink."

"Yes, Purlis, I'm sad to say, almost every day for thirty years, 'til I became a Christian."

"Was you a' alcoholic?"

"Some would say 'yes,' Purlis, some 'no.' There are two kinds of alcoholics and we'll talk about that and lots more when you come back to see me. Okay?"

Purlis smiled, a very dim, very faint smile as though somehow he had been granted a small measure of hope. He would be looking forward to that visit.

Patie found Fern sitting on the low wall surrounding a flower bed outside the church. The tall man looked up at Patie with gratefulness for the coffee, emitting a quiet "thank you."

"You're welcome, Fern. Millaree and I are almost ready for you to come back in, okay?"

Fern nodded.

"I'll come back and get you."

Handing the mug of black coffee to his lady visitor, the preacher asked politely, "What's the verdict, Millaree?"

"I guess I need to tell ye', Brother Corbin."

Patie nodded.

Millaree swallowed hard. Her eyes narrowed and a frown replaced the smile. She shifted her weight in the chair, crossed her legs and shifted her weight again. "This here is the hard part to do, Brother Corbin. I mean, hits' real hard to do!"

"I can see it is, Millaree. Would you like for me to pray and ask God to give you strength?"

"Yas' Sir, would je' please?"

After the prayer, Millaree lifted her eyes to the counselor's face. "I had a' affair with Mr. Ellis at the glove factory."

"Mr. Ellis? Who is he?"

"Mr. Sam Ellis. He was my foreman at the glove factory."

"While Fern was in prison?"

"Yes, Sir, but me'n Fern, we wuz'nt married then."

"Millaree, was Ellis married?"

The woman suddenly dropped her head, leaned over, her elbows resting on her knees, and nodded her head. She appeared to be shamed.

"Does Fern know about the affair?"

"Yas, sir. Ever'body in Tishomingo County knowed' about it rite' after it quit hap'nin."

"How did they find out, I mean, how did it become public?"

"Miz' Ellis, she caught us outrite' an' went to the plant man'ger, Mr. Collins, to git' me fared'. But both of us got fared'."

"What happened to you after that?" Patie quizzed, which would lead him comfortably to the next question.

"I went back home to Mama's house and got me a job in the little trailer factory. "Wuzn't makin' near the money, but I didn't have to pay no rent, neither."

"What happened to Mr. Ellis?"

"Wal', he moved to Memphis, I hear tell, and put in him a tar' shop to own."

179

"A tire shop?"

"Yas', Sir."

"Have you had any contact with him?'

Patie not only listened very carefully to Millaree's answer but he also watched her very carefully. She continued to look downward; her shoulders slumped, and she uncrossed her legs. Her answer, slow in coming, was very weak, almost inaudible. "Naw', Sir."

Patie did not believe her but neither did he challenge her. He did, however, insist that she look up at him. Millaree did it, but with difficulty.

"Millaree, I want you to know, what I'm about to say, I'm saying in love," Corbin promised, "I want you to know that. You understand?"

"Yas', Sir."

"For some reason, Fern must not trust you, at least about going to Memphis. In a minute, I'm going to bring him back in here. If you have anything you need to tell me, please do it now, okay?"

"Thar' ain't nothin', Brother Corbin."

"Alright, Millaree. Now, tell me why Fern didn't want to talk, either at your house or when you first came into my office. Can you do that?"

"Yas', Sir, I thank' so. Hit' goes back to him a hurtin' my Daddy, on accident surely. Fern was total mad—"

"Angry?"

"Yas', Sir, total mad. He's a'feared thet' iffen' he starts talkin', he'll start arguin' and he'll get mad agin'. Mite' hurt me or somebody else. So he said he's never do at' agin'.''

Patie nodded. "I understand. Now, Millaree, can you think of any reason, except Mr. Ellis, that Fern may not want you to go to Memphis?"

"Naw', sir."

"Do I have your permission to ask Fern if the problem is the fact that Mr. Ellis is in Memphis?" Millaree began shaking her head almost as hard as her husband had shaken his earlier. "Wal', I don't know 'bout thet' now, Brother Corbin."

"Millaree, we have to find out why he doesn't want you to go. Mr.

Ellis being there is our only lead. At the very least, we have to eliminate him as a reason. You agree?

Millaree said nothing for a full minute. When she answered, the preacher , it was with an uncertain tone of voice. "Wal', I don't lik' it, Brother Corbin."

"Do I have your permission, Millaree?"

Reluctantly, the wife nodded.

"If he loses his temper, Millaree, I promise you–I'll get between him and you, okay?"

Millaree nodded again.

"Fern, it's obvious you don't want your wife to go to Memphis. But what's not obvious is 'why'? She has given me permission to ask you about a man with whom she was involved before y'all were married and who lives in Memphis, Sam Ellis. Is he the reason you don't want her to go to Memphis?"

Immediately Fern nodded his head. "He's the reason, alright."

"Well, Fern, Millaree has assured me that is NOT the reason she is going to Memphis. Do you believe her?"

"No, Sir."

"You don't believe me, Fern? You thank' I'm lyin' to you!"

"I love you Millaree. No, I don't _thank'_ you're lyin' to me. I _know_ you are..."

"I am NOT lyin'! How dare ye' call me a liar. Ye' better have proof a' thet!" Millaree screeched, springing from her chair and facing her husband.

With that, Fern unsnapped the middle pocket of his overalls' bib and extracted a letter. It was addressed to Mr. Sam Ellis. He unfolded it and began to read: _Dear Sam, it was very good to hear from you. Yes, I_ *would like to come to Memphis to see you and, yes, I would like to talk to you about working for..."*

"Quit readin', Fern, quit readin'!" the anguished wife screamed. "How could ye' do thet' to me, Fern? How coud'ju steal thet' letter? Iffin' you loved me, ye' couldn't do thet'. You don't love me, Fern." Millaree stood in front of her husband, her fists clinched, stomping one foot on the floor, tears streaming down her red face. "How could ju' do thet'? How could ju' do thet'?"

Without looking at his wife, Fern slowly folded the letter and placed it back into the middle pocket of his overalls bib and snapped the pocket closed. He lifted his eyes and looked directly into the eyes of the pastor. Outside, he had told the preacher that he held proof that Millaree was planning to leave him. He had told the truth.

CHAPTER FIFTEEN
A CURVE BALL THROWN

The viciousness with which Millaree attacked her husband for somehow gaining possession of her letter to Mr. Sam Ellis while, apparently, completely ignoring her own sin of going to see the old "lover," unsettled the new preacher a little. He thought he had seen and heard just about everything regarding the behavior of man. He would need to ease into this counsel carefully—not only with Millaree but also with Fern.

Five minutes after her husband's "revelation," the wife was standing by the window, gazing out at the Tishrock town square in the distance. Her hands seemed embedded into her hips, and she was shaking her head in obvious disbelief. Patie was about to speak when the agitated wife wheeled around and stared at her husband. "How could je' do this to me, Fern? I thought you loved me. You broke the law, stealin' the letter lik' ye' did, you know thet'? I could have ye' put in jail—I mean rite' smack in the middle of the jail!"

With those errrant words, Corbin knew he had to re-enter the counseling. He couldn't afford to allow Fern and Millaree to square off at one another. He looked at Fern. If the man was angry, it did not register on his face. His eyes seemed to be fixed on a point somewhere between his knees and the top of the preacher's desk. He made no effort to refute his wife's accusation or even to look at her, a fact not unnoticed by the preacher—and not unappreciated, given his history of anger.

Patie spoke first to the woman. "Millaree, please come sit back down."

She didn't move, standing ten feet away, her feet planted defiantly on the floor, her hands on her hips, her eyes locked onto the side of her husband's head.

"Millaree? Please!" Patie exhorted and waited.

Momentarily, the wife stalked over to her chair, yanked it several feet farther from Fern's chair and sat down tempestously, her gaze remaining on her husband, who still had not moved.

"Millaree?"

The incensed woman did not answer.

"Millaree, please look at me," Corbin requested.

At Patie's entreaty, the counselee jerked her eyes from her husband and bored them into the preacher; fire blazing from them. If ever a female believed her husband had wronged her, the preacher thought, she's sitting directly in front of me now!

"Millaree—and you, too, Fern—you remember in the questionnaire you filled out last week, there was a section in which I alerted you to the fact that I do directive counseling and the questionnaire itself explained what directive counseling is. You remember that?"

Both counselees nodded, Millaree's eyes fixed upon him, Fern's still lingering somewhere between his knees and the top of Patie's desk.

"And both of you agreed to allow me to counsel you that way, didn't you? You signed your names saying I could."

Both nodded again.

"Well, now, directive counseling means that you agree to let me give you directions about your problem and to prove those directions from the Bible. Are you still willing to let me do that?"

Fern nodded. Millaree did not respond.

"Millaree?" Patie asked, his voice gentle.

The novice counselor knew Millaree was experiencing a little psychological pressure. To answer "no" would place her into a position of admitting a lack of desire to see the problem solved, or even worse, denying the authority of Scripture. To answer "yes" would allow her wrongs to be made evident. She liked neither of her choices so she said nothing, but she knew in order to save face before her family and friends, she was compelled to receive instruction from the man whom she had visited to gain it.

"Millaree?" Patie repeated.

"I guess."

The preacher maintained softness in his voice. "Millaree, you need to make certain that's what you want. I'm saying this in love—this isn't a guessing game." Then, with a tone of voice even more gentle, he asked again. "Millaree, is that what you want—or, at least, are willing to listen to?"

Millaree started to speak, hesitated, then spoke. "Yas', Sir."

"Good. Then I need to ask you a question," Patie declared, careful to speak softly. "Do you really believe that opening a letter which isn't yours and reading it is a worse sin than a married woman planning to meet a former lover behind her husband's back in a town far away?"

"Ain't nothin' wrong with 'at iffen' the woman wuzn't gonna' do nothin' wrong."

Millaree's sudden and spontaneous answer left the unsuspecting counselor speechless, although a thought immediately ricocheted through his frustrated mind; that is the kind of statement which might cause a frustrated listener to hit himself on the side of his head with the heel of his hand a couple of times.

The preacher shook his head and asked, "Then why didn't you tell Fern the reason you were going to Memphis, Millaree, if there was nothing wrong with it?"

"'Cause he'd a' got vi'lent, thet's' how come," the woman screamed, thrusting herself up from her chair again. Walking quickly to the door leading from Patie's office into the hallway, she flung it open and disappeared through it.

"It 'pears that I'm not the only one with a temper, Brother Corbin,"

Fern observed. "What do I do?"

"Well, Fern, first let me say I'm sorry Millaree stormed out angry. She knows she was wrong. That's why she left like that. When ya'll get home, tell her that my office door is always open to her— as it is, of course, to you. But you have no choice about her trip to Memphis. You have to insist that she not go—but, Fern, be careful–you need to do it gently—in love. Don't lose your temper."

The counselee nodded. "If she's bent on going, do I give her any money?"

"Absolutely not, Fern. You can't finance her sins."

"Do I tell anybody about the letter?"

The preacher considered the husband's question. "Fern, I can't think of a reason to tell anyone about it right now, but situations change. Call me if you do tell anyone. Call me and let me know what Millaree does, too."

"What about the letter itself. Ought I to keep it?"

"Absolutely. Do you think there's any chance Millaree will try to leave you? I mean move out?"

"Two weeks ago, I wouldn't a' thought it. But then, two weeks ago, I didn't know she would slip off to Memphis to see Sam Ellis, either."

Patie nodded. "Fern, I think you ought to come in again. I'd like to talk to you about this situation—but I'd like to talk to you about you, too. You have a college degree. I'd like to hear why you aren't using it."

"Mornin', Patie," Dimples greeted, bustling through the doorway between her office and his. "Here's Otis' questionnaire."

"Dimples, how are you this morning?" Patie responded, taking the forms from his secretary's hand.

"Fine. But I hate funerals."

"Humm! Hate funerals, huh?"

"Yes, Sir, don't you?"

"Wal', I never—" the preacher stammered, then realized he was already pronouncing "well" like most of the natives. He started over. "Well, I never really thought about either hating them or not hating them. Are the funerals today?"

"Yes, Sir, an' I sure don't want to go."

"Do you have to?"

Dimples nodded. "I knew the Johnsons. They weren't close friends but I knew them pretty well."

"Dimples, what you just said puts me to wondering. Do you think I ought to go? I mean as a preacher?"

"Yes, Sir," Dimples answered, turning and starting toward her office.

"Wait, talk to me about this a little, Dimples."

The secretary stopped and turned back around, her eyes twinkling, as usual a smile on her face.

"Is that the custom here, Dimples? I mean, are all the pastors expected to go to all the funerals?"

"No, sir."

The preacher waited for her to explain. She didn't. "Aren't you going to explain the custom to me?"

'Wal', 'course if someone in our church dies, you are expected to go, but if—"

"I know that much, Dimples," Patie interrupted. "I would think I'd probably preach the funeral service."

"Not necessarily. The family might want somebody else to do it."

"What about people from other churches who die? Am I expected to—"

"Wal', I was about to say that best as I can figure it, if somebody important dies like the mayor or a doctor or the school superintendent or somebody like that dies, then all the preachers usually attend."

187

"Dimples, I know when you say "somebody important" dies, you're not saying that those deaths are more important than the deaths of other people, are you?"

"Oh, no Sir," Dimples explained. "No, Sir. It's showin' respct for the leaders in the town and it would figure that all preachers would know them, where you might not know other folks."

"I see."

"Then, too," Dimples continued, "most preachers attend funerals when there's a tragedy, like a car wreck or a tornado."

"Oookay," the preacher exclaimed, "I think I have it. So I need to be at the funeral this afternoon, you think?"

"Yes, Sir."

"Dimples, do you reckon it bothers Purlis to be called Otis?"

The secretary looked surprised. "Wal', I reckon not. He never said it did. I think he's kinda' proud of bein' called by the name of a famous person. How come you asked?"

"When I asked him which name he wanted me to call him by, he said 'Purlis.'"

"Aw, shoot, Patie, that's 'cause you're a preacher. I bet he'd a' told anybody else to call him Otis."

"Humm, you may be right. You think maybe Cricket is ready to see me?" Patie teased, changing subjects suddenly, giving his secretary a "sniff of her own perfume."

Dimples turned again to go into her office, wheeled back toward her boss. "You better stay away from Cricket, Patie, not to tell you what to do. She likes preachers." When she saw Patie's grin, she quickly disappeared into her office.

"Good mornin', Aunt Winnie and Miss Minnie," Patie greeted the one twin he saw who was either seated on a stool or standing behind the cash register. He figured the other one was within hearing distance. The Hole Donut wasn't *that* big. "Rose!" the preacher yelled.

"Too late," Miss Minnie called back. "Brother Jerry Ferguson already named it."

Patie looked over at the preachers' gathering table. Jerry Ferguson had extended both arms into the air, like a referee signaling touchdown, a sign of victory. He was the first one today to notice that a rose had been placed in a small vase on each table. "When it comes to winning food, you can't beat the Methodists."

Patie grinned back at the Methodist preacher as he walked back toward the table. "I grew up Methodist. I know exactly what you're talking about."

Patie was the fifth pastor to arrive. Before long, Gerald Collins, First Pres, had gotten there and all six preachers were seated around the table.

"All of you want coffee and donut holes?" The call came from behind the counter. It was Miss Minnie.

"Yes'm," floated back the unanimous reply. Before long, each minister faced a mug of hot coffee and a platter filled with donut holes. After a season of prayer, the ministerial conversation moved directly and naturally to the tornado and the funeral that afternoon. It would be held at 3:00 o'clock at the Church of Christ, where the Johnsons were members. "It was really, really sad," Dave Smith, minister of the church described, "an entire family wiped out. All of your people have responded unbelievably well, fellows," Dave expressed. "I can't tell you how grateful I am. Please convey our church's deep appreciation to your people."

"We will," Ralph Wellmon, pastor of First Baptist concurred. The other men nodded.

"By the way, Patie," Ralph commented, "Your sermon Sunday morning must have touched a lot of hearts. Word about it has exploded out of your church into the community."

189

Ralph's statement surprised Patie. He preached on why bad things, like tornadoes, floods, hurricanes, car wrecks, etc., happen to Christians. His primary text had been Romans 8:18-25, with help from Genesis 3 and Romans 8:28, illustrated by the life of Job; Paul in II Corinthians 12:7; Peter in John 21:18 and others. But he had no idea that it had been anything other than a normal enablement sermon following a natural catastrophe, one which any preacher could preach. A moment of consideration led Patie to realize that Ralph's comment was perhaps the preacher's way, and maybe the group's way, of delegating the new pastor into a role of equality and acceptance—probably.

"Thank you, Ralph," Patie responded. "I imagine I would have done well, though, to have taken my congregation into any of your services Sunday morning."

"No, not really," Ralph continued. "I'm serious. From time to time, we take turns sharing with each other special sermons which we preach— in capsule form, of course," he grinned.

"Kinda' like, three main points and a cloud of dust?" the new preacher asked.

"Yeah, kinda' like that," one of the others agreed.

"Wait, before you preachers get to a'preachin' to one 'nother, let me pull up a chair," Miss Minnie called, walking around the counter and sliding a chair up near the preacher's table, "Come on, Winnie," the business owner yelled to her sister. "Preachin's 'bout to start."

A few minutes later, Corbin found himself in the middle of a small audience, consisting of preachers, shop owners, and customers. Only in Mississippi, he thought! The event touched his appreciative heart.

"Well," he smiled, "y'all asked for it. But if you had called Dimples and asked her about the sermon, she might have warned you against doing this. Oh, by the way," Patie challenged, "which one of y'all can I get to call Dimples and congratulate her for coming to church even though the water and electricity were off and she couldn't fix her hair? Whatever that means."

190

"Not me," Aunt Winnie quickly retorted, eyebrows raised, "I ain't gonna' touch Dimples' hair. I can't run fast enough anymore."

"Me neither," Miss Minnie agreed. "An' you *better* not," she warned, pointing a long bony finger at Patie, "if you know what's good for you."

Everyone there including Patie and the other preacher's agreed. Then thoughtfully, Aunt Winnie surmised, " But I hafta' admit, I woulda' bet against it."

"You would have bet, Aunt Winnie?" Stanley Day, the Assembly pastor asked. "I didn't know you bet. You do that often?" his serious expression concealing the 'jest.'

Aunt Winnie was half way through her explanation of how she used the word "bet" as an illustration before she realized Stanley was teasing her. "AW, SHAW," she exploded, "you're a' foolin' with me, Preacher. You oughta' know bettern' to fool with a' old lady, 'specially 'bout bettin'."

"And hair," Ralph added.

"'Ats rite'! 'An hair!"

After the laughter subsided, Patie asked. "You all seem serious! You really want me to talk about my sermon?"

"You got ten minutes, Patie. Then we're all gonna' start doing what my members start doing to me about11:50," Ralph promised.

"What's that?" one of the other customers asked, grinning.

Ralph threw his left arm up in front of his face, pulled his left sleeve up, and started looking hard at his watch. "It's a Baptist's way of saying, 'Wind it down, Preacher. My wife's got a roast on!'"

"The Baptists don't have a corner on that market, Ralph," Jerry argued, "the Methodists know how to look at a watch, too. I mean," Jerry emphasized, "a Methodist can look at a watch—I mean Methodists can *really* look at a watch!"

"I'm glad to hear the Community Church members aren't the only ones," Patie quipped, a smile on his face. "We seem to be in good company. Well, anyway, as far as my sermon was concerned, I'm not sure my preaching could be rated even mediocre, but since the sermon came from Scripture, and since all Scripture is inspired and profitable, I can share with you how I applied it to the horror of the tornado. Though to be honest, my sharing these things with you who having been standing in the pulpit for so long puts me in mind of a first year junior high school football coach, trying to coach Bear Bryant."

"Well, now, Patie," Dave Smith, minister of the Church of Christ declared, "we didn't say we would agree with your sermon—only that we'd like to hear it." A wry, but friendly, smile occupied his face.

Patie laughed. He hoped Dave was teasing him, but he suspected, though, perhaps spoken partly in jest, it contained more than a nugget of truth. "Okay, on the basis of Dave's statement, I will seek the courage to proceed—but only on the basis of it. I promise, it will be a very quick review."

"First, we know from Genesis 3 that sin entering Adam worked its evil way through him and into every person to be born after him. We, of course, know the same truth from Romans 3: 9-23, most of which is a quote from various Psalms. That deed, of course, polluted the nature of man, killing the spirit in him which in the beginning was a clear communication link to Almighty God. Then from Romans 8:18 through 25 and other places, we learn that all nature has been polluted with sin and its evil consequence—death. Man, animals, trees, vegetation, all die. Sin introduced Satanic behavior to man—and—it introduced hellish activity to nature. Had there been no sin, for example, tornadoes and hurricanes and earthquakes apparently would never have occurred."

The speaker glanced around at his audience. None of them said anything though they seemed to be listening intently

"But since 'All things work together for good,'" Patie continued, "even bad things, like tornadoes, may cause us to look up toward God. Anyway, nature, now polluted with sin, groans and suffers and longs with anxiousness to be set free from the slavery. But in the meantime, secondly, that same nature or creation, operating presently, to a degree, by the evil

one, John 12:31 and 14:30 under the permissive will of God, shoots catastrophic events at people—all people—even God's people, causing unbelievers to either open their hearts to God or curse Him, clearly establishing
their true positions. That same horrific event allows believers to deepen
their faith.

"Finally, we see from Scripture and history, that as I mentioned
above, true believers are not exempt from the ravages of the terrible event.
When Nubuchadnezzar carried Judah captive in 606, 597, and 586 B. C.,
Ezekiel and Daniel were enslaved, too, along with many other believers.
When tornadoes and hurricanes and wildfires occur, Christians may be
killed along with the unbelievers. Scripture nowhere guarantees that Christians, who have been regenerated by the Holy Spirit into new life, are pro-
tected from a creation which hasn't been regenerated yet, but some day,
will be.

"Now, as an addendum which I cannot prove from Scripture," Patie
added, "as we grow close to the end time, I personally believe that God
will allow catastrophic events to be hurled toward especially evil areas of
the earth, as He begins to bring justice into full view of all men. That, however," Patie smiled carefully, "is a personal opinion which, as I said, I cannot prove from Scripture."

"In conclusion," Patie finished, "I asked the people to consider a
Christian's response to catastrophic, so called natural, events. I suggested
six things: Thank God that he saw fit to spare us; Reconsider our relationship with Him; Pray for the loved ones and friends of the victims; Ask God
to show us what He would have us learn from the momentous occurrence;
Ask him to protect us from such future happenings and finally Pray that His
Person might be glorified and His name hallowed through the event."

Patie was seated at his desk before Dimples realized he had returned from Holie Preacher's Club. She had been waiting for him to get back. "Patie, how long's it been since you cut sorghum?" she yelled from her office through the open doorway.

"What, Dimples?"

"How long has it been" she restated more slowly, "since you cut sorghum?"

"I've never cut it," he answered, looking at the phone notes stacked up on his desk.

"You've never cut it?"

"Cut a little cane, but not sorghum," he repeated. "Is there an echo in here?" remembering Johnny Carson's oft-used comment to his mate, Ed McMahon.

Dimples ignored his tease. "You'd better think twice about doin' it."

"Doing what?"

"Cuttin' sorghum," the secretary explained, sticking her head into the pastor's office, then pulling it back.

"I have thought about it. I thought about it twice the first time."

"Wal', you'd better," she warned, ignoring his insensible remark.

"Why?"

"It's hard work."

"You think no preacher can work hard, or is it just me."

"That's hard work for anybody, even young men," the secretary continued to caution.

Placing his stack of notes back on his desk, the preacher looked up toward Dimples' office. "Harder than two-a-days?"

"What's two-a-days?"

"Well, that's what two practices a day—oh—that—doesn't matter. How'd you know about me cuttin' sorghum? Wait, don't tell me. I know. It's Tishrock."

"That's not how I know," she denied.

"It's not?" Patie asked, getting up and walking to the open doorway between the two offices. "How'd you know?"

"Lester called."

"So he told you?"

The secretary nodded.

"Gosh, Dimples, I'm sorry you had to learn it from the horses' mouth rather than from the Tishrock Communication System. I know how disappointing that must be for you."

Dimples glared back at her boss from across her desk. She did not respond concerning Lester and the sorghum. Patie turned to go back into his office when the secretary's voice caught up with him. "The preachers, Aunt Winnie, Miss Minnie, and the other folks really enjoyed your mini - sermon."

The pastor stopped, turned and went back to the doorway. "How did you know about my mini-sermon?" Before Dimples could answer, he knew he had left himself open again.

"This is Tishrock."

Corbin was still shaking his head when he walked back to his desk, picked up the small box of doughnut holes, and carried them back to his secretary.

CHAPTER SIXTEEN

SORGHUM

"**A**nn, this is Patie."

"Patie! How are you?"

"Fine. Just wanted to call and brag on your coverage of the tornado."

"Well, thank you, Neighbor. That is an extremely appreciated comment, coming from a man who's been interviewed by newspapers like the New York Times and Commercial Appeal."

"And the Tishrock Boulder!" The preacher added.

"Yeah, right," the editor laughed. "Thank you. By the way," she asserted, changing the subject, "you know what I'm stirring on the stove right now?"

"No idea."

"A big pot of stew. You eaten supper yet?"

"No," Patie answered truthfully. He thought about saying 'yes,' but that would have been a lie. He knew Ann was about to invite him to come over. The words of Turk Burley tore into his consciousness and a slight touch of resentment suddenly contaminated his emotions. He wanted to go. There was nothing wrong with going. He enjoyed fellowshipping with Ann. Yet he desperately did not want to weaken his reputation nor ministry in Tishrock. But on the other hand, he was hungry. "You aren't going to the football game tonight?"

"No," Ann answered quickly. "My sports writer is covering it. It's been a long week, so I decided I'd just stay home tonight. I had frozen some stew and to keep from cooking, I thawed it out. Want some?"

"Sure you have enough?"

"I'm sure. Come on."

"Right now?" Patie asked.

"Right now!"

Ten minutes later the preacher stopped his SUV in Ann's driveway. An hour after that, the two friends had eaten and were placing the dirty dishes in the dishwasher.

"Thank you, Ann. The stew was delicious!"

"You're welcome, Patie. Thank you for the compliment. Would you like some hot chocolate?"

"Yes, I sure would. Thank you."

Handing Patie a mug of the delicious drink with marshmallows melting on top, Ann invited, "Let's go sit in the den."

Sitting in the leather easy chair across from Ann, with some reservation, Patie decided he would mention his social dilemma to his neighbor. At first, he had thought he wouldn't, but the longer he stayed in her house, the more his mind tricked him into concern. He was about to bring it up when she asked him a question.

"You didn't want to go to the game tonight?"

"Well, I kinda' thought about it, but this has been a long week for me, too. Maybe I'll go next week. Do they play here?"

"No, at Red Bay."

"That's not very far, is it?"

Ann shifted her weight on the leather couch, leaned over and placed her mug of hot chocolate on the coffee table. She glanced up at her neighbor, lowered her eyes, and looked up at him again. "No, not far. Only about fifteen miles. Patie, I had another reason for inviting you over here tonight."

The preacher said nothing. It sounded serious. He tried to hold his eyes onto hers, but she kept dropping her head and raising it again.

"Patie, have you heard the rumors—I mean—about—" Ann was struggling to push the words from her throat.

Corbin decided to make it easier for her. After all he was just about to broach the subject, anyway.

"You mean about us—you and me?"

Ann nodded.

"I've heard, Ann. Heard I was wearing a path out between my place and yours."

"I'm so sorry, Patie. I'm so sorry. I wouldn't have that happen for—"

"You don't have to apologize to me, Ann. It affects you as much as it affects me."

Slowly the attractive woman shook her head. "Not really, Patie. You're in the ministry. I'm so sorry. I'm afraid at least part of it has been my fault."

"How's that, Ann?"

"Well, I've been a little loose with my tongue, Patie, especially with close friends."

Corbin could see Ann's embarrassment, not only in the grimace on her face, but in the quietness of her speech. She spoke slightly louder than a whisper. He would have loved to have ended the conversation, but he needed to know what Ann had said. Nothing sinful had happened and only if she had lied to her friends, would her conversation impact the ministry. Gently, he asked, "What did you say to them?"

"It's not so much *what* I said as how often I said it," the publisher whispered. "I've just been talking about you too much, repeating things you have said, bragging on your athletic accomplishments, telling stories about you which circulated around Laurel and Ellisville. I don't know, Patie, just acting like you and I are special friends. A woman can't do all of that in a little town without raising eyebrows, especially when she lives next door to the man and took a bath in the spring under his house."

By the time Ann finished her mini-monologue, the preacher was beginning to feel ignorant. Nothing she had said seemed evil to him, although as a Christian, he might have reminded Ann that all honor goes to the Savior, not some old broken-down ex-football player, regenerated though he may be. Patie learned one certain thing from Ann's discourse, though. As an adult, there was still an awful lot he needed to know about living in a little town, something he had never done. His voice was compassionate when he responded, "Ann, I've never lived in a small town since I've been grown, so I yield to you concerning its mores and standards. Maybe I need to apologize to you. I *do* promise to adjust my behavior where you think it's necessary. But, also, thank you for the compliment."

Ann lifted her face toward Patie. Her smile was warm and her voice soft, "You're welcome, Patie. I guess I, along with many other people in town, was excited and astonished that you would actually make your home in Tishrock. You could have lived anywhere, but you chose to live here, and—"

"Ann," the preacher interrupted, "I really, really appreciate what you are saying, but I believe the Lord brought me here. I chose to live where He wanted me to live. To be honest, I may never have chosen to come here otherwise."

Ann smiled again, not quite so anemically this time. "Of course, Patie. I should have phrased it like that. Anyway, I guess I fed my ego by letting all my friends know you and I are good friends."

Patie laughed. "If you knew me just a little better, Ann, you would know there is absolutely nothing about me worthy of an ego build. When I got off my knees from praying to receive Christ four years ago in Eagle Pass, Texas, I learned that truth for a fact. By the way," Patie changed the subject, "you do have a microwave, don't you?"

"Your hot chocolate not hot anymore?" Ann queried, anticipating correctly the reason for his question.

"Yes! How did you know that?"

Ann quickly stood, her own mug in one hand, pointing at her head with the other. "Female intuition." Then, reaching, the lady took Corbin's mug and started toward the kitchen. Halfway there she stopped and turned back toward her visitor. "I'm going to stop running my mouth, Patie, but I'm not giving you up as a friend."

Corbin glanced around at his hostess. He owed her an answer. The only one which quickly came to his mind consisted of only one syllable. "Good!"

The sound of Patie's alarm clock detonated in his ears at exactly 5:00 a. m. For four or five seconds, which seemed like an hour to the sleeping man, he couldn't identify the noise. When finally he recognized it and found the necessary button to stop it, he grunted, pulled the covers back over his head and rued the promise he had made to Lester. An un-planned "dad-gummit" exploded from his mouth. A minute later, he threw the covers back and gazed at the ceiling of his bedroom, his mind, however, still wallowing in the mire of a stupid promise. Saturdays in Mississippi in September weren't made for cutting sorghum! They were made for leisurely getting out of bed; restfully drinking a large mug of hot coffee; maybe eating a bowl of cereal or a sausage and biscuit; relaxing with a newspaper in hand; strolling into the office around 9:00 o'clock; watching a good college football game or two on television in the afternoon, perhaps with friends. Saturdays in a Mississippi September weren't created for cut-ting sorghum.

The dark dot on Patie's otherwise off-white bedroom ceiling, upon which his eyes were unconsciously fixed, moved. Squinting, the preacher looked hard at the crawling spot. It was some kind of bug, a big black bug. Bugs didn't normally excite the old athlete, but he had never liked the idea of sleeping with one and this one looked as though he might nose-dive onto him. Suddenly, with a burst of energy, the pastor jumped out of bed, hustled into the kitchen and retrieved the fly flapper, as Mississippi people refer to it. He dashed back to his bed, balanced upon its quivering springs and ended the invader's misery. Nudging the dead insect from the sheet, where it had fallen, onto the fly flapper, he carried it to his front door and slung it. After ambling back to the kitchen, he poured himself a mug of coffee, and carried it out into the sunrise of his front porch. "Another day which you have made, Lord, another day which you have made. Help me rejoice and be glad in it, even in a sorghum patch. And Lord, thank you for the bug which kicked my lazy body out of bed!"

Clothed in a pair of old faded blue jeans, an old Giants tee shirt, an old pair of Nike shoes and a brand new Tishomingo Chiefs cap which someone had given him, the preacher flipped his hand-drawn map into the passenger seat of his SUV and brought the vehicle to a stop on a grassy area between the deep dust dirt road and the sorghum patch. Lester and the two other men stood in the shade of a sweet gum tree thirty feet away near a pickup truck with its tailgate down. All three were looking at the motorist and grinning. The preacher possessed no ability by which he could determine the purpose for the grins. Perhaps they were social banners of friendliness; or maybe smiles of delight knowing extra help had come; or perhaps indicators revealing a knowledge of what life would be like after eight hours in the sorghum patch. "'Git' out an' come in, Preach," a loud voice echoed before Patie could get out of his truck. It was Lester. "Better give me the keys," the big man quipped, walking toward the SUV, his hand outstretched.

Knowing he was being "jested" but not why, Corbin, adding a little extra aggression to his voice, asked "And why is that, Lester?"

"So you can't git' away 'bout a' hour from now!"

That statement identified the source of the big grins. Maybe Dimples was right. In his ignorance, he had no choice but to return the grin.

"Come on over here, Preach, and meet the other fellows," leading Patie toward the other two men. "This here's my Unca' Dink Junkin, my daddy's youngest brother, only two yer' oldern' me."

Dink was a smaller man than his nephew, perhaps five feet, eight inches tall. His earlier grin had quietened down to a wry smile and he actually looked younger than Lester. He wore a felt hat, which earlier in its life had been a dress hat. Numerous holes had been cut in it for ventilation purposes, the preacher supposed. A greasy pink headband encircled it. Like Lester, Dink wore overalls but unlike his nephew who wore a short-sleeved khaki shirt, he wore a long-sleeved pink dress shirt. Very noticeably, one eye looked larger than the other. The farmer extended his hand toward Patie, but said nothing.

"This here's his boy, Dip," Lester introduced, turning toward the younger and larger man. "Dip's called 'at 'cause since he 'uz a chap, he's been a' dippin' snuff, mostly Skoal, makin' no matter to'im, does it, Dip?"

Dip Junkin wasn't offended by his cousin's introduction. In fact, in some inordinate way, he seemed proud of it, a personal badge which apparently provided identification.

Like his father, Dip wore a large hat, but unlike his dad's, it was a straw hat. It, too, was riddled with holes and was discolored by dark stains of dried sweat. He wore old blue jeans, large holes revealing his two white knees, and an army drab-colored short-sleeved shirt. He looked the preacher in the eye and extended his right hand. "Glad to have you come out'n hep' us, Brother Corbin."

"Thank you, Dip. I'm glad to be here—ah—I think."

Dip and Lester laughed. Dink didn't.

"'Wal, Preacher, we need to get started, so let me kinely' 'splain whut' we're gonna' do. As ye' ken' see, we got 'bout a acre of sorghum, an' as ye' ken' see, we done cut 'bout half of it," Lester pointed. "We done toted whut' we cut to the mill."

"Where's the mill?"

"'Rite 'chonder," Lester pointed, "on th' side a' thet' hill under 'em sweet gum an' oak trees."

Corbin saw what Lester pointed to, though he could not have identified it as a sorghum mill—two tractors, both with wide belt-looking things attached to what appeared from that distance, to be rollers. About twenty feet farther up the hill, Patie could see a large silver container. Probably what they cook the sorghum in, he figured.

The preacher thought the tractors might turn the rollers but he ventured the question anyway, more to hear Lester's response than to gain information. "Where's the mule?"

"MULE! Whut' mule?" Surprise and a little disdain contorted Lester's face.

"The one on the end of the pole that turns the rollers that squeezes the juice out of the stalks."

"Preacher, we ain't used mules since tractors come' out!" Lester responded quickly. When he saw the smile on Patie's face, he bellowed, "Ye' a' joshin' me, ain't 'che, Preach?"

"Maybe a little bit, Lester. But I have seen mules turning the mill."

"Whur' ye' seen thet'?"

"South Mississippi, near Gloster on my uncle's farm."

"Bet thet' wuz' sugar cane, reckon?"

"I think so" Patie surmised.

"'Wal, Preach, 'bout six o'clock this even'nin', I don't 'spect yore' gonna' have much joshin' left in ye'." Lester's big teasing smirk added credence to his troubling words.

Patie glanced past Lester at Dink and Dip. Dip was smiling. Dink wasn't.

"Now," Lester continued, "we need to git' started. These here four thangs' a' layin' in th' truck here are sorghum blades. We give ye' first pick, Preacher, an' put these gloves on," he commanded, handing the pastor a pair of leather work gloves.

Patie looked at the blades. All of them were about eighteen inches long, about four inches wide, a handle on one end, like the ones he had seen in Harkum Hector's shop. One side of the blade was very sharp. One of the blades had a hole in the upper corner, probably for hanging on a nail. He choose that one. The others picked up the remaining three blades and quickly walked to the end of the rows and immediately began cutting the stalks down, each working one row.

"Say you never cut sorghum 'afore, huh, Preach?"

"Never have, Lester. A little sugar cane—not sorghum."

"'Wal, there's four thangs' ye' got to do. Cut the stalk down, strip them leaf lookin' thangs' offen' it, cut them seeds offen' th' top an' stack th' stalks in a tollible good stack, all th' tops an' bottoms a' pointin' the same way. Watch Dink fer' a minute. He's the fastest sorghum cutter in th' county, 'sides bein' the cooker. When ye' thank' ye' ready, thet's' your row rite' thar' lessen ye' want 'nother one."

"No, that one's fine," Patie replied, silently asking himself if it made any difference. Deciding it didn't, he studied the sorghum stalks. Most of them seemed to be about two inches thick at the base and maybe one forth of an inch thick at the top. Leaves protruded thickly out of the stalks from the ground to the top and the stalks themselves seemed to be about seven feet to nine feet tall. Each stalk was topped with a six inch long stem of seed, a crown insuring future crops, and the stalks grew in a row, almost touching one another.

"One other thang' Preach. See thet' sweet gum tree, thar'?" he pointed.

"Umh humh," Patie grunted.

"Thar's' a water cooler in the shade under it an' four stire'-foam cups."

"I see it. Thanks. Lester, where do we go to the bathroom?"

Lester laughed. "Anywhur' ye' want to, Preach, cept' in the sorghum. You in the woods now."

For a minute, Patie watched Dink and Dip. Dink started from the top, gathering several stalks in his hand, pulling them over and removing the seed stems. Then he slid the blade quickly down the stalk, slicing the leaves off. Last, he cut the several stalks with one swipe, stacking them neatly in small piles.

Dip, on the other hand, cut the stalks down first. Then he stripped the leaves from them, and finally the seeds.

Lester, Patie noticed, stripped the leaves first, cut the stalks down and then, with the stalks lying on the ground, topped the seeds off. Well, the pastor thought, one thing's sure, there is no set way of doing this. He decided he would imitate Dink first.

Soon, the preacher had flowed into the rhythm of cutting sorghum with the three other men, albeit about ten yards behind Dink, eight yards behind Dip and about three or four yards behind Lester.

Thirty minute after starting, Patie's clothes were soaking wet, including his athletic socks. A deep ache had developed across the lower part of his back, a pain in his right elbow from swinging the blade.

Dimples was right!

At 7:30, an hour and a half after starting, Lester yelled "water break." Lester, Dip and the preacher immediately dropped their blades and turned toward the water cooler.

"Dink not coming?" Patie asked.

"Not 'chet," Dip answered. "He slows down gradual. He'll come along in a minute or two." The others had finished their first cup of water and were sitting in the shade of the sweet gum tree when finally Dink stopped cutting and arrived at the water cooler. Patie noticed that Dink wasn't breathing as hard nor seemed to be as wet as he and the other two men were.

"How ye' makin' it, Preach?" Lester, the first one to speak, asked.

"Fine. Thinking I'm about to get the hang of it."

"I believe you are," agreed Dip, taking a small round can from his back pocket and depositing a pinch of snuff between his bottom lip and his lower teeth. "You gonna' blow past the rest of us here in a little while."

Patie wanted to laugh but he was hurting too badly. He managed a moderate grin. "I don't think there's any danger of that." Changing the subject, he asked, "How long are these rows?"

No one answered at first. Finally Lester said, "I don't recken' I know, Preach. 'Spect they close to a hunnard' yards though."

Corbin nodded.

"Whut' we gonna' do, Preach, is cut to dinnertime. They'll give us 'bout enough sorghum fer' a cookin', countin' whut' we already got up at th' mill plus whut' we squeezed out this mornin'."

Patie was baffled. "Y'all have already squeezed juice this morning?"

Lester ndded. "Unh hunh."

"When?"

"From 'bout 4:00 to jest 'afore ye' got here."

Corbin shook his head. "Y'all must have lights up there."

"We do," Dip explained. "A string of overhead lights."

"Time to cut!" It was Dink. It was the first thing he had said.

Patie Corbin had not hurt this badly, nor been this tired nor thirsty since his last two-a-day practice almost thirty years earlier. When Lester yelled, "Dinnertime," he immediately dropped his blade and bent over, resting his hands on his knees, sucking air, as he and his old teammates once described the action, trying to loosen the "kink" from his throbbing back. The three other men were standing upright, apparently suffering little pain. They seemed to be oblivious of their visitor's agony.

"Ye' recken' we got 'nough, Unca' Dink?"

"I 'spect so," Dink affirmed, nodding his head and looking around at what they had done. "'Pears to be. We got 'bout six rows, total. Ourghta' be 'nough."

The other men were almost to the water cooler by the time the preacher had untangled enough of his cramps so that he could walk comfortably. Lester was waiting on him. Dink and Dip were already turning their vehicles around.

"Preach, whur' ye' gonna' eat?"

"Don't know, Lester. I hadn't thought about it much," Patie grunted. That was almost a lie. He had figured someone would bring food to the field.

"Ye' wanta' go to Purple Rock?"

Lester's question surprised the preacher. He would never have considered walking into a restaurant as sweaty and dirty as he now found himself. "No, I don't believe, Lester. Rufus wouldn't let me in the front door."

"Shoot, whut' you talkin' 'bout, Preach. Thar'll' be folks thar' dirtiern' us!"

"You reckon?"

"Yes, Sir, I know so."

"Naw,' I reckon I'll go home, Lester. It's only four miles to the house." Truth is, the preacher wanted desperately to lie down in the spring water which flowed from beneath the cabin.

By the time Patie got back, a little before 1:30 that afternoon, Lester, Dink and Dip had already carried the morning's cutting to the mill where it sat piled near the two rollers. The preacher got a much better view of the "muleless" syrup mill.

The two tractors sat side by side, perhaps six feet apart. Large wide rubber-band shaped belts ran from fly wheels on the sides of the tractor to wheels on the two mills, some eight feet behind the tractors. When the tractors were running, the belts moved, turning the rollers, through which the sorghum was shoved. The juice then ran down a chute into two barrels, one barrel per mill, which were half-buried in the ground. From the barrels, the juice was dipped out with five gallon buckets and carried to the large cooking pan some twenty feet farther up the hill.

The silver-colored cooking container, probably stainless steel, Patie figured, was about eight feet long, three feet wide and about eighteen inches deep. It was separated into three sections by metal dividers. Each divider contained small doors with could be opened to allow the juice to flow from one compartment into another as it cooked.

By the time Patie had fully surveyed the area, Dink had built a raging fire under the silver pan.

"Ye' ready, Preach?"

"I don't know, Lester. Ready for what?"

"To start the squeezing?"

Suddenly a loud noise jerked the pastor's head around. Dip had started one of the tractors. A minute later he had cranked the other one. The belts were running.

"What do I do?" Corbin yelled into the ear of his friend.

"'Wal'," Lester yelled back, "me an' Dip's gonna' feed the cane through them rollers. Ye' gona' catch th' stalks after they come through the rollers, an' stack em' perpin'dicklar cross' 'em chains a' layin' on th' ground, rat' thar'," he pointed.

Patie looked at the two chains.

"Later on," Lester continued, "when th' two stacks o' squeezed stalks git' 'bout five feet high, we'll cut the' tractors off, wrap em' chains total 'round 'em, an' drag em' off with thet' tractor rite' thar'."

Corbin had not noticed the third tractor parked in the edge of the woods.

"An' we'll too tote juice to the pan," Lester pointed. "Dink'll have th' fare' 'agoin' hot by then."

"I've got to catch both mills?" Corbin asked, skeptically.

"Yeah. Now 'hits gonna' work ye' some, Preach, but with ye' a' bein' a football player an' all, I figure ye' can hannel' it."

Lester wasn't smiling, Patie noticed, but there surely were some mighty big Dimple-like twinkles in his eyes. Behind the farmer, Dip *was* smiling.

"That means I've got to run from one mill to the other, all the way 'round a tractor?"

Lester nodded. "But 'hit don't matter none iffen' th' squeezed-out stalks pile up a mite', 'cept' be keerful' 'bout them belts. We don't want no squeezed-out preacher-juice in our cookin'."

Dimples was right!! Fer' shore'–ah–for sure, Patie thought, Dimples was right!

CHAPTER SEVENTEEN
ANOTHER LESSON

Patie Corbin had more than a little trouble getting out of his truck. Every muscle in his body was sore, including the ones which ran up his neck into the back of his head. When finally he had anchored both feet onto the ground, legs bent, he placed the heels of his hands upon his knees and pushed, straightening his tortured body into an upright position, the only way he knew how to do it. He certainly could not have done it with only his back muscles, he figured. Slowly he inched his way around to the other side of his SUV and opened the passenger door. "Umh," he breathed out loud. Even reaching for the door handle pained him. Keeping his back straight, he bent his throbbing knees into a half-squat again and retrieved his Bible from the front seat.

"Pastor, you alright?"

The preacher turned slowly toward the sound of the voice. It was Mark Hoffman, the youth pastor. In spite of his torment, Corbin was relived to see that Mark was wearing a shirt and tie, rather than the attire which he was wearing when the two met two weeks ago. The young man had missed the first two Sundays Patie had been there. He was on vacation the first Sunday. Last week he had attended his grandmother's funeral in Florence, Alabama. Corbin had never seen him in Sunday dress.

"Not really," Corbin grunted. "Good morning."

"What happened?"

Patie glared at his assistant and for a moment, wondered if the youth pastor was teasing him. After all, this is Tishrock! "You really don't know?"

Mark looked surprised and a little guilty, as though he had forgotten something he should have remembered. "No, Sir."

"Been helping Lester cut, strip, top, pile, and haul, and make sorghum molasses all day—yesterday."

By the time the preacher painfully wheezed his explanation, the two pastors were walking slowly into the church building. Corbin spoke, looking straight ahead. His neck was too sore to turn his head toward his listener.

Mark chuckled. "We should have warned you. I'm surprised Dimples didn't."

"She did!"

"She did?' Mark repeated. "And you—ah—you—"

" I did it anyway. I didn't listen."

"Humh!" the young youth leader exclaimed. Though Mark didn't verbalize it, Patie thought he could hear his intelligence being questioned.

"Yep! I did it anyway. Shore' did," Patie answered deliberately corrupting the word "sure." It was the new preacher's way of indirectly agreeing with his co-worker concerning intelligence.

Patie was sitting at his desk studying his sermon notes when he heard the door into Dimples' office open. He painfully lifted his head. Dimples stood just inside his office. She was shaking *her* head.

"I saw you trying to lift your Bible out of your truck."

"You did? I didn't see you. Where were you?"

Dimples was still shaking her head. "Just pulling into the parking lot. Pitiful."

"Dimples," Corbin responded, trying to speak with volume, "I don't think you're pitiful. Why do you say that about yourself?"

"Wadn't talkin' 'bout me. I was talkin' 'bout you. Pitiful."

Determined to stand without revealing his pain, the preacher pushed himself up from his chair. It hurt. "Dimples, I can't remember when I've had a better workout. I want to thank you for recommending it," Patie teased. "Lester and the others really appreciated it. And I *certainly* do."

Dimples ignored his comment. "I told you so. You think you're gonna' be able to preach today?"

"Oh, sure. If I can get you and someone else, maybe Mark, to help."

"Help? Help do what?"

"Well," the preacher explained, trying to manufacture some vocal force in spite of his sensitive rib-cage, "you remember what the Bible says about Israel fighting the Amalekites in Exodus? When Moses held his hand up, Israel prevailed. But when he dropped his hands, Amalek prevailed. Moses was old and his hands grew heavy so Aaron and Hur held his hands up. Israel won the battle. Now, if I could just get you and Mark to—" Patie stopped talking in mid-sentence, giving Dimples' imagination time to develop.

The secretary gazed at her pastor for fully thirty seconds. "Humh," she finally responded. "I think somebody's gonna' have to hold moren' your hands up."

Patie laughed. The laughter hurt his sides. "I think you're right, my sister," he agreed as the secretary turned to walk into her office. "I think you're right!

"Dimples?"

The secretary stopped and slowly turned her head over her shoulder back toward her boss. She said nothing.

"You were right."

The same wall of noise met Patie this day which had met him the last two Sundays. It exploded from the SINO Sunday School Class room, the twenty-five class members catching up on news, acting as though they had talked to no one for a week, discussing everything from the tornado through football to—sorghum making. When the afflicted pastor entered the room, the cacophony of sound quickly died, held its quiet place for a moment, then discharged again in cheers and ovations.

Hattie Peak, the class president, hastened over to her visitor, who was struggling to walk without obvious pain and who was forcing a weak smile through the discomfort of his stiffness. "Welcome to the SINO class, Brother Corbin. Your mug of coffee awaits you."

"Thank you, Madam President. I, too, have been looking forward to my mug of coffee, perhaps more for its warmth this morning than for its taste. I may want to rub it over my sore muscles," he replied, focusing his eyes upon Lester, who stood grinning back at him out of a group of men standing near the coffee urn. A moment later, the preacher had indeed gathered his mug of coffee and a blueberry muffin. Lester was still grinning.

"Would you like to say something to the class, Brother Corbin?"

"Thank you, Madam President. I believe I would," Patie nodded. "Thank you. Yesterday, at the invitation of Tom Sawyer, whom most of you know, I think, as Lester Junkin, I was allowed to experience the joy of making sorghum molasses. Under the loving tutelage of said member of your class, I learned to cut sorghum, to strip it, to top it, and to stack it properly. I learned how to haul it to the mill. But, most of all, I learned how to catch the stalks of pulp from TWO mills at the same time after the juice had been squeezed out—and how to stack those stalks on a chain so they could be pulled away at the appropriate time. In other words, *two* men were pushing the sorghum through the rollers of *two* mills and only *one* man was catching and stacking those *two* separate squeezings of stalks on *two* chains. Best as I can figure it, I sprinted about nine and one-half miles in four hours with arm loads of squeezed-out sorghum stalks."

The SINO Sunday School Class members erupted in laughter, alternating their gazes between Lester and the preacher, the latter trying desperately to maintain a serious expression upon his face.

Then—above the din of the crowd—Lester's loud booming voice could be heard. "Wal', all 'ats goodn' proper an' mitey' interestin', Preach, but th' main thang' is how ye' feel this mornnin'?"

When finally the laughter died down, Patie answered, his gaze burning into the man's face. "Well, now, Lester, I feel pretty good considering. It hurts a right smart lifting this awful heavy mug full o' coffee up to my mouth. It took me awhile this morning to put my shoes on, and if they had been lace-ups, I don't know whether I'd a' made it or not. Then, o'course I had to drive my SUV this mornin' holding onto the bottom of the steering wheel 'cause I couldn't lift my hands up to the top of it. But all in all, I feel right pert, I reckon. Main thing is–my vocal cords are a little sore, and a preacher's whole life is built on his vocal cords. I hear tell exercise gets rid o' soreness, so I guess I'm just gonna' have to exercise my vocal cords a long time this mornin' startin' about 11:00 o'clock to get rid of the soreness in 'em"

By the time Patie finished his monologue, he was smiling, all the class members were laughing, and half of them were shaking their fingers or fists at Lester, who responded by holding both of his large hands up in the air, trying to quiet them down. When finally they hushed, he spoke. "Folks, this here preacher rite' 'cher' in front a' us got worked lik' a rented mule yesterdy' an' done a' rite' decent job. But th' only thang' is, he left 'fore Dink got thru' with his cookin."

"How much did y'all make, Lester?" came a male voice from the crowd.

"Forty-two gallon'. 'Enyhow, Preach left 'fore he got his pay so I brung' it to church this mornin'."

Turning around, the large man picked up four gallon cans, two with each hand. Facing his preacher, he proclaimed, "Preach, first thang' I want to say is much obliged fer' a' helpin' us. The second thang' I want to say is, it gives me fun to give ye' these four gallon' o' pure Tish'mingo sorghum

215

molasses. An' th' third thang' I wanta' say is more a question. How come ye' left 'afore th' cookin' wuz' done?"

Corbin knew Lester understood why he left, but he also knew Lester was continuing to joke with him. "Well, Lester, about the time those two rollers squeezed out the last few stalks, I was pretty near death. On a scale of one to ten, I 'spect' about a nine and a half! I wanted to die in my own bed with my own sorghum juice-soaked Nikes on. I figured I could just make it back home before it happened."

"Wal', I'm shore' glad ye' didn't die, Preach. We got a big hog killin' planned fer' th' first cold spell in December. I shore' wouldn't want 'che to miss 'at."

"Come on, Brother Corbin, when you get through shaking hands. I want to buy your dinner at the Purple Rock." The invitation belonged to Miss D. J. Crisp.

"Well, thank you, Miss D. J. I'll meet you there—about 12:30?"

"That will be fine. Some others are going. We'll pull some tables together."

Patie nodded to her as he shook other hands. Five minutes later he had gotten back to his office. Dropping his Bible on his desk, he eased into his chair, trying to ignore the pain in his sore legs as he sat down. "Lord," he prayed out loud, referring to his sermon that morning, "thank you for the account of the Caananite woman. Please help us in this church to have the determination to come into your presence which she had and the God-given ability to humble ourselves before you which she exhibited. Lord, I trust I preached about her and her relationship with you in a way which was pleasing to you. If I didn't, please show me my problem this afternoon and I'll correct it before your people tonight."

The preacher ambled slowly through the door of the Purple Rock Café. Standing to preach the sermon had stiffened his strained back muscles even more, causing him to feel them more when he was walking than when he was sitting *or* standing. Seeing the long table at which Miss D. J. was sitting, the preacher began making his way toward it. His movement was slowed by his soreness but also by the several people who asked him about his molasses making experience. Apparently, the entire town knew about it, he thought. They were probably laughing. To be honest, he said to himself, it is funny. Talking about getting sucked in along a trail of ignorance!!

"You planning to start farming?" Miss D. J.'s question was terse and the gentle smile on her face belied the caustic state of her heart in asking it.

"Not if I can help it, Miss D. J. If I had ever had the notion, it is gone now."

Miss D. J. was seated at the end of a long table made by shoving two smaller tables together. Six other people sat with her and there was one empty chair. It sat next to her. "Sit down, Preacher."

"Thank you, Miss D. J.," Patie humbly responded, easing into the vacant chair. He suspected Miss D. J. had orchestrated the seating arrangement. He knew a lecture was coming and he suspected he knew what it was going to be about.

"You know everyone here?" the widow for twenty years and retired pharmacy owner asked.

Patie turned and looked at the others sitting around the table, recognizing all their faces, remembering none of their names, yet certain they were all members of his church. Smiling, he asked, "Yes'm, I think so. But I have to admit, I haven't learned everyone's name just yet." Then nodding to everyone, he asked, "If y'all will tell me your names again, it will help this ol' preacher some."

Seconds later all the diners had identified themselves to their pastor. As soon as Patie heard their names, he remembered having heard them before, but he had not assigned those particular names to those particular faces. That was a fact somewhat distressing to the new preacher, though not altogether surprising. Several months would pass before he would learn to identify all his members by their names

"All these folks are relatives, Pastor," Miss D. J. explained. "Dot there is my niece Missy's mother. Cal and Rex are my nephews."

"Oh, a family reunion," remarked Corbin. "Thank y'all for inviting me." Then turning toward Dot and Henry, her husband, Patie asked rhetorically, "So you're Missy's mom and dad?"

Henry smiled and nodded. "Yes, though we don't always claim her."

"Henry," Dot corrected, "that's not true." Looking at the preacher, she elaborated. "Yes, she is Brother Corbin and we're real proud of her."

"Of course we are," growing serious, Henry joyfully admitted.

Patie was about to agree that Dot and Henry had ample reason to be proud of Missy when Miss D. J. quickly spoke. "Missy is a sweet young lady–almost perfect and will be as soon as she learns not to interrupt other people when they are talking."

Because neither Dot nor Henry asked their aunt to explain, Patie reasoned that Missy had told her parents about Miss D. J.'s gentle scolding last week at the Purple Rock.

"Now, are we all ready to order?" the elderly lady asked. Everyone nodded. Turning her head over her left shoulder toward the counter where the cash register sat, she called out in an authoritative voice, "Rufus, we're ready to order."

Rufus, the owner of the purple Rock Café, wasn't behind the counter. He was taking the order of other customers behind Miss D. J. And to her right. She couldn't see him or had not, although knowing he was waiting on other people would not have silenced the long-time patron.

"Just a minute, Miss D. J., please M'am."

Patie glanced at the people from whom Rufus was taking an order. Two of them glared at Miss D. J. One, a younger lady dressed in church clothes shook her head.

"Missy not working today?" Patie quickly asked, as much to move everyone's mind to something else as to gain information.

"No, we prefer that she not work on Sundays," her dad explained. Patie nodded.

A minute later, the owner had taken the eight orders. After he finished writing, he looked at Patie. "Got that special order coming in Thursday, Brother Corbin."

"What time you gonna' shuck 'em, Rufus?"

Rufus glanced nervously around the table, "'Bout nine—rite' after we close, I reckon."

"Great. I'll see you then."

Rufus walked quickly toward the kitchen but before he got out of hearing range, he heard Miss D. J.'s crusty voice. "You like raw oysters on the half-shell, huh, Pastor?"

"Love 'em, Miss D. J. I grew up pretty close to the coast and New Orleans. Been eating them most of my life."

"Humh!" she breathed. "You would do well, I believe, my Pastor, to think through that invitation a little before indulging Thursday night." Patie was surprised at Miss D. J.'s statement and he frowned. "You mean eating raw oysters?"

"No, I don't mean eating raw oysters! I mean eating raw oysters or anything else with Rufus and his friends back there in the kitchen after this café is closed!"

The preacher's mind whirled. He glanced around at Miss D. J.'s relatives. Three of them, two men and a woman, were looking down. The other three were watching him, anxious, he imagined, to hear how he would reply. Patie looked at Miss D. J. again—intently. He supposed what her disapproval might be, but he did not know for certain. He would know shortly.

"Do you know Rufus and the others drink when they eat raw oysters?" Miss D. J.'s voice was sharp, precise. Her face reflected no apology for asking the question.

"Well—ah—no, I don't, Miss D. J. I don't know for certain. I've never eaten oysters with them. But I don't know for certain that they *don't* drink either, I reckon."

"Well, they drink!"

Patie felt his sore shoulders slouch a little. He drew his eyes from Miss D. J. and dropped them to the place mat lying before him on the table. Strangely, with his mind stirring, he noticed the pictures on it—the Swinging Bridge—the entrance—the old log cabin—the lake—Bear Creek. From what Rufus had said last week, he suspected the men might have a drink, but that fact had not personally bothered the preacher, not much, not now. Immediately after salvation, he had noticed within himself a reluctance to frequent restaurants which sold liquor. But he no longer drank and that truth coupled with the fact that spiritual growth literally killed all desire for alcohol, had freed him to be in its presence without temptation or guilt or judgement.

The very last thing in this world which the preacher wanted was a confrontation with a church member, especially one like Miss D. J. in a public place, about Biblical interpretation. He did not want to say what he was about to say but he was forced to—his role as pastor demanding it. Disciplining a pleasant expression on his face and making certain love resided in his heart, he lifted his skeptical eyes back onto his spiritual sister's face. "Miss D. J., I'm not being argumentative, I promise you, but are you certain the men drink alcohol back there?"

Without hesitation or timidity she answered, "Yes."

Patie gently nodded, maintaining eye contact with his new friend. There was no wavering in either person. "May I ask you how you know for certain?"

Again, without hesitation, she answered. "Yes, you may, but I will not tell you."

Corbin, who had been leaning up slightly, slowly sat back in his chair, his narrowing eyes still fixed upon the face of his friendly antagonist. He consciously fought the resentment which he found easing its way into his thoughts. He would not allow the discussion to degenerate into argument, but he needed information. "Miss D. J., are you familiar with Colossians 2:16 which says, "Therefore, let no man judge you in respect to food or drink or in respect to a festival or a new moon or a Sabbath day?"

"Yes, I am, Preacher. But that verse doesn't apply to this situation, unless you plan to drink alcohol." Miss D. J.'s voice had lost none of its assertiveness. "You don't plan to drink, do you?"

Patie's eyes flew wide open. "Of course not, Miss D. J."

"Then that verse doesn't apply to you, does it?"

"No," Patie speculated, speaking slowly and thoughtfully, "I suppose it doesn't, Miss D. J. You're right. It doesn't"

It was there that Corbin saw the love and compassion in his opposer's face. "Thank you, Patie, for not trying to force that verse of Scripture into the discussion. You are an honest Christian and an honest preacher. Please don't ever lose that."

Patie smiled. The encroaching resentment had dissipated. "Thank you, Miss D. J. Every Christian needs strong loving people who will tell them the truth. I can see that you and I are going to have some interesting discussions through the years."

Corbin glanced around at the others. None of them seemed especially worried nor especially relieved, apparently expecting the conversation between their aunt and the pastor to proceed exactly as it had. Patie chuckled at that thought. They had been there before—!!

"Now, my pastor, since you invoked Scripture, let me ask you a question," The committed Christian stopped there. She was obviously waiting for Patie's permission to proceed.

Patie nodded, appreciating Miss D. J.'s respect, if not for him, then for the office which he occupied. Had the preacher possessed the ability to

221

read his companion's heart, he would have seen respect for both.

"Are you familiar with First Thessalonians 5:22, where God tells us to abstain from every appearance of evil?"

Patie nodded. He was, of course, familiar with the passage, but in fact, he also knew the verse as interpreted by some translations contained a little problem. The Greek word translated "appearance" is "eidous." The great preponderance of Greek scholars would translate the verse "abstain from every *form* of evil—in other words, from doing everything which might be considered evil. But the new preacher and pastor did not want to descend into that kind of discussion with his beloved church member either. To do so would sound arrogant and place her into a great disadvantage before her family, since she probably had not been afforded the opportunity to study Koine' Greek, or the Greek of the common man in which the New Testament was originally written. He knew he must remain silent, for now, on that issue. He would discover through his ministerial years that one of his greatest lessons would be recognizing the proper time to speak and the proper time to simply shut up. "Yes, M'am, I'm familiar with the verse, a great verse for all Christians. Do you think, my Sister, that I would be giving an appearance of evil by eating oysters in a setting where others are drinking liquor?"

"Yes, I do. Everyone in town knows what they do in that kitchen when the oysters come in, although Rufus and his friends, of course, would deny it. You go back there," Miss D. J. nodded toward the kitchen, "and do it with them, everybody in town will know it and many people will assume you're drinking with them. Whether you like it or not, you'll become a stumbling block."

Corbin looked down again and nodded. He was not accustomed to life in small towns, especially the Christian life—especially the pastoral life. "I understand, Miss D. J., I understand."

"One more thing, Pastor. Did you know Tishomingo is a dry county?"

Patie's eyes and mouth flew open—again. No, he did not know it!

He had not even thought about it! He had lived in areas of alcohol drinking, and partying for so long, the concept of living in a dry county wasn't even relevant to him. As soon as the lady asked Patie the question, he remembered that he had not seen alcoholic beverages advertised anywhere in Tishrock. "No, I didn't, Miss D. J. I hadn't really thought about it."

"That means, of course," the lady continued, "when Rufus and his friends drink in his kitchen Thursday night they will be breaking the law? Do you really want to be locked up in that kitchen with a group of men who are breaking the law?"

Corbin, remembering Romans 13:1 and 2, flinched. From that moment the preacher realized he still had a lot to learn—that seminary, even a great one, could not prepare him completely for everything he would face in his ministry. It would be a valuable lesson following him all the remaining days of his life.

CHAPTER EIGHTEEN
The House on the Hill

Patie Corbin had been asleep on the couch about ten minutes when two soft knocks on his front door jerked him into a partial consciousness. He sat up quickly, looking at the Colts-Eagles football game on television and wondered if the sound had come from there. Two more gentle knocks answered that question and the preacher stood up in his sock-covered feet, his faded blue jeans and a tee shirt and walked swiftly to his front door. He was surprised and elated when he saw his visitor. It was Mr. Hampton Crimm, whom he had met at dinner-on-the-ground two weeks ago, his first Sunday at Tishrock Church. Patie quickly shook the old Eighth Air Force veteran's hand. "Come on in, Mr. Hamp. How in the world are you?"

Mr. Hamp smiled, revealing his darkened and snaggled teeth, rendered thus, at least in part, by chewing tobacco. He wore overalls, a khaki work shirt, and work boots. The same Ole Miss baseball cap which he had worn two weeks ago was in his hands. His parted hair had been cut recently and he had shaved, allowing the preacher to notice his strong nose and chin. Lines of age cut across his face and a slight twinkle brightened his pale blue eyes. "Thank you, Brother Corbin, but my boots are muddy. I 'spect I'd better stay out here."

"Well, have a seat, Mr. Hamp. You want the swing or a chair?" Corbin asked, walking out on the porch and pointing. "Take your pick."

Without answering, the man sat in the nearest rocking chair. Patie moved to the swing.

"I hope I'm not botherin' you on a Sunday afternoon, Brother Corbin. I know Sunday afternoons are made for nappin'."

Corbin marveled at the dichotomy of his visitor. On one hand, if looks were the only indicators, one would assume the World War II veteran was an uneducated, unpolished, non-traveled, backwoods hillbilly; his clothes, his teeth, his retiring disposition—and two weeks ago, the beard and hair. The fact that he had groomed his hair and shaved his beard did not go unnoticed by the preacher. On the other hand, Mr. Hamp spoke and acted like a highly intelligent, well-versed educated man. "Mr. Hamp, I can think of nothing I'd rather do than visit with you this afternoon. I really appreciate you coming. I've been wanting to talk to you. Like I said two weeks ago when we met, I have an extremely high opinion of all you World War II—"

"Brother Corbin, I'm sorry to interrupt you. I really 'preciate what you said when we met and what you were about to say, but I don't feel like much of a man to be admired. And, begging your pardon, I'm not a hero, like you said at church. I do have a problem I'd like to talk to you about, though, if you have the time to listen."

The pastor glanced at his watch. It was 2:40. He wouldn't need to be at church until 6:40—no—6:15. A Deacon's meeting had been called for 6:30, but I can miss that, he quickly considered. I'll call Dimples and have her call the chairman, Brother–ah—Lucious, if need be.

Patie studied the old man. His guest's agony was very apparent and akin to his own anguish the day he walked into Jess Gingrich's office almost five years ago. The old man leaned forward in the rocking chair, his elbows resting upon his knees, his head bowed as though he were praying or, for some unexplained reason, exploring the tops of his boots, or the floor under them. His eyes were open, but at that moment Patie did not know it, The only thing the man could see was the travail of his own soul.

"Mr. Hamp, I have time to listen to you and then some, if need be."

The man, without lifting his head, quietly nodded. He whispered,

"Thank you, Brother Corbin."

Patie nodded, though his new friend could not see it. "Before you talk to me, Mr. Hamp, in order for me to better understand, may I ask you a few questions?"

The tormented man slowly turned his face toward his host. For a moment he did not speak and when he did, his words were slow and tortured. "Yes, Sir—but I—but I need to talk to you very–very badly."

The preacher further explained. "The reason I need to ask you a few questions, Mr. Hamp, is to keep from interrupting you too often when I have a question. I may have to do it anyway, from time to time, but not as often, probably."

The struggling visitor nodded again and then lowered his head back toward the floor. "I just have a few questions, Mr. Hamp. It won't take too long."

The traumatized man nodded even again, in understanding.

"First, would you call the event about which you want to talk to me a serious problem?"

"Yes, Sir, a problem. A very big serious problem."

"Mr. Hamp, is it something which you did to someone else? Or did someone else do something to you?"

"Both," he replied, taking a deep breath, "but what I did was much worse than what they did."

Corbin continued. "Was what you did recent?"

"No, Sir. It was more than fifty years ago."

"Did it happen here or somewhere else?"

With that question, the old man slowly pushed himself from the rocking chair. He carefully walked to the far corner of the porch and gazed into the distance, silently. In slow motion, he removed the cap from his head and drew a large red bandana from his rear overalls pocket. Holding the Ole Miss cap in his left hand and the bandana in his right one, he lifted his right arm and pointed toward the hills at the rear of the cabin. He tried to speak—his voice choked—he stopped. He tried again, pointing with his right hand, the large red handkerchief dangling from it. "It happened up there—in the Distant Hills where I live—about two miles from here."

For a moment, the elderly man stood as though in a hypnotic trance, frozen into his own timeless memory, psychological pain covering his aging face. Then he turned and walked unsteadily down the porch steps.

Patie, who thought the man was leaving, stood. "Mr. Hamp?"

The man did not answer. He walked to the edge of the small sandy bed through which the spring water flowed from under Patie's cabin into Bear Creek. He dropped his cap to the ground and then his bandana. Carefully, he knelt, supporting himself with his arms and hands, until he was on his knees. Lethargically he grasped the bandana and dipped it into the cold spring water. Turning his face toward Heaven, he called out to a God whom he seemed to know. "Oh, God, forgive me! Please forgive me! Please forgive me!" For a moment or two he stayed in that position. Then he spread the piece of wet cloth around his neck and picked up his cap. Cautiously, he pushed himself back into an upright position and began to make his way falteringly back up the steps. When finally he reached the porch again, he stopped and turned toward the pastor. "Brother Corbin, when I was a boy, I squirrel hunted all around this spring and up and down Bear Creek. I set out many a hook in the creek. I knew all this land like the back of my hand." Moving somberly, the troubled man sat back down in the rocking chair and leaned back, lifting his face toward the ceiling. He spread the wet handkerchief across his contorted face and grew silent.

Patie watched that entire event with great concern and more than a little interest. And he tried, though mostly in vain, to determine what it meant, if anything. Perhaps Mr. Crimm was mentally casting himself back into his younger and more innocent days. Maybe he was simply hot and wanted to cool off a little. Or could it be that the cool spring water somehow made him feel closer to God—an aid to faith, in the same way that Christ helped a blind man to have faith by making clay from His spittle and applying it to the man's eyes. Or maybe it was none of these. Maybe it was something else.

"Mr. Hamp, I have just one other question. Obviously you have a great burden upon your heart. My I ask you—in love—how would you have me help you? Something I want very much to do."

At first the old man did not answer. He continued rocking gently in the chair but otherwise remained motionless, his face turned upward, the cool cloth spread across it. Corbin was considering asking him the question again but was stopped by the low moan of the man's voice. The preacher heard the sound but could not understand what he said.

"Sir?" Patie asked.

Slowly the distressed visitor slid the bandana from his face. He leaned up in the chair, gripping the wet cloth so hard that water ran from it, repositioning his elbows upon his knees. Turning his head toward the preacher, a pitiful expression twisting his face, he spoke again. His voice was low but his tone was definite. "I have to make something right with God and with man. I want you to help me to do that before I die."

The preacher's impulse was to place an arm around the hurting man's shoulder, to try to comfort him and assure him that he had not committed the unpardonable sin, that no matter what he had done, God could forgive him. But this was not the time to do that. Comfort *would* come after Biblical confession was made and restitution, if need be, was given. "Mr. Hamp, I want to hear what you have to say and when you leave here today, I promise you will know what God, in His Word, says to do. I promise you that."

Patie was aware that his statement might sound arrogant to the ears of a third party but he believed his statement was true. Pain needs promise! Anguish needs authority! And sin needs a Savior. "Please, my friend, start at the beginning and tell me everything."

The following minutes would shock the preacher's Christian sensitivities, touch his compassionate heart and test his commitment to the authority of God's Word, a commitment which he had pledged to keep, as God the Holy Spirit gave him power.

"Preacher, it's gonna' be kind of a long story. I know you have services tonight and I don't—"

"Mr. Hamp," Patie interrupted, " please don't worry about that. I don't have to prepare a sermon on Sunday nights. I answer questions. Please tell me the whole story."

The old man nodded and started to speak. Patie interrupted him again. "Before you do, though, would you allow me to pray?"

"Yes, Sir."

The preacher prayed that their compassionate God would grant to Mr. Hamp the ability to remember details; that He would give Mr. Hamp courage; that He would bestow upon him, Patie, the ability to discover from God's Word the wisdom necessary to help Mr. Hamp find his solution; and that God might be glorified in the process.

When Patie finished praying, his guest whispered an almost inaudible "Amen."

"I was born and raised in those hills," he pointed, "and other than when I was in the war, I have lived there all my life. I was the only child. Something happened to Mama when I was born and she couldn't have more children. When I graduated from high school I got a football scholarship to Northeast Junior College. The war broke out at the end of my second season, and—"

"Mr. Hamp, from time to time, I need to interrupt you to ask questions. Is that gonna' be alright with you?"

"Oh, yes, Sir, of course."

"What kind of work did your parents do?"

"Farm and sharecrop. Daddy owned seventy-five acres but half of it was high hill. Only about thirty acres was low. He helped farm other folks' places."

Patie nodded.

"Well, when the war broke out, a bunch of my friends and I joined up. I was fascinated with airplanes, so I joined the Air Force and was sent to Blytheville, Arkansas, for training in B-17's. Two big things happened to me while I was at Blytheville. First, my Daddy, who had never public-worked got the offer of a job at the shell plant in Natchez, and—"

"Sorry, Mr. Hamp. The shell plant? What was that?"

"They made 105 Howitzer shells. One of Daddy's brothers was a foreman down there."

"I see. Sorry. Please go ahead."

Mr. Hamp nodded. "Well, they moved down there and Mama got a job in a café near the plant. Mama was a really good cook.

"The second thing that happened to me was meeting a girl. Her name was Mandy Lynn Carmody. She worked in the Officer's Club mixin' drinks, waitin' tables. Anyway, we started goin' steady."

"Sorry, Mr. Hamp! Was she from around there?"

"No, Sir. Turns out she grew up down in Calhoun County, a little place called Derma, not too far from here. That was one of the main things which—ah— which—kinda' drew us together," Hamp Crimm pondered, his speech growing noticeably slower and weaker, then trailing off into silence. He sat that way for a few moments. Then gradually, he started sobbing, softly and quietly at first, but soon the sobs increased in frequency and intensity, jerking his aged body as though he were being touched with an electric wire.

Patie, beginning to be a little concerned, stood quickly from the swing and hustled over to his chair. "Mr. Hamp, are you alright?"

The man nodded.

"Can I do anything for you?"

He shook his head.

"You sure? A glass of water? A Coke?"

He shook his head again. When finally he spoke, his voice was soft, his speech broken. "I'm alright—just—give—me a minute—thank you–I'm sorry."

Patie walked back to the swing. "That's okay, Mr. Hamp. Take your time."

Presently, the sobs slowed as gradually as they had started. And then they stopped and the grieving man continued talking. "When I finished training at Blytheville, I was transferred to Minot, North Dakota for pilot training. Mandy kept her job at Blytheville and on my next furlough, we married. I didn't want her to keep tending bar at Blytheville, so I brought her here to live and she found a job in a grocery store down at Tupelo. She and a soldier's wife got an apartment in an older couple's home, and she was making it fine. 'Course I was sending her most of my pay. I didn't need that much in England."

"Were you all flying combat missions when you first went over?"

"No, Sir, not at first. We trained some more for a couple or three months, I guess. Then we started flying combat—daylight—missions. No fighter protection past a hundred miles into the mainland. It was pretty rough. We lost lots of planes. Several of my buddies were killed early on! Then one day we got hit."

"You mean your plane?"

Hamp nodded. "Yes, Sir, the "Goal Line Stand.""

"Name of your plane? Goal Line Stand?"

Hamp nodded again. "The pilot and I loved football. Anyway, we were hit over France on our twenty-first mission, eight months after I got to England. Took heavy flak on my side. Knocked out two engines and got me pretty good. We limped back to England."

"You were wounded, Mr. Hamp?" Patie asked, surprised. No one had told him the veteran had been wounded.

Hamp nodded again but did not elaborate. "Well, I stayed in the hospital two months in England and then I was transferred to Bethesda. I stayed there three months."

"Was Mandy still working in Tupelo?"

"Yes, Sir."

"Did she have a car?"

"No, Sir."

"Mr. Hamp, if you don't mind me asking—what were your injuries?"

Patie half expected his visitor to decline answering that question but he didn't. Without hesitation he said, "I lost three ribs on my right side, some internal injuries. I lost the hearing in my right ear and I lost my right leg just below the knee."

"I'm sorry, Mr. Hamp. I had no idea."

"That's alright, Brother Corbin. Bethesda fixed me up pretty good." he smiled wryly. "Doesn't hurt at all to stump my right toe."

"Did Mandy come to Bethesda?"

"No, sir, and that was part of my problem. I couldn't understand why she wouldn't come. The government would have paid her train fare or bus fare. She kept saying she would lose her job."

"Did you talk to her—I mean on the telephone?"

"Just when she was at work every once in a while. 'Course we didn't have a phone up there," he motioned with his head, meaning in the hills. "But I wrote her every day. She wrote about once a week, I reckon."

"Umh," the old ex-football player grunted. "I know that *really* bothered you."

"Yes, sir. To tell you the truth, I got real worried and suspicious. Remembering Mandy and thinking about coming home to her was about all that got me through it—I mean through the missions and the hospital stay and the pain.

"Well, when I got to where I could walk real well, I came home without letting Mandy know, on a weekend that she was supposed to be at our house. I got off the train in Iuka about noon and hired a fellow to drive me to our mail box up there." he gestured with his hand. "Our house sits on a high hill about a quarter-mile off the county road and the driveway didn't go all the way up the hill. When I got to the end of the driveway, about a hundred yards below the house, an A-Model Ford was parked there."

"Mandy's room mate?" Corbin asked.

Hamp did not answer. It was as though his mind was so mired down by the jumbled mass of emotions, he could not hear. "They didn't even know I was there until I stepped onto the front porch," he said, his voice barely audible. Patie was forced to sit still in the swing in order to hear.

Strangely, Mr. Crimm turned them and looked at his host. His face softened and his voice mellowed. "If ol' Rock had still been alive, they would have known I was coming long before my boot hit the front porch."

"Ol' Rock?' Was he—"

"My hound dog. Best coon dog in the country. Good squirrel dog, too, 'til he picked up the scent of a coon." The benign smile on Hamp's face indicated a heart which apparently needed temporary respite from the horror of the tale, a touch of shelter in the midst of a storm.

After a moment of reflective silence, he continued. "I saw Mandy peep through the window, saw her full face, and I knew something was bad wrong. I had seen that look before, on the faces of my friends who died in the war—a look of fear an' of horror. When I opened the door, Mandy was —she was—" the old veteran choked, struggling to say the words. "She was cowered against the far wall. I didn't see the man at first. He was standin' to my left over by the fireplace. When I looked back at Mandy, she looked different, a lot bigger, standin' there in that blue rayon dress I bought her. And then I could tell. She was with child."

The heartbroken old man sobbed loudly again. Patie waited in silence.

"Then," he continued, "I walked past her into my bedroom, took my 12 gauge shotgun down from the gun rack and loaded it, with her screamin' and askin' what I was going to do. It was then I said the only thing I said that day—I asked her if she was goin' to have a baby. When she said 'yes,' I put the shotgun to her belly and pulled the trigger. Then I walked over to where the man was crouchin' behind the settee and I shot him in the back."

Patie stood with Mr. Crimm upon the north slope of the high hill where his log house stood. They were glaring at the small patch of ground, which looked exactly like the earth surrounding it except for the four partially buried grey stones, forming about a six foot square.

"I buried them right here, Brother Corbin, behind the house, 'cause I knew nobody'd ever come back here, at least not very often. There was no one *to* come back here. Mama and Papa were in Natchez and we didn't have any close kin living around here. Mandy had a few folks in Arkansas somewhere, and I never did know where the man was from."

Remarkably, Mr. Hamp's voice had grown stronger, perhaps rendered thus by the cleansing confession. To Patie, however, the creases of age and worry across the old man's face seemed to cut more deeply than an hour ago.

"Did you know him?"

"No, Sir. I didn't know his name. I didn't want to know it. He had a billfold. I took the money and the ration stamps out of it without looking at anything else. I buried it with him."

"Mr. Hamp," Patie gently asked, "would you allow me to pray while we're here at the grave? I sense a real strong need for you and me to be in close touch with the Lord about now."

"Yes, sir. Please pray, Brother Corbin. I wish you would."

When the preacher finished, the two men walked back to the house; Patie more burdened than he was two hours before; the old pilot seemingly less burdened. He was beginning to make a terrible fifty-seven year old sin right with God and with man.

Even in the midst of all the trauma, the preacher could not help but marvel at the beauty of the place. The log house, slightly larger than his cabin, it appeared, was almost square. It was surrounded by small boulders, some no more than six feet high. Large oak and hickory trees formed a green canopy over the house and a log barn squatted thirty yards to the right. The house, the barn and the space in between filled the entire peak of the hill, the ground falling away sharply on every side. Patie could easily understand why no one had ever attempted to build a road up to the top, especially before these present years of large construction equipment. It was too steep.

"You want to sit on the porch, Brother Corbin?" Hamp asked, as the two men reached the house.

"Yes, if it's alright with you. But I would like to see inside the house, too, if I may."

The pastor knew little about home furnishings and furniture, but it appeared to him that everything in the house might be called primitive. Most of it appeared to be hand-made.

"I imagine you want to see where they—they—died, Brother Corbin—to see if there's still any sign?" Mr. Crimm's voice had grown weak, his face wrenched again, his eyes moist. "I cleaned everything up good. Where Mandy died, it was in the middle of the floor. Wear and tear helped destroy all that sign. I pulled the settee over the spot where the man died. There's still a little stain under there."

Patie nodded. "You have a beautiful and different place here, Mr. Hamp. I have some more questions, though. Do you mind me askin' them?"

"No, Sir."

A moment later, the two men continued their strange conversation, each of them sitting in a rocking chair. Patie spoke first.

"Mr. Hamp, did anyone ever ask you about Mandy, where she was?"

"No, Sir. She had already quit her job, her being with child, I found out later."

"What about the man? Did no one ever ask about him?"

"No, Sir. I reckon no one knew he was here. By the way he was dressed, he didn't seem to be from around here. His car had an Arkansas tag on it. I figured he was from over there."

Patie nodded. "What happened to the car?"

"I drove it back to Maryland and sold it."

"If this question bothers you, Mr. Hamp, please don't answer it, but I really need to know the answer. Are you sure the baby wasn't yours?"

236

"I don't mind answering it, Brother Corbin," the old airman murmured. "I want all the truth to come out now. I'm sick of holding it in. I hadn't seen Mandy in a year—a little over a year. It couldn't have been mine."

Patie only nodded.

"But I thought about it—just—just before," Mr. Hamp added, his voice trailing away.

"What about your parents? Did they ever know?"

"Yes, Sir," Hamp acknowledged. "When the war ended, the shell factory went back to making rubber tires. Daddy and Mama stayed in Natchez. Before I left here to go back to Bethesda after what I did, I called them. I had planned to pick up Mandy and catch the train to Brookhaven and they would pick us up there, but after what happened, Mama got off from work and came up here. I told her and she helped me clean the floor. 'Course, I had already seen them once when I first got back stateside."

"You didn't want to drive down there in the man's car?"

"No, Sir, I couldn't. I didn't have enough gas coupons to get me down there and to Maryland, too. Plus, I needed to get back to Bethesda for some more work on my leg—you know—the prosthesis. And I wanted to drive back up there to sell the car. I thought about giving it to Daddy but that woulda' been dangerous, prob'ably."

Patie gazed out over the hills and slowly shook his head. He had not been prepared for such a story. Remembering the service at church, he glanced at his watch. It was almost 5:00 o'clock. He nudged the rocking chair back and forth and wasn't even conscious of the squeaking one of the rockers made as it rolled across a loose board. For the next fifteen minutes, the wounded airman finished the story; his mother and dad were both dead and buried down the hill in the graveyard at Rocky Mount Baptist Church; he came out of the war on one hundred percent disability; he got an education degree from Ole Miss after the war and tried to teach. In the early 1950's he came back home and became a recluse, living in fear of having his sin discovered by the authorities. Six months ago, while watching Billy

237

Graham preach on confession, he bowed his head and in front of the television set asked Christ to save him. From that time he knew he had to make right what he did—with God and with man.

And the new preacher knew he had to help him.

CHAPTER NINETEEN
PULLED INTO CONTROVERSY

It was 7:30 P. M., midpoint in the Sunday night service, time for the drawing of the card which would tell Patie the subject he would teach tonight. He was reaching into the back of the pulpit for the box which contained the cards when a man's voice rang out. "Pastor, may I say a few words to the church before you start?"

The preacher, who was bending down, looking into the back of the podium, straightened up. It was Larry Steeg, the father of the little Ole Miss girl, Cindy, who two weeks ago had jumped up and offered to the church her rendition of the yell, "Hotty Totty." "Of course, Brother Steeg."

Larry slid out of his pew and stood in the center aisle at the front of the church. He was a young man and handsome, narrow of face, a strong nose, clear grey eyes, pronounced eyebrows. His hair was blond and neatly cut. An attorney, his office was in Iuka, the county seat.

"Folks," Larry addressed the church, "A couple of weeks ago an event happened here, which at first was humorous to everyone, except Cheryl and me—and would have been to us if it had happened to any of you. You all were wonderful in your love and understanding and forgiveness. To be honest, Cheryl and I were tempted to pass it off as one of the funny things that an offspring might do in his or her youth, a saying which needs to be recorded in a book of remembrances. But upon more serious reflection we took a closer look at the issue. That closer look forced us to examine our priorities and ask ourselves some tough questions. Our children mirror and repeat what they see and hear from us, so you know where it came from. The episode has forced us to realign our priorities. Loving our college is good, but it isn't nearly as GOOD as loving and serving our Lord. We realize now we went wild when Ole Miss won a football game and yawned when told of Christ winning victory for us over death and the grave. By His Grace, we've rearranged all of that. Thank y'all for listening."

Larry sat down as quickly as the stood. A healthy chorus of "amens" followed him.

When Patie, who had sat down while Larry spoke, stood again, he saw a hand waving at the rear of the church. It was Lester. The preacher recognized him.

"Larry, I just wanta' say amen to whut' ye' jest' said an' I 'spect we all need to make thet' same commitment. I'm serious in sayin' 'at. But let me ast' ye' this. Thet' mean ye' gonna' yell fer' State now?"

Patie shook his head. He believed he understood Lester, though he had known him only two weeks. Some people, Lester seeming to be one of them, occasionally want to add a little levity to the emotional state of a gathering, in case someone might be embarrassed, a back door version of some sort of ministry as they perceive it.

After the smattering of laughter subsided, the grateful preacher, circumventing Lester's comment, spoke to the father. "Thank you, Larry. If no one else needed to be reminded of that truth, I'm certain I did."

While Larry was speaking, the pastor realized he had not been aware of the fact that the young father was an attorney. Following the service tonight, he would try to talk to him about Mr. Hamp.

Holding the question box low, Patie asked, "Cindy, Honey, would you come and draw the piece of paper out of the box for me again?"

Without hesitation, the pretty little girl, a big smile on her cute face dashed to the platform, drew the note from the box and handed it to the pastor. After Cindy ran back to her seat, the preacher unfolded and read the message. It caused him to smile, then laugh.

Preacher, would you explain to me (one more time) election and the freedom of man when it comes to personal salvation? It has been explained in this church before and just about the time I think I have it, I lose it again.

"I laughed," Patie quickly explained, "because this great and complex issue produces the same question in my mind, too. How can both Biblical teachings be true? I wrestle with it, as I'm certain all Christians have, from the birth of the church at Pentecost until now. Well, let's get into it, but before we do, please allow me to warn all of us, this topic can be and often is very controversial. You know why?"

"Because it's hard to understand?" a tentative female voice immediately asked.

"Exactly!" Patie responded. "And not only hard but impossible. And that creates frustration in the human mind. I think most of us are about the same. We dislike being forced to accept anything as fact which we cannot understand, though without realizing it, we do it all the time. How many of us accept the concept that space is infinite, that it has no end?"

Most of the hands in the audience shot up.

"Now, how many of us can explain it? That space goes on forever? And if it doesn't go on forever, if it has a boundary, what's on the other side of that boundary?"

Patie hesitated a moment for that concept to sink in. "You see, with finite minds working through temporary brain cells, we try in vain to comprehend infinite truth. We cannot *comprehend* it but as Christians, we can *accept* it. The distance between a finite mind and an infinite truth is traversed through what?" he asked.

No one answered, though everyone seemed to be considering Patie's question.

"Let me give you a hint," the preacher offered. "Much of science scoffs at it."

"FAITH?" The voice was loud and the answer formed as a question.

"Yes," Patie agreed. "Faith. We keep waiting for science to destroy the concept of eternity when looking at space. But even with strong telescopes and spaceships, science cannot refute the concept of eternity, yet *they* cannot explain it. Rather, science confirms it. Scripture taught the concept of eternity four thousand years ago. God is eternal–no beginning and no end. And His ways, for finite beings like us, are past finding out. We could not even know God exists, except for the fact that He has revealed Himself to us—in our consciences, in nature, and finally in His Son, according to Romans I and Colossians I. And of course, the written Word explains Him. But even then, we finite Christians, though endowed with the indwelling Holy Spirit, cannot understand all about God. And aren't we glad of that?"

"Why is that, Pastor? Why would we be glad we can't understand all about God?" The lady's voice was tentative, humble.

"Let's think about that worthy question for a moment. Would we want to worship a god with no more complexity or intelligence than we possess?"

Most everyone shook their heads. A few said, "no," including the person who asked the question.

"By the way," Patie continued, "the early idol worshipers would answer "yes" to that question. That's why they fashioned their own idols and then fell down upon their knees and worshiped them. They were in essence worshiping their own intelligence and creative abilities."

Corbin hesitated a moment before he proceeded, permitting that information to be digested. Presently, he continued.

"Now, occasionally in the Bible, God allowed His infinite knowledge to dip down into the pages of Scripture, arranging for earnest finite minds to read of these unsearchable riches. We read of these things and we try to understand them, but we cannot. How then do we respond to these things clearly written in Scripture? Things we cannot understand? The carnal mind will tend to reject them because the carnal mind will usually not accept that which it cannot understand. But the spiritual mind, that is, the mind yielded to the Spirit of God, will accept even "opposing" truths, though it cannot understand one or the other of them, through what ingredient?"

Corbin waited for an answer, searching the faces of his listeners. Finally a familiar voice asked "Faith?" the same voice which answered "faith" earlier.

"Exactly," the preacher welcomed, excitedly. "Good. You all agree?"

Almost everyone in the auditorium concurred. A few exhibited quizzical expressions.

"That's why Scripture teaches, or at least one of the reasons why Scripture teaches, 'Without faith, it is —' Corbin hesitated again.

"Impossible to please God, Hebrews 11:6," Lester sounded out from the rear of the building. "Mama made me memorize that verse when I was a chap."

"Your mama did well, Lester. Without faith it is impossible to please God. You see, it's faith, simple trust in God, trust in His willingness to leave us a roadmap called the Bible, and trust in His Omniscience, which traverses the space between infinite truth and a finite mind."

"Preacher?"

"Yes, Lester."

"I wanted to ast' 'ye 'afore when ye' said tray'verse what th' meanin' 'o thet' word wuz', but 'chu'us 'agoin purty' good, so I didn't wanna' stop ye'. Whut' does it mean?'

"I'm sorry Lester. I didn't mean to use a word that—well–that some might not—"

"Thets' one 'em sem'nary' words, Preach?" Lester interrupted.

The entire church erupted with laughter, including Patie, remembering what Lester had said two weeks earlier. When the laughter slowed, Patie answered, "'Fraid so, Lester, though it might be used outside of seminary, too. It means moving or passing from one point to another."

"Um-hunh," the farmer grunted. "Kinda' like ye' a' movin' from

243

not being sore to a' bein' real sore?"

When finally the mirth diminished—for the second time in less than a minute—the preacher confessed, "Folks, I think that Brother Lester back there on the back row just broadsided me for the second time in two days. I believe he might have known the meaning of traverse and set me up!"

With laughter, smiles, and nods, many of the other church members confirmed the pastor's suspicions. He would remember that!

"Okay, Lester and all y'all, back to the subject," Patie grinned, smothering his desire to laugh. "It's faith, given to earnest, truth-seeking people—Ephesians 2:8 and 9—which enables a finite mind to accept infinite information as truth. Without that faith, we cannot please God and we cannot often accept spiritual truth which we do not understand. In fact, to the unbeliever, the message of the cross is foolishness, I Corinthians I:18 and 23. Now, let's look at some of these infinite truths, two opposites which in a finite mind cannot both be true but both of which Scripture teaches as true, a term which theology calls *antinomy*, Lester."

Lester waved.

"The Trinity itself is an antinomy. God is three Persons but one substance at the same time. Nothing on the face of this finite world can be used as a perfect example of that. In our world, nothing can be one substance yet three separate distinct items at the same time."

"Brother Corbin," a man asked, "what about a cup of water? It can be either liquid, ice or gas."

"Very true, my Brother, but not at the same precise time."

"What about a basketball team?" Patie did not notice who asked the question, nor did he try to determine it. "Five people, one team, at the same time?"

"A good illustration but not a perfect one. The five team members are of a *like* substance but they are not the exact *same* substance. You see, there are no finite examples of this great infinite truth. But do we accept the Bible's definition of the Trinity as truth?"

Almost everyone nodded.

"Well, so it is with election and the freedom of man, as the two pertain to personal salvation. The Bible clearly teaches election—that God elects us to be saved before we are ever born into this world. But it also teaches that every person is totally free to become an elect— that is, to be saved. Do I understand how both can be true? Absolutely not! Do I accept both as true? Absolutely! Why? Because God's Word says it. Election and the freedom of man are just one antinomy out of many which the Scriptures teach. Do I understand any of them? No, I don't understand a single one of them! I don't, for example, understand how God can be everywhere present in all His fullness at the same time, but He is! I don't understand how ALL of God the Holy Spirit can be in me and ALL of God the Holy Spirit can be in you at the same time, but He is! And I don't understand how God can elect me to salvation before I'm ever born and yet grant to me the freedom to either be saved or not be saved after I'm born. Does not being able to comprehend both frustrate me? Not now, but you better believe it did before I finally accepted the fact that our infinite God might actually know more than I do."

"Pastor, can you give us some Scripture?" The unrecognized voice seemed sincere.

"Yes, of course. I'll give you numerous verses, and if you care to write them down, I'll speak slowly. In regard to election—I Peter 1:1-2; Matthew 22:14; Romans 8:29; II Thessalonians 2:13 and I Timothy 4:10 and these are only a few.

"In relation to the freedom of man–II Corinthians 5:14-15; Titus 2:11; John 1: 7 and 29; I Timothy 2:6 and 4:10, and there are many, many other verses which clearly tell us to be saved.

"Now, let's look at Romans 8:29 and II Corinthians 5:14-15. First Romans 8:29 and 30 which speak of election. Scripture says: "For whom He foreknew, he predestined to become conformed to the image of His son—and—whom He predestined, He also called and whom He called, He justified and whom He justified, He glorified."

"Now, clearly those verses teach—"

"Pastor," a voice interrupted. It was Anselm Frompton. "Don't you recken' those verses mean thet' God looks down through the tunnel o' time an' sees who's gonna' git' saved an' then they become the elect?"

"That's one way to interpret it so that it makes sense to us, Anselm, but when we think through it, it doesn't seem to solve the problem."

"Whut' do ye' mean, Paster?"

"May I ask you a question, Anselm?"

"Why, shore. Anythang' ye' want to, Paster'."

"You remember when you were saved?"

"March thirty-first, 1971," Myrtle, Anselm's wife, answered. "Three-thirty in the afternoon."

"Best day o' her life," Anselm laughed.

Patie grinned and Myrtle, smiling, concurred.

"Well, let's take a close hard look at Anselm's question, church," Patie suggested. "The problem most of us have with election, I think, is that in our finite minds, it eliminates the possibility of man's freedom. And so, we tend to reject it, claiming that the words must mean something else, since, again, in our finite minds, both election and freedom cannot be true. Anselm, I'm not speaking of just you, I'm speaking of all of us. When we assume both sides of the antinomy cannot be true, we consciously or subconsciously tend to reject one or the other teachings, perhaps, without malice, actually changing the meaning of words in the process, which, of course, makes my interpretation of the Bible rather than the Bible itself, my final authority.

"Now, Anselm, you were saved March thirty-first, 1971, at three-thirty in the afternoon. God looked down through the tunnel of time and saw that, right?"

"Right," Anselm agreed. "Thet's' whut' I b'lieve!"

"I agree. He did. He's omniscient. Now, is there any possibility that at three-thirty p. m. on March thirty-first, 1971, you WERE NOT going to be saved?"

Anselm was thinking and so was everyone else in the audience. "Wal', ah, wal', I reckon, ah, Preacher, thet's' a good querstion, I reckon'. I coulda' changed my mind, don'tcha' reckon'?"

"Anselm, that seems logical to everyone of us in here, including me, I imagine, but let's look closer at the problem. We are trying to pre-serve your freedom either to receive Christ or not receive Christ, aren't we?"

Anselm nodded. "Yes, Sir, I recken'!"

"Could God have looked down through the tunnel of time and seen a mirage, something which might not happen?"

Patie could see the man's struggle. He had been there.

"Wal', oh, no, Preach, I—wouldn't exactly say thet'."

"Tough problem, isn't it, Brothers and Sisters?" The pastor asked gently. "Hard to understand, isn't it. But the fact of the matter is, God can't foreknow, that is to say, look down through the tunnel of time and see a lie or even an uncertainty. Once God looked down through the tunnel of time and saw that at three-thirty p. m. on March thirty-first, 1971, Anselm Frompton would be saved, there was absolutely no doubt Anselm Frompton would be saved right then. Well, in that case, where is his freedom? Is Anselm free, if God's foreknowledge locks him into certain behavior? Now, seeing the certainty of Anselm's salvation, March thirty-one, 1971, at three-thirty, our finite minds might deny Anselm freedom, because we now can't see that freedom, which would make what theologians call Hyper-Calvinists out of us. Was Anselm free to be saved that day? Of course. Why? Because I understand how he could be? No, because Scrip-ture teaches it in every place it exhorts us to be saved.

"Now, let me say this before we look at some verses which teach the freedom of man. As I said before, if we deny individual freedom, we become Hyper-Calvinists. If we deny God's sovereignty in election, then we become what the theologians call Armenians. Some people and some churches deny election and some deny man's freedom. But as a people and a church we must accept both, not because the preacher said it, but be-

247

cause the Bible does. As I said, since we cannot understand both parts of an antinomy, our tendency is to reject one part or the other. If we did that to the Trinity, which is another antinomy, reject either the fact that God is three persons or the fact that the three Persons are the exact same substance at the exact same time, we would be called heretics and rightly so. So we must be careful not to reject God's teachings even though we cannot understand them. By the way, as I said, the antinomy allows us a glimpse into God's infinite wisdom and omniscience."

The preacher hesitated, looking around his audience, "Are there any questions before we look back at Man's freedom?"

A booming voice issued from the rear of the church. It was Lester again. "I got lots o' questions, Preach, but I don't ritely' know how to 'ast 'em."

Patie laughed. So did many of the others.

"Now, concerning the freedom of man," Patie elaborated, "that issue is determined by answering the question, "For whom did Christ die?" Obviously, if Christ died for *all* men, then *all* men are free to become an elect, or to say it another way, free to be saved. So, not only the verses which teach that Christ died for all, but the numerous verses, as I said before, which implore men, and women, of course, to repent and be saved, coupled with the very nature of God, teach that man is free. Some of the verses where Christ and others command sinners to repent and be saved are Matthew 3:2; Mark 1:15; Acts 2:38; 17:30 and many, many others. II Corinthians 5:14 and 15 tell us that Christ died for all people, and the word "for" means in place of or on behalf of all people! So Christ died for all people and He invites all people to be saved. Do I understand that, in light of what Scripture says about election? Of course not. It's an infinite truth being considered by a finite mind. Do I accept it as truth? You bet'cha! Why? Because I—"

"Preacher," Lester called out again. "How much you gonna' bet?"

For the first time, even considering the sorghum patch, the preacher sensed slight frustration toward his large friend. And for the second time tonight, he did not answer. But he did forge a slight smile onto his face, as much to conceal his modest irritation as to placate Lester in lieu of his lack of reply.

"Do I accept the freedom of man as truth, in light of that which the Bible teaches about election? Yes! Why? Because I understand it? No, not because I understand it, but because God says it—in His Word."

"AMEN, Preacher." The voice was Lester's again.

"For me to deny that which Scripture teaches, frankly, is to position my intelligence higher than God's. Folks, for me to do that would be akin to a Tishomingo mosquito attacking an Air Force F-16 fighter plane—or worse."

"Brother Corbin," an anonymous voice asked, "Do you have any kind of illustration which would make trying to reconcile election with the freedom of man a little easier? I mean, is there anything?" A hungry pleading was evident in the question.

"Yes, I do, my brother, at least in part, but you all are gonna' have to use your imaginations. Will you help?" The expressions which the preacher saw on his parishioner's faces almost produced pity in him. They were struggling to understand truths which were impossible for the finite mind to grasp. And the intellectual conflict was producing impatience in some, irritation in others, and even some passive indifference. The subject needed to be broached because it involved personal salvation, but had it not been written on the slip of paper pulled from the box tonight, it would have been done in the distant future, perhaps at least a year from now. The church members needed to know and trust their preacher better, much better, before he delved into this kind of controversial issue.

"With those imaginations, pretend I have a large blackboard here beside me," Patie proposed, motioning with his hands. " On that blackboard, I'm going to draw a large square pasture."

"Pasture?" a voice asked. "Like with cows?"

"Yes, pasture, like with cows. In the middle of that large pasture, I'm going to draw a small catch pen. From that catch pen, I'm going to draw four fences, one due north, one east, one south, and one west, so that the large pasture is actually divided into four smaller pastures. Now, each of these pastures; the northwest pasture, the northeast pasture, the southeast pasture and the southwest pasture has a gate leading into the catch pen. Then, picture this. I have a cow in the catch pen which I want to go into the northwest pasture. How do I get her there?" The preacher waited a moment for all that he had said to register with his listeners and for the question he asked to be considered. Then he repeated the description which he had given. When he finished, he asked, "Can you see my four imaginary pastures, each connected to the catch pen by a gate?"

A preponderance of the heads nodded, including Lester, who bellowed, "We know pastures, Preach. Go 'head."

"How do I get that cow from the catch pen into the northwest pasture? Well, the first thing I do is close the three gates to the other three pastures and I open the gate to the northwest pasture. Then I get into the catch pen with the cow, and start yelling, waving my arms and slapping my legs with my hat. The cow spooks and starts looking for a place to run. She spots the open gate and lopes through it into the northwest pasture." The preacher hesitated again. Looking around the congregation at his people's faces, searching for nods and smiles, he asked, "Y'all with me?" Again, a majority of the people nodded. A few, including Lester, concurred with "amens."

"Now, let me ask you this. Did I elect that cow to go into the northwest pasture? I think you will agree that I did. But was that cow free?" Again he waited, looking for understanding. Lester again gave it to him.

"I recken' she wuz', Preach, seein' as how you didn't pick er' up or pull 'er through with a rope or nothin'."

"You're absolutely right, Lester. She could have lain down and I could not have gotten her into the northwest pasture. But you see, I know the mind of a cow better than the cow does. I knew when I started making certain noises, that cow would panic and look for a place to run. But she was absolutely free. I elected her but she was free. Now, God's mind and knowledge of us are infinitely greater than our knowledge of the cow and He brings circumstances into our lives by which we come to Him. He elects us but we are free to be an elect. Do I understand that infinite truth with my finite mine? Of course not! Do I accept both teachings? Absolutely! Why? Because God's Word teaches both."

"Preacher, you said that illustration only partly described election and the freedom of man!" a lady asked.

"Yes, thank you. I'd almost forgotten. Although it describes how a thing might be elected and free at the same time, that illustration does not explain why some cows are elected to go into the northwest pasture and some are not. That's the infinite truth which we must leave in the hands of our Sovereign God. And, by the way, God *is* sovereign, you know. That, of course, means there is nothing over which he does not posses authority. If there should be anything, then He would not be sovereign.

"Folks, please don't try to *understand* these infinite truths. Like mine, your minds are finite. We cannot understand, we can only accept— and thank our just and holy and loving God that He is in control. You may get very, very frustrated and discouraged if you insist on understanding these truths before accepting them. And that frustration may pressure you to reject one or the other truths—election or the freedom of man, and I don't think we would want to do that. Remember, ninety-five per cent of the Bible we may be able to understand with our finite minds. The other five per cent, we accept by what?"

"FAITH," someone shouted.

"Exactly. Faith," the preacher agreed. "We accept it by faith— grateful faith—that our God is infinitely more intelligent than we."

"Finally, I want to give you some more verses where the word "elect" is used synonymously with those who are saved. You may want to write some of these verses down. Pardon me for getting technical with you, but the English word "elect" whether it's used as a noun or a verb, comes from the Greek word *EKLEKTOS,* which, according to the Greek lexicon, dictionary, literally means "picked out or chosen." Here are some of the verses: Matthew 24:22; Matthew 24:24; Mark 13:20; Luke 18:7; Romans 8:33; Colossians 3:12; I Timothy 5:21; II Timothy 2:10; Titus 1:1; and I Peter 1:2. There are others, of course.

"Brother Abe Goodson, would you dismiss us?"

As soon as Abe finished praying, Patie walked quickly to Larry Steeg. "Brother, do you know off-hand whether you are free for lunch tomorrow?"

"I'm free, Brother Corbin."

"May I take you to lunch with a friend? He needs to see you very badly."

"Certainly."

"Good, good," the pastor murmured. "Twelve noon at Hilda's alright?"

Larry nodded. "Yes. I'll look forward to it."

CHAPTER TWENTY
A SECOND WIND

"**D**imples, could you come in here a minute, please?"

Patie looked at his desk clock. It was 9:00 a. m. His large flat desk calendar announced no appointments for today, but he wanted to make certain that Dimples had not scheduled him anywhere or with anyone. "Dimples?" he called out again.

"Brother Corbin—ah—Pastor—ah—Patie," the secretary replied, her voice muffled. "What day is it?"

"Monday–why?"

"No, sir, I mean what's the date?" she yelled, her voice muffled.

"September10, 2001," Patie answered, walking into the secretary's office. Dimples was bent over in the large storage room adjacent to her office, her backside protruding from the doorway. "What are you doing?"

"Trying to get my files straightened out." She sounded a little frustrated.

The preacher walked to her side and looked over her shoulder into the storage room. With both her hands, she seemed to be holding places in her crowded file cabinet.

"What are—"

The secretary jumped, which in turn made the preacher jump.

"Sorry. I forgot you are–" he hesitated. "What are you doing?

You got your fingers caught in a rat trap?"

"I can't let go."

"Why not?"

"I think I filed a whole month's reports with the wrong dates on them."

"Can I help you?" Patie asked.

"Yes, Sir. Hand me two pencils outa' my desk drawer." A few moments later, with the two pencils stuck into the file drawer marking the questionable reports, Dimples stood up. "Thank you."

"You're welcome. Nothing's written on my calendar for today. You know anything I need to do?"

Quickly, the secretary answered. "No, Sir."

"'No, Sir, you don't know of anything' or 'No, sir, you don't have anything?'"

"Yes, Sir," she answered, moving toward her desk.

"Yes, Sir? What does that mean," Patie questioned, admitting to himself that he could *never* have figured out the meaning of *that* answer.

"Yes, Sir, both. You takin' Mr. Hamp to see Larry today?"

The bewildered preacher, shaking his head and frowning, backed up a few feet and sat down hard on the chair in front of Dimples' desk. His mind raced. How in the world could Dimples have known he was taking Mr. Hamp to see Larry Steeg today? He decided not to ask. "That's what I wanted to talk to you about. I'm going to be leaving in a little while. I should be back around 3:00 o'clock."

"Yes, Sir," she answered, pulling a desk drawer out and fumbling for something inside it.

"Did you already know that?"

"Oh, no, Sir," she blurted out. "How in the world could I know you were getting back at 3:00 o'clock?"

Not once did the pastor even consider responding to that comment. "You're eating at Hilda's?"

"Yes. Did you know that or did you just guess?"

"Guessed. Remember!"

"Remember? Remember what, Dimples?" The preacher had already remembered but he wanted to let the conversation ramble a little—see if the secretary would just come right out and say it.

"Just remember. That's all. Just remember," she reminded him again, leaning over and looking into a desk drawer.

"Remember. Just remember," Patie spoke slowly. "She tells me 'Just remember!' Humh!"

"Peach cobbler."

"Peach cobbler? What about peach?—oh—heh, heh, peach cobbler!"

Dimples cut an accusing eye at him.

"Peach cobbler!" Patie repeated emphatically. "You want me to bring you another pint?"

"Whatever you think."

Patie glanced at his desk clock again. It was 9:20. He took Larry Steeg's business card from his shirt pocket and dialed his number. A moment later Larry was on the phone. "Good morning, Larry."

"Mornin, Brother Corbin."

"We're still on for Hilda's at noon?"

"Yes. I'm looking forward to it."

"Good! Larry, do you know who I'm bringing with me?"

"No, I don't."

"It's Mr. Hamp Crimm. I thought it might be wise to talk to you about his problem before we got there. Are you comfortable discussing it on the phone?"

Larry answered quickly. "I think so, Pastor. I've never had a problem with it before."

"Good." Patie told the attorney the story, touching only the major points. When he finished, he asked, "Do you think he needs to bring a suit-case–I mean–his personal items? I told him yesterday to have it packed just in case."

Larry hesitated. The sounds on the telephone indicated to Patie that the lawyer was considering it. "Oh, Pastor," he spoke calmly, "I don't think so. I know the sheriff real well, a personal friend, great guy. He'll want to see the crime scene and the grave. That means he'll be taking Mr. Hamp back down there, or maybe he'll let you take him back. He'll know, of course, Mr. Hamp won't try to run." The attorney hesitated again. "On second thought, better tell him to bring it, just in case the sheriff is tied up and can't get down there today."

"Okay," Patie confirmed, "I'll tell him. One other thing, Larry, will you want Mr. Hamp to start telling you the story at Hilda's? While we are eating?"

The attorney answered quickly. "No, better not, Brother Corbin. Too close quarters. We'll come back to the office."

Mr. Hamp had finished telling Larry the entire story. Larry had listened patiently, making extensive notes, asking an occasional question. Patie's cell phone rang. The preacher excused himself and walked quickly from the attorney's office into the outer reception area. On the caller ID he saw it was the church.

"Hello, Dimples."

"Patie," Dimples sharply answered, her voice low but sounding extremely frantic, "when are you gettin' back?"

"Oh, I don't know. I have to go back by Hilda's and pick up your peach cobbler. Why do you—"

"Patie," the secretary interrupted, whispering. "We have a bad

256

problem down here."

"Where are you?"

"In your office. You need to come back."

"Right now?"

"Yes, Sir. You need to come back." Her voice was still frantic, her speech rapid and little more than a whisper.

"Dimples, is it *that* serious?"

"Yes, Sir," she breathed.

"You know what I'm involved in up here. This is pretty serious, too. Is *that* serious enough to draw me away from this?"

"Yes, sir, I think it might be."

"Can you tell me what it is?"

"No, sir, it's too involved but it's serious."

"Okay, okay. I'll see what I can do. Does that serious problem involve someone else?"

"Yes, Sir."

"Are they there? I mean, at the church?"

"Yes, Sir, in my office."

"How many people?"

"Two."

"Okay. Tell them I'll be there shortly. Let them wait in my office."

Patie walked back into Larry's office. The attorney was talking. When the preacher continued standing, Larry stopped. Both men looked at him.

"Y'all, that was Dimples. She told me we have a serious crisis at church. Do you need me here? If you do, I'll call Dimples back and stay here."

"No, Pastor," Larry answered, "we would love for you to stay but we don't need you. In a few minutes, Mr. Hamp and I are going to the sheriff's office. Then, I imagine we'll all go talk to the judge. If Mr. Hamp is allowed to go home tonight, as I believe he may be, I'll take him."

"Mr. Hamp," Patie asked, "is that alright with you?"

The old man looked up at the pastor. Dropping his head again, he struggled to his feet. He extended his right hand toward the preacher and when Patie grasped his hand, the old man spoke. His voice was strong and definite, a dim smile was on his face.

"Brother Corbin, I thank you for what you have done for me."

"You're welcome, Mr. Hamp, but I haven't done very much for you. I'll see you soon, though, I promise you that"

The old veteran nodded, relaxed his hand out of Patie's grip and sat back down. It was still easy for the preacher to see he had really decided to make his crime right with man and his sin right with God—by the determination in his voice and on his face.

The drive back down State Highway 25 toward Tishrock was a fairly quick one, only about twenty minutes, usually. In spite of the urgency in Dimples voice, though, Patie Corbin was in no hurry. He needed time to think–not only about Mr. Hamp–but about everything–the myriad of catastrophic events which had challenged him since moving to Tishrock–the lack of a close and continuous relationship with his children and grandchildren—the stark contrast in the lifestyle which he lived now, compared to that which he had lived before, especially since pro football, including living alone—his relationship with Ann. His children and grandchildren had naturally moved away from him and toward their mother and her family, a fact which existed before Mom's death, but certainly true now. His grandchildren were growing up and he didn't even know them, not well. And he hardly ever saw them. Occasional phone calls, birthday cards and exchanged Christmas presents were about the only contact, he brooded, and most of it was his own fault. Because of all the things he did wrong before becoming a Christian, he figured he didn't deserve a relationship with them. Now, he yearned for it. But now, all of them were four years older than they were on the day he prayed to receive Christ—four years of having separated even farther from each other. There was no hostility, of course, but there was very little family closeness either.

And what about Ann? They had become good friends, perhaps too good, although absolutely nothing physical had occurred. But he had begun to notice more thoughts of her springing up in his mind and a few nights ago, he had dreamed about her. It woke him up in a cold sweat and forced him out of bed and onto his knees. And what about her? Is she having thoughts? In shame, he tried not to hope she was and he prayed she wasn't, all at the same time.

Then, there are these problems, Lord, he thought within himself. Is this natural? A typical state of ministry? Lord, my lifestyle has been faster in ministry here in rural Tishomingo County, Mississippi than it was in New York or Memphis.

The preacher did not expect God to speak orally to him and God didn't. But, he thought, Lord, it sure would be wonderful to hear your voice. Am I where you want me to be? Am I doing what you want me to do ? Are you allowing all these problems into my life for a reason? Or is it Satan trying to weaken me?"

The seminary graduate knew the Biblical answers to his questions before they were framed in his mind. He pulled his SUV over into the parking lot of a Baptist church and prayed, re-committng himself to the Lord and to His will. Before the audible prayer echoed from his mouth, the preacher began to mentally, spiritually and physically feel it—the awesome and incomprehensible peace of God—the peace which passes all under-standing. Fifteen minutes later he pulled his SUV into the parking lot of Tishrock Community Church and hustled inside, walking boldly straight to his office. Dimples was there with a woman.

"Patie," the secretary immediately introduced, even before the preacher had an opportunity to speak. "This is Inez McAdams."

Inez was a short stocky woman with curly grey hair. As the world measures beauty, she wasn't a beautiful woman in the face, a face contorted and streaked with tears, but she was attractive, or would be, without the pain. Her reddened eyes were blue and spaced far apart and indeed, were mirrors into her tortured soul. She wore a fashionable pants suit.

"Inez, I'm very glad to meet you," the preacher softly spoke, granting deference to the torment so visible in her, extending his hand.

Inez shook Patie's hand, looking up at him as she did so. She seemed to have no strength in her grip.

Before the pastor could walk around his desk and sit down, Dimples continued, "Patie, Inez and her husband Alex are members of the church, but you haven't met them yet. They—"

"I thought someone else was with you," the preacher interrupted, then realized what he had done.

"I'm sorry, Dimples, I shouldn't have interrupted you, but I expected to see two people."

"Alex left," the secretary explained. "He didn't want to wait on you."

Patie nodded in understanding. "You were saying, Dimples?"

"Oh—oh yes—Inez and Alex have been out of town—on a cruise. That's why you haven't met them."

The secretary took the woman's hand. "Inez and I have known each other all our lives. We were in the same class. We lived rite' down the street from one another. We double dated together an' we married our husbands who are friends, too, six months apart. She's got a bad, bad problem, Patie, an' I'm hurtin' almost as much as she is.

"Honey," Dimples asked, "you want me to tell Patie or do you want to?"

"You tell him, Dimples, if it's alrite'," Inez sobbed deeply. "If—it's—alrite' with him."

"It's alright with me, Inez, but I need to ask you a question before we start. Dimples, have they filled out the questionnaire?"

Patie was relieved to discover that Inez had. Alex wouldn't.

260

"Since she has filled it out, Dimples," the preacher clarified, "why don't you explain the situation, hitting only the high points, if you understand what I mean. I may have to stop you every once in a while, though, to ask you a question. That okay?"

Both women nodded.

"Wal', Alex travels in his job, and—"

"I'm sorry Dimples. Who does he work for?"

"A heavy equipment company out of Memphis, and lik' I was sayin', he travels. Wal', when they got home off their—"

"Sorry again. How big of an area does he travel in?"

"From Little Rock to Nashville to Birmingham to Jackson and back to Little Rock an' all the area in between. That right, Inez?"

The suffering wife nodded.

"Obviously, he can't come home every night," Patie surmised. "Is that right?"

"Yes, Sir," Inez whispered, her voice hoarse. "That's rite'."

"How many nights is he back home each week, about?" Corbin asked.

"Wal', he usually gets home Wednesday nite' an' leaves on Sunday afternoons—usually—but sometimes he changes that up a little bit. Is that rite', Honey?" Dimples asked.

Inez nodded.

Dimples continued. "Wal', yesterday when Inez and Alex got off the boat in New Orleans, a woman was waitin' for em', holdin' a little boy and a little girl by the hand. When the woman saw Inez and Alex, the little boy and girl broke away from the woman, who Inez found out later was their Mama, and ran up to Alex yelling, "Daddy, Daddy."

Patie walked into his cabin at exactly 6:00 o'clock. Not often in his life had he felt like he had been run through a wringer mentally. Physically, many times, but not mentally. He did today.

The preacher had spent two hours with Inez. From all the information which he gathered directly and from the questionnaire, he determined that Alex had married Inez at least eighteen years before he "married" Connie, the other woman. He assured Inez that she was her husband's legitimate wife, even though he had gone through a justice-of-the-peace ceremony with Connie—and—he had presented her with numerous other salient counseling principles. That exercise, coupled with Mr. Hamp's tragedy had just about depleted him of desire to do anything the rest of the day.

Exchanging his dress clothes for a pair of workout shorts, a Giants tee shirt, and a pair of Nikes, the ones with embedded dried sorghum juice, he turned his television on to see who was playing on Monday night football. Then he poured himself a half glass of Diet Coke and walked out onto his porch only to be met by the whine of mosquitoes. Setting his Diet Coke back inside the cabin, he grabbed his Yard Guard and sprayed it up into the air around the edge of the porch. Then he reached back into his house, retrieved his Diet Coke and slouched to the swing. He had no more than sat down when he took a deep breath, looked through the few trees which were left standing toward the sunset and murmured, "Lord, if there ever has been a day of my life when I didn't want to talk to anyone else nor work out, it's today." Immediately, he shook his head, breathed deeply, retrieved his cell phone and phone book from inside the house, repositioned himself in the swing and dialed Ann's house. She didn't answer. He decided not to leave a message. He found the number for the Boulder in the phone book and dialed it.

Ann answered.

"Hi, Ann. This is Patie."

"Hi. How are you?"

"Fine. Ann, have you heard about Mr. Hamp?"

"Mr. Hamp Crimm?"

"Yes."

"No. I haven't heard a thing. Why? Has something happened?"

262

"Yes, It has—not physically–he's alright physically. May I ask you a question? I mean about the Boulder's publishing policy?"

"Of course, Patie."

"Do y'all print legal matters, like arrests, court sessions, trials, things like that?"

"Yes, we do."

"Well, I need to talk to you about Mr. Hamp, Ann. Something's about to happen to him legally. I may want to ask a favor of you."

"I'm leaving here around 7:00 o'clock. Want me to come by?"

Patie's conscience screamed at him. With every fiber of his spiritual being, he needed to say "no." But he needed to talk to her about Mr. Hamp, too. She might be able to help the old vet. She certainly could be implored not to hurt him. "If you don't mind! I'm going to be working out on my Healthrider in my bedroom for the next forty-five minutes or so. Just come on in."

CONCLUSION

Patie Corbin made no mad dash to his bedroom this night. Had he the energy, he might have. But he was tired—more tired than he ever remembered being.

Fatigue was no stranger to the old retired ex-pro football player turned minister. College football two-a-days were exhausting, but they wore you out physically, not mentally, and the same could be said about pro football two-a-days. Tiring, but not totally depleting of energy. Besides, he was much younger then and "tired" to a twenty-five year old is different from "tired" now.

The preacher had gotten intellectually tired during his years in seminary. But a good grade on an exam after having truly learned the material, coupled with a good night's sleep usually brought complete recovery. The Holy Spirit seemed to see to it.

But tonight, the night of September 10, 2001, the preacher was completely sapped of physical energy and intellectual energy. Little did he know that the next day, September 11, 2001, would horribly and grotesquely thrust upon the minister of the Gospel another evil adversary— a problem which would not be so easily solved in three hours of counsel or two expository sermons. A problem first presented to him four years ago by an ex-New York Giants teammate and a Christian Arab in Eagle Pass, Texas, named Musai Mohammed.

The preacher finally dozed off, the words "husband of one wife" whirling about in his subconscious mind.

A PERSONAL NOTE

For almost twenty-five years, by God's grace, I, along with other men and women counselors whom I had trained, ministered to about fifteen hundred counseling units per year at Directive Counseling Center in Memphis and the Mid-South area. God developed great counseling principles from His Word as they applied to people's lives literally faster than I could write them down.

For years, I taught these Biblical principles in counseling classes called The Directive Counseling Institute, and from teaching podiums. But our Lord stopped me from teaching these in-depth Biblical truths when I allowed my life to become extremely contrary to His righteousness.

BUT—I don't want to take these truths to the grave. Since I can no longer pass them on in the ways I once did, understandably, I am passing them on another way.

SO, I am passing the literal truths on through a fictitious preacher by the name of Patie Corbin and his make-believe counselees. While Patie and his counselees are fictitious, the Biblical truths which he counsels aren't. Everything you read in the Patie Corbin series of Christian novels has occurred in a counseling office, most of them at Directive Counseling Center, a few in other offices.

Likewise, all the humorous stories have literally happened, too. For example, I personally spent three days in September, 2006, cutting, stripping, topping, stacking and cooking sorghum molasses for my brother-in-law, Donald Orr, in Vaiden, Misissippi. Everything Patie Corbin experienced in Chapter 16 of this book, I experienced—and then some.

I do more than *hope* you enjoy these books. I *pray* to our gracious Lord that you will.

The third Patie Corbin Christin novel will be on the market in summer, 2008, the Lord willing. You will be able to read about Patie's counsel to Maggie, to Millaree and Fern, to Inez and Alex and to others.

Other Books By Paige Cothren

1. *LET NONE DEAL TREACHEROUSLY* (Christian) A look at Christian marriage principles for husband and wife. $12.00, includes shipping

2. *SEEKING TO KNOW HER* (Christian) Written primarily for husbands, giving them deep insight into the nature of their wives. $10.00, includes shipping.

3. *WALK CAREFULLY AROUND THE DEAD* (Football) Dozens of funny football stories during the time when coaches "held the players by the throats." $20.00, includes shipping.

4. *HOME SWEET HOMOCHITTO* (Christian and historical) About a very unusual community near Natchez in Southwest Mississippi. Non-fiction and humorous. $20.00, includes shipping.

5. *SO GREAT THE PRETENDER* (Fiction) Set primarily on the Mississippi and Florida Gulf Coasts. The novel about Patie Corbin is a love story-murder mystery. $24.00, includes shipping.

6. *THE ECHO OF SILENCE* (Fiction) Set on Sugar Mountain in North Carolina, Laurel Mississippi and the swamps of Pontchartrain, north of New Orleans. A second murder mystery novel featuring Patie Corbin. $24.00 includes shipping.

7. *THE CRY OF THE CAMEL* (Fiction) An adventure-murder mystery set along the Rio Grande River and in San Antonio. The third novel

in the Patie Corbin series deals with the invasion of Muslim terrorists flowing from Mexico into the USA. $24.00, includes shipping.

8. *AN ACADEMY CALLED PAIN* (Currently out of print.)

9. *AT THE END OF THE SWINGING BRIDGE* (Christian fiction)
    The fourth Patie Corbin novel, which is the first in the Patie Corbin Christian novel series. An in-depth, but humorous look at the life of Patie Corbin the preacher as he preaches, teaches and counsels the word of God in rural Mississippi. Softcover. $20.00, includes shipping.

10. *AT WHAT PRICE LAW* (Theological) A Biblical examination of the Mosaic Law, the New Law of Christ, and the relationship between the two, written to enable Christians to know exactly which law we are to obey. Softcover. $20.00, includes shipping.

11. *A LAMP UNTO MY FEET—A LIGHT UNTO MY PATH, 1,216 expository sermon outlines, with commentary, 651 from the Old Testament and 565 from the New Testament (Almost 10 years of sermons)* Softcover plastic-spine workbook. $25.00, includes shipping.

   TO ORDER: Please send a check or money order to:

   Swinging Bridge Publications
   1332 Hwy 15 South
   Woodland, MS 39776